CONVICTION

CONVICTION
Mark Daniel

MICHAEL JOSEPH
LONDON

First published in Great Britain by
Michael Joseph Limited
44 Bedford Square London WC1
1980

ISBN 0 7181 1910 X

Typeset in Great Britain by
Granada Typesetting, Redhill

Printed and bound by
Billing and Sons Ltd, Guildford

The peculiar circumstances in which this book was researched and written make me more than ever indebted to those who have given me their constant love and support. To June Stuart-Routledge, to Edward Stigant, Andrew Rolla, Sonia Goodman, Claire Elliot, John and Judith-Rose, Leo Yanez, John Tucker, Jane Walwyn, Michael Brook, Charles Lea, Emma Russell, Mignonne, and to Clare George, my love and thanks.

For
Nick Robinson

GLOSSARY

Alkie	Alcoholic
Bender	Suspended sentence
Bird	Imprisonment
Bird drag	A state of mind in which the time seems to stand still, and no end to the sentence is in sight
Birdman	Experienced prisoner
Blade	Any sort of knife
Blagging (doing a blag)	Armed robbery
Burn	Tobacco
Cons	Convicts, prisoners
Creeping (doing a creep)	Burglary
Dear John	Letter from mistress or wife, telling of her infidelity
Divvy	Idiot
Doorbangers	Warders
Duff	The ballast of prison meals, a heavy sponge pudding
Fencing	Selling stolen goods
Fistful	A five-year sentence
Gobbling Behind Hedges	Grievous bodily harm
Goulash	Any meat or fish stew, and thus any prison meal, per se
Grass	Informer
Handling Swollen Goods	Handling stolen goods
Headbanger	Madman
Jam-roll	Parole
J. Arthur	Wank
John Law	The police
Lagging	A three-year sentence
Nick	Prison – divided into 'The big house' and 'open nick'

Nonce (nonceing)	Sexual offender
Old Bill	The police, or a policeman. The term 'cop' or 'copper' is never used
Old lag	Inveterate prisoner – a perjorative term
Paraffin lamp	Alcoholic
Peter	Cell (or safe)
Screw	Warder
Shanghaied	Returned to closed prison from open prison
Smoke, Snout	Tobacco
Stair-crazy	Mentally unbalanced by imprisonment
Star	First offender
Stoat the ball	Sexual offender (Scot.)
Stretch	A twelve-month sentence
Tramp's lagging	A three-month sentence
Turd burglar	Homosexual

Part One
THE GREATER GOOD

1

Georgie Barnett had bird drag. Two and a half months out of a five-year sentence still to go, and he could not sleep. The wind whipped at the walls of the block and rattled the panes of the windows, bearing with it the faint smell of home, and the memories that he had learned to subdue.

'Bugger!' he grunted, and sat up in bed.

By the moonlight, he found four dog ends and, carefully laying out his last cigarette paper, he broke them up, rolled a cigarette and licked it lightly. He struck a match, took a deep drag and lay back with a sigh.

No one could say that Georgie Barnett couldn't do his bird. He'd been in Walton, Wandsworth and the Ville. He'd done a two, a three and a five, and he couldn't understand why now, in this parody of a prison, he should be finding it tough.

After all, this wasn't even a nick as he understood it. An ex R.A.F. base in the Lincolnshire dales, made up of white painted billet sheds, Nissen huts and playing fields that had once been airfields, scarcely constituted a prison. You worked all day as a brickie. You played snooker in the evenings and football on Saturdays, and at night you returned to your dormitory or, if you were doing longer than eighteen months, to your own little room like this one. The only people that this sort of prison hurt were your wife, your kids.

Barnett thought of closed nicks. Of the days when there weren't even any blankets in the cells, and you slept on bare boards. Of spending twenty-three hours a day for two and a half years 'banged up' in a stinking cell. It was still like that for most cons.

11

The cigarette burned down fast. He snatched a last drag from the remaining quarter-inch and dropped the butt by the side of his bed. Tomorrow morning he'd pick it up and put it in his tin.

He settled down and heaved the bedclothes up over his head. It took a certain amount of delicate judgment to ensure that the too narrow blanket completely enclosed him, and he had only just achieved it when he heard the doorknob turn. He did not move. The door opened and clicked shut again. Someone was now in the room. His hand moved imperceptibly to grasp the razorblade under the pillow. He didn't owe tobacco to anyone, but you can never be too careful in nick.

Then a voice at the foot of the bed said, 'Georgie ...' An anxious voice, almost keening. 'Georgie, are you awake?'

'No, who's there?'

'It's me, Trevor. Can I turn on the light?'

'No, you bloody cannot. Fuck off, Trev.'

'I've got to talk to you', said the Yorkshire voice. 'I'm just off.

'You're what?' Barnett said, astonished, and sat up. 'All right,' he sighed, 'turn on the light.'

There was a faint scratching sound as fingers fumbled for the switch, then the light juddered and came on with a buzzing. Two men screwed up their eyes and blinked at one another.

Barnett was naked in bed. He was a broad and powerfully-built man, with a simian head. The cranium was almost completely flat, while the lower jaw jutted forward. He had the usual quota of messy, half-accomplished tattoos on his arms – daggers, scorpions and messages of hate which he had stabbed out with his own hand in long days of confinement, together with more professional work proclaiming undying love for his mother and for Doreen.

By contrast, the other man appeared mild and defenceless. He was small and plump and had a round red face. His pate gleamed brightly between two patches of sprouting white hair above each ear. He could have been a Yorkshire greengrocer were it not for the distinctive blue and white striped shirt under a grey pullover and the tracksuit trousers.

'Give us a smoke,' said Barnett.

The older man reached into his pocket and threw a tobacco tin onto the bed. As Barnett rolled a cigarette he asked, 'What

12

the hell do you mean, you're off, Trev?'

'I'm off. I'm going. I've got to.'

'Absconding, you mean? You're crazy. You've cracked up, Trev. You're a headbanger. You've only got a month to go.'

'I know, but I've got to.' The little man shifted from one foot to the other and fidgeted with the beret in his hands.

'Was that a Dear John you got today, then?' Trevor did not answer. Barnett sniffed and shook his head. 'Look. No woman's worth that, Trev. No one. I mean, in a month's time, you can sort it all out if there's something wrong. But you won't achieve anything this way. You'll get picked up before you get there and then you'll lose a hundred and twenty days and be put back in a closed nick.'

'It wasn't a Dear John,' bleated the little Northerner. 'Cindy's all right. She's very all right. It's something else.'

'For Christ's sake, Trev, what else can there be? A hundred and twenty days, you'll get, and . . . Look. The Big 'Ouse is all right for us lot. We're suited to it. But not you, Trev. I don't think you'd survive that long in there. For God's sake, listen to your Uncle Georgie. He knows what he's talking about.'

'I've got to go, Georgie.' Trevor walked over to the window and gazed out into the dark. 'I wish I didn't have to. I can't stay here. There's trouble this end too.'

'Oh, Jesus!' cried Barnett in exasperation. 'You're tougher than this lot. Sure, they've had it in for you recently. It makes me puke. They've had it in for you more than anyone I've ever known in a nick. But you'll survive for a month. You will.'

'It's no good. I'm going. I have a duty.' Suddenly, Trevor was assertive and sure. Barnett did not bother to argue. 'I just want you to make sure, when you get out, that Cindy gets a message. Just in case something happens to me.'

'You mean you're not going back home to yer missus? Christ, Trev, I've known some morons – but you . . . ?'

'It's not like that,' Trevor said appeasingly. 'I said, "If something happens to me." If I haven't got back to her.'

'I don't understand.' Barnett shook his head wearily. 'What's the message, then?'

'You'll take it?'

'I'll take it.'

'Just tell her, from me . . . Tell her . . . Oh, the usual things.

Tell her "Thank you for being a good mate" and . . .'

'The usual things.'

'The usual things.'

'O.K. Trev. I'll tell her. But nothing's going to happen. Right?'

'Right.' Trevor smiled and held out his hand. 'And thanks to you, Georgie. I'd never have made it in here without your help.'

'Piss off.' Barnett grinned. 'Now let me give you one more bit of advice from my vast store of ill-gotten experience. If you're going to run, keep running. Don't quit on it. Just run. If anything or anyone gets in your way, run over it or through it. Once you're over that fence you've got nothing to lose. Just never stop running.'

The older man smiled. 'I won't,' he said. 'You'll be hearing from me.'

He pulled up the grey woollen pullover until it covered his mouth and nose and pulled the beret onto his bald head. He switched off the light. His voice came muffled, 'Goodbye.' Then a gust of wind passed through the room and he was gone.

Trevor Abbott padded down the stairs, on guard. Sideways, his back to the wall, he slid around the hallway to the ablutions door. Then he was in. The night was suddenly very quiet, and when the urinal suddenly hissed into life as it cleared itself, he jumped.

He climbed onto a basin, and reached for the window ledge just above his head. He smelt his own sweat as he reached up. Nerves. He pulled himself up. For a moment his feet kicked for a hold, then he was lying flat, half in and half out. He dragged himself agonisingly through. There was a ten foot drop from the window to the grass and no ledge on which he could squat before jumping. He just had to slide through like a worm, falling when the weight became too great.

He landed untidily, and cursed under his breath. He had scraped his hands in trying to cling to the brick walls and had torn his trousers on the window catch. He unfolded himself and struggled to his feet. A huge blow from the wind almost knocked him back over again. He licked his lips, and leaning forward, moved on. Before him lay the parade square. On the right a light shone in the P.O.'s block. The duty screw lay back with his feet on the table. He was flicking over the pages of a comic.

14

Beyond the parade-ground, there were flowerbeds. Beyond them, the playing fields. Somewhere out there in the darkness, beneath the bucking trees, four more screws patrolled. Each could run faster than he. And screws did not like runners. Open prison, after all, is founded upon trust.

Alert to the slightest movement, Trevor Abbott scuttled out onto the moonlit parade ground. A few seconds later, a swift skidding shadow cast by a cloud caught up with him and he vanished into the darkness.

It was September 10th 1976.

Open prison offers a wide variety of occupations and training courses, unlike the closed prisons in which a convict is considered lucky if he can sew mailbags for a few hours each day. The inmates of Ravenhill could be trained in electrical engineering, in building operations, in bricklaying, plumbing and plastering. They could work in the prison kitchens, on the nearby home farm, in the maintenance of the vehicles and buildings, or on the gardens. Mickey Rourke had chosen the gardens. Mickey Rourke sought peace.

Sometimes Mickey would shake his head and reflect that he was the unluckiest person that had ever been born. He'd been to prison seven times since he'd come to England at the age of sixteen. He had only been out of Ravenhill for two days when they'd nicked him again. He had already done the plumbing course and the plastering course, and still the police kept picking him up and pulling him in.

It had only been for twenty-four lousy pounds this time. One month for every two pounds.

The prisoners called him 'divvy', 'headbanger' or, more affectionately, 'soft'. His mother had always called him soft. They wound him up. They provoked him and made him lose his temper, and when he lost his temper, Mickey lost time. Each time that he was discharged, Mickey thought that perhaps they would leave him alone and that the cycle would be broken. But the police seemed to want him. He kept returning.

At least out here in the gardens he was left alone for most of the day. He could sing his songs and do something that he understood. In the recent sweltering summer, he had been grateful to have been working outside. It had been a bitch of a summer. The heat had been merciless and had caused throats to ache and rasp for a pint of beer, bodies to vibrate with longing for a shared heat. The cons had run in their droves, only to be captured and returned – but when they came back, it was to closed nicks, and Mickey could not bring himself to imagine what those tiny, stinking, cockroach-ridden cells must have been like in that creeping heat.

Only two had got away for good. One was a merchant seaman. He would not be recovered. The other had just disappeared. But then no one was surprised at that. Runners were expected to disappear, the lucky ones.

The weather was almost cold now. It evoked few yearnings save, occasionally, the lifelong dream of a warm hearth and companionship. The wind was high and soupy. It came in muffled body blows like gloved punches, speckled now by rain. The trees strained and tossed their heads, releasing dark leaves that spun like darts against the tie-dyed grey.

If you were caught smoking out in the open you'd be nicked and lose days. So in a minute, Mickey promised himself, he'd take shelter in the gym and have a well-earned cigarette in the warm. He had a small space of this bed yet to dig, no more than eight foot square. Easily, mechanically, he lifted the spade, crunched it down, heaved, turned and started again. An easy rhythm. Accent on the down beat. One two three, one two three.

The spade struck and rasped.

Mickey saw the things lying in the soil that he had turned. He'd already lifted the spade before he realised. The song checked on his lips and turned to a dribbling sound.

He could not stop the downward stroke, but he let go the handle as though burned, and the earth suddenly shifted like the scudding clouds.

'Jeesus,' Mickey gulped. 'Jeesus, Mary.' He looked over his shoulder. Guilt and wariness accompanied any shock. Then he squatted, steadying himself with one hand. With the other he reached out and touched.

He crooned, 'Oh no, Jesus.' It was prayer, not profanation.

For his hand returned holding two severed fingers, dry as leather and thick with grime, and from under the earth where the spade had sliced, there sprouted dry white hair.

2

I jumped from the taxi at the Temple tube station, paid the driver, and turned to walk up to Fleet Street.

My condition was satisfactory. I knew that because the radio had just identified it. They'd been talking about a UDR man who had lost both legs the previous night. His condition was satisfactory. I didn't know to whom. Right then, my condition was satisfactory, too, in so far as I was not dead or dying. The sun was shining.

No one ever believed that I worked at school, because I enjoyed my studies and could as well synthesise data with a fly-rod in my hand as I could crouched diligently over a desk. In the same way, no one ever believed that my life was less than perfect, because I loved life despite some of its constituents, because I would rather smile than cry, rather skip than walk, rather prattle than sink into gloomy silence.

One aspect of my life was indeed black, but I saw no purpose in tarring the rest of my existence with the brush which had coloured it. I couldn't afford gloom. I knew what it was to lie gazing at the ceiling day after day, allowing the world to crumble and rot all around me. I knew what it was to live in a world of total darkness, with no visible means of escape. Leaden-limbed lethargy. The private prison of the depressive.

So I waved to Rob, the newspaper seller on the corner, and swanned into Lord Chesterfield Buildings, where Sir James Crashaw, QC, had his chambers. On my right as I entered was a glass partition through which I could see the clerk at her desk. I tapped on the door. She looked up, and grinned.

Catherine Clifford, commonly known as Catkin, was not cast

17

in the usual mould of barristers' clerks. Clerks should be rotund, eager and bespectacled. Catkin was slender, had a complexion which, in the middle of London, glowed like a rose amongst orchids, and long Bob Martin's hair which people called 'red' at their own risk. She wore black silk jersey and, far from being eager, she did not move as I entered, but simply said, 'Morning, Foy.'

'Morning, ma petite, you look obscenely lovely today.'

'Shut up, Foy.'

'You've destroyed any chance that I might have had of doing any work today. I'll have to ask his judgeship for an adjournment on the grounds of counsel's concupiscence. Can't you arrange to be fat and white and ugly, darling?'

'Ta gueule,' said Catkin, and grinned. She pushed back her chair and stretched her legs. The black silk softly swooped and gripped her mons veneris. I growled. She picked up *Law Reports of 1932* and threatened to throw it at me. 'Did you have a good time last night?' she asked.

'Oh, quite amusing. Same old crew.'

'And you got drunk again.'

I raised an eyebrow and tried to look superior. 'No, I was on quite good form.'

'And you went to bed sober? Bloody liar.'

'All right,' I smiled, 'but it's the best way I know of getting to sleep. Turn out the light and then turn out the light.'

'Poor darling Foy, you are an idiot. She can't be worth it.'

'Maybe not. Who is? I didn't choose to be English, and I don't like what's happening to England, yet English I am, and ever more shall be so. I don't choose where I belong, I just know. There's no pragmatism involved. Oh, damn you, woman, why do you start me off every morning like this?'

'Sorry.'

'Idiot.' I sat on the corner of her desk and looked down at her. 'What about your famous ducal dinner party?'

'Gruesome,' she shuddered. 'Rugger buggers and intense young men with more money than manners.'

'I know the type. Heavies. I trust that you put the grockles in their place?'

'I did. Went home at half-past eleven. Still, the lobster was lovely. Stop doing that.'

I stopped doing that (running the tip of my brolly up her leg) and asked, 'Is the monster in yet?'

'What do you think? It's ten o'clock of a Wednesday morning and he's been bellowing down the stairs for you every ten minutes for the last hour. You're in court at mid-day. Mmmmm. No! Stop that, Sebastian! Here, take your brief and get out of here. Here's your *Times*.'

'Thank you, my dear. Time to do at least two clues before mid-day. Oh, is that *Vogue*?'

'Yes, and no you can't have it yet. I haven't even looked at it myself.'

'I should hope not, indeed. You're supposed to be working. Must have a look at my horoscope and decide what to buy you for your birthday. Give it back to you at lunchtime.' I picked up the magazine and headed for the door.

'No!' squeaked Catkin. 'Foy, you insufferable queen!'

I waved to her and climbed the worn stone stairs to my little office. It was a bare, panelled room, rather like my college rooms at Trinity. A large anonymous desk with a green top stood in the centre. There were two shiny green armchairs for clients, a cabinet in the corner, and a rather nasty picture of mammarian pink chrysanthemums above the filing cabinet. A high window looked out onto a little grassy courtyard where illustrious eighteenth-century advocates and poets lay entombed. The pale November light split and splayed through little leaded panes and splashed on a parquet floor which was always dull, despite the pervasive smell of lavender. A bleached streak, dry and white as fishbones, marked the daily path of sunlight across the room.

I sat at my desk and revolved the revolving chair. Across the landing were the offices of my boss, a huge, wild, bearded Scot who had taken me on as his junior because, though he would never have admitted it, he had wanted and never had a son, and I amused him.

Sir James's reputation as counsel was formidable and well-deserved. He knew and used rhetorical tricks which pass unrecognised by modern college lawyers. Juries made up of just men and true were composed of geniuses when Sir James had finished with them. They were privy to self-evident revelations which were beyond the comprehension even of the learned

19

judge.

He could destroy a witness's credibility without giving the slightest impression of bullying, could flatter and cajole without giving the slightest inkling of subversion.

But outside the courts, for all his blustering grandiloquence, he was essentially soft. He enjoyed the youth of his subordinates, he enjoyed our constant flirtation, 'damned poodle-faking' as he called it, and he enjoyed it when we bammed and outraged the more sedate members of the profession. He often growled and muttered disapproval and blew out his moustaches, but he, and we, acknowledged our several obligations and fulfilled them as much from affection as from duty.

That is, we *had* fulfilled them until a few months before. Catkin was not the only critic of my lifestyle at that time. Sir James had now given me five final warnings on days when I had not come in or had arrived so hungover as to be useless. I had relied on charm to hold onto the job, but I knew it couldn't last. On the last occasion, I had played truant for five days, and he had written his warning. Its terms were unequivocal:

'You've got a considerable talent and you're throwing it away, together with your health. Quite frankly, you're damned near totally burned out. Someone's got to tell you, and it might as well be me since my interests co-incide with yours. On those nights when you are not paralytic, you're involved in your other sordid escapades. If, in other words, you're not trying to destroy your body, you're attacking your sensibilities.

'You may be cracking up. That's something which could happen to any one of us. But, for God's sake, in that case, see a psycho-therapist. I've been in this game long enough to have overcome those prejudices which once I had against psychoanalysis. It can do a power of good. See a good doctor. I want you to succeed, as undoubtedly you still can, but I cannot carry you. You're sick. Do something about it, or resign your position. There are plenty of young barristers who would be only too grateful to take your place.'

I had engaged a psycho-analyst. She, in turn, had sent me to a psychologist for a series of tests.

The night before the appointment had been a good night, and I had no sleep. I arrived on time at nine-thirty in the morning. The psychologist handed me a load of Rorschach ink blots and asked me to tell him what they reminded me of. I was still warm and comfortable and well-pleased with myself. The smell of her was still in my nostrils. Every one of those forms reminded me of just one thing.

The psychologist had concluded that I was 'of above average intelligence', but that I 'depended excessively upon women for happiness'. Which brilliant observation cost me fifty pounds.

Any minute now, I expected Sir James to be in, demanding to know where I had been. Still, in the time to spare . . . I unfolded *The Times* and checked on the forthcoming marriages. Fiona was not betrothed to anyone else. I sighed with relief and turned back to the news pages.

I checked as I turned a page and, suddenly alert, I smoothed the paper out on the desk top. A photograph – a familiar face – stood out.

JOURNALIST FOUND DEAD

Trevor Abbott, former journalist with the *North Riding Courier*, was found dead yesterday in the grounds of Ravenhill Open Prison in Lincolnshire. The police are investigating his death but are not yet prepared to issue any statement.

Abbott was sentenced to two years' imprisonment at Leeds County Court in April 1975. The well-publicised case was called the 'Yorkshire Watergate'. Abbott was caught rifling the offices of the Housing Department of Ripley Borough Council and planting bugs at a private meeting of the Housing Committee.

Abbott only had a few months of his sentence to serve.

I ran my finger down the columns as though it could bring me closer to the dead man.

'Oh, bugger!' I said quietly, and had to blink. 'How the hell did that happen?'

Trevor Abbott had begun his career as a journalist on the staff of the *Manchester Evening News*, the training ground of so many distinguished journalists. It soon became clear that he had a natural crusading talent and he joined the *Daily Mail* in 1955 as an investigative reporter. When the *Mail/Sketch* merger took place,

21

Trevor returned to his native Yorkshire and joined the *North Riding Courier*. He was passionately interested in the affairs of local government.

I had met him in the course of a case in which an eighteen-year-old girl was accused of soliciting and various drug offences in Gateshead. The police had made her statement for her, but by then the girl was too tired to care or worry.

Then a passionate, hardy little Yorkshireman had stuck his nose in where it wasn't wanted. Convinced of the truth of her tale, he had sought the best counsel in the business. Four policemen were subjected to the vituperous brilliance of Trevor's pen and to the brutal cross-questioning of a man whose 'team', when it closed ranks, was as formidable as any on earth.

Sir James, Catkin and I had been on our feet all day, at our desks all night and, for a while, it seemed that old-fashioned rhetoric would prevail over latter-day third degree.

It didn't. The policemen fell back on the essential trustworthiness of those in a position of trust. Shortly afterwards, the girl was mysteriously released from prison and the policemen went into premature retirement. On full pension. The *North Riding Courier* hounded them south.

I often visited Trevor and his wife at their cottage near Thirsk. I suppose that we were incongruous friends – the young 'sophisticate' and the tactiturn, hospitable northerner – but we hit it off.

Trevor had been a quiet man, and asked no more of life than his wife, his floozie in Leeds, his dog with which to walk the Dales, and a pub to whose clients he was always 'Our Trev'. But let there be one mention of an abuse of privilege and he reddened beyond his conjectural hairline. His accent became hard and abrasive. He bit off words in sharp-edged, foul-tasting chunks.

As the newspaper report said, he had been sent to prison for burgling the council offices. Certain people were being left homeless while large sums of money were being voted for the construction and maintenance of their homes. Trevor had to know why and decided to collect the evidence for himself.

He burgled badly and was caught in the act. The council prosecuted and he was put on probation for a year. The *North Riding Courier* turned a blind eye to their favourite son, but

Trevor didn't know when to stop. He tried again, making it worse this time by planting bugs, and it was almost as if they were waiting for him. On both occasions, he defended himself, and the first that I had known about it was the account of the second trial in the papers.

I opened the drawer and reached for a sheet of the Montpelier Square paper. My first thought was for his widow, Cindy, and I wrote to her offering the usual sympathies and my help, should it be needed.

The inquest on Trevor Abbott's death took place the next day in Lincoln. I asked that I should be informed of the outcome. As the courtroom darkened and the roar of the rush hour swept into the Old Bailey with the dusk, Catkin leaned over the wooden partition. She handed me a single sheet of paper. I read it, and nodded gloomily. It was what I had expected.

'Cause of death: head injuries. One major fracture and multiple contusions. Knuckles scarred. Minor spleen haemorrage. Assumed *killed* September having declared intention to escape. Found buried in flowerbed at Ravenhill.

'Open verdict recorded.

'P.S. Police have not sought permission to investigate further within the prison. Internal Investigation fruitless. It stinks. Love C.'

Yes, it stinks. The police are rarely allowed into a prison, and any evidence supplied by other prisoners would be disbelieved, even if it got past the governor. Any prisoner could be murdered and his body hidden in the prison grounds, and no one need be any the wiser. It would merely be assumed that he had escaped and successfully changed his identity. He would exist no more.

For Cindy's sake, I was grateful that Trevor had been found, but I could not help suspecting that for someone, Trevor had once more caused a great deal of trouble.

23

3

I had arranged to dine with Verena, and looked forward to it.

Verena von Kauz was one of Europe's most beautiful women. All right, I'm biased, but Salvador Dali, for one, agrees with me. We had met while I was at Cambridge and she at the Slade, and we had fallen in love in a nice, diffident, happy way. We enjoyed one another. Sex was a pleasure and an inevitable consequence of our sharing so much, a means of communication which we used. It was not our master, so there were never the problems of rows and resentment which possessiveness engenders.

And when, one night, we found ourselves incapacitated by giggles at the silly things which sex had caused us to say, we decided that we were far too alike for an affair, so gave up sex and took to dining and the theatre instead.

But Verena had a huge circle of friends and we didn't see each other often. Occasionally, when things weren't going right for her, she got in touch. Then, last month, when Fiona had bolted and I was nearer to breaking point than ever before, I found myself heading for Eaton Terrace. I was tight. I let myself in with the old key, climbed the stairs and crept into the bedroom in the darkness. Undressing, I slipped in beside her without a word. She awoke, whispered, 'Darling, you're drunk,' and kissed me.

She turned over, laid her head on my chest and her thigh over mine, and we slept. In the morning, when we awoke, she simply said, 'Good morning, you self-indulgent pig. Is life terribly beastly?', kissed my chest and my forehead, and cooked breakfast.

Tonight promised flirtation and fun, with no threats.

I sat back with my feet on the desk. The metallic grey leaves tapped and bustled at the window. The dusk swarmed in the corners of the room and mounted like smoke. I sat in my shirt-sleeves, a brief in one hand and a large chunk of amethyst in the other.

The brief concerned a man who had castrated himself whilst uncorking a bottle of wine. The bottle had been flawed, but the shippers blamed the bottlers and vice versa. Furthermore, since the plaintiff was a forty-eight-year-old bachelor, it was claimed that damages should be minimal, just as a solicitor would receive less for the loss of a hand than would a concert pianist.

It was all very silly, and I was grateful when Catkin interrupted me with a cup of tea. Only when I saw her did I realise how dark it had become. I grasped her hand and kissed it. She smiled and ruffled my hair.

'You've got a visitor,' she said. 'A very sad, very sweet old dear.'

'Cindy,' I said, suddenly sure.

'Yup. I've just given her a cup of tea because I thought you still had those clients up here. She seems very tired, but very together.'

'That's Cindy,' I grinned, and jumped to my feet. I reached automatically for the jacket on the back of the chair, thought better of it, and walked to the door. 'Oh, I do hope she's all right. Thank you, my love,' I said, and clattered down the spiral stairs.

I swung into Catkin's office and saw Cindy Abbott sitting in the only armchair. She sipped tea rather studiously and stared at an old *Country Life*. She was a short, stocky woman with a face of startling serenity. I always thought of her as plump, but she never had been. It was the general air of ready laughter and protectiveness, realism rather than cynicism, provincialism rather than rusticity, which padded her in the memory. Her hair, piled in a bun, was of pewter grey and she wore grey. Camouflage for the evening.

'Cindy,' I said softly. She looked up. Her eyes were wide and bloodshot, but she smiled. I took her hands and drew her to her feet. I kissed her on both cheeks. She wore too much powder.

'Poor girl,' I murmured, 'come on up and talk to me. It's

25

good to see you.'

'Good to see you,' she smiled and patted my arm. 'You're looking fit.'

'Surviving,' I said. 'Come on. Bring your tea with you.'

I followed her up the stairs, ushered her into the office and shut the door.

'Now, Cindy,' I said, 'tell me all about it and *do* tell me that I can do something. The news just came out of the blue.'

She folded her hands in her lap and looked down at them. 'It was quite a shock,' she said, 'and I'm hoping that you *can* help, or at least advise me. Trevor thought so much of you, even though he did think you were quite mad. He always said, you know –' she turned her head towards the window and set her face and her voice – 'he always said you'd die for loving life too much. He used to quote that song. "You may have been a headache, but you never were a bore", then he'd say, "Damn his eyes!" ' She laughed. 'Eh, but you did drive him wild sometimes.'

'Mmm,' I said, 'I know.'

'The way he died—' She stopped, blinking.

'So horrible . . .'

'The way he died was so very strange,' her voice continued in a dreamy monotone. 'He was on to something. He told me so, he told me that it was dangerous. He knew something like this was on the cards.'

'He knew?' I urged gently.

'Yes. He was on to something big in the prison. Trevor was killed for a good reason, for something he knew and was trying to tell us. It might have been something he'd discovered from another prisoner or maybe something about the system itself.

'Something worth killing a man for? Surely . . . Well, Cindy, I imagine that fights and vendettas are pretty common in prison.'

'Yes, but it wasn't that. Trevor could fit in anywhere. He liked the professional villains. He told me so at the beginning. He said that many of them had a rather splendid code of honour, and he admired their vigour. Anyhow, can you imagine Trevor making mortal enemies with anyone unless he knew of some injustice?'

No, I admitted, I could not, and injustices Trevor would surely have witnessed in a system not known for its Christian

26

virtues. But no officer would kill to protect that system.

Cindy rummaged in her shapeless black handbag. 'You see,' she went on, 'about four months ago, last July, it would be, he started to hint during visits that something was up. Then I got these letters, all excited, you know, but saying nothing because all the letters were censored, and he could only be vague. Look, look at this one.

' "My dearest love, I am back in the chase at last. This one's going to prove the fiercest quarry to date – and the biggest." And in this one . . . Where is it now?' She scanned another letter. ' "This is going to be tricky, Cindy. I'm so damned impotent in here. I cannot tell you anything, but this is the big one." You see?' She handed the letters over to me. 'You see he knew there was danger, yet the silly stubborn bugger could never keep his nose out of trouble once he was on to something. Here is the last letter that I got. There's a message in it for you.'

I took the letter from her. It was grubbier than the others, so I had no desire to read more than was necessary. I looked where she had pointed.

'There's a particularly laidly worm to be dug out and dealt with. Tell the boy then that this place is really worth a visit for these roses I've been working on, the old moss roses. He'll know how much they mean. He should see them next summer. It really is worth it. Si monumentum requiris, look at them.'

'Bloody hell,' I said.

'Does it mean anything to you?'

'Not a thing.'

'Nor me.'

We were both lying.

'He was allowed visits once every three weeks. At first, it was all right. We used to talk about home and that, and he seemed fine. Then a change came over him. They'd always put him at the table nearest to the security officers – at least, that's how it seemed to me. Maybe I was just getting paranoid. He was jumpy. He kept looking over his shoulder, and then suddenly he'd bang his fist on the table and curse out of sheer frustration. I knew that look. Eh, Sebastian, we've seen it enough times before, haven't we?'

'We have.' I smiled, remembering those fits of fury. 'When did you last see him, love?'

'Six weeks before he ran. Beginning of August, it must have been. We'd broken its back, you know, and we hadn't long to go. Not really long. And he was still all nervous and he said that he was going to have to do something dangerous, something that would worry me a bit. But I wasn't to get all worked up and so on. I argued with him, of course. Didn't know what he was on about, but I just begged him to wait till the sentence was over. I went on at him as I have done a thousand times, and he always came back at me with the same old line. Always.' She smiled and mouthed the words carefully. Her lip trembled. 'I could not love thee 'alf so much ...'

'Loved I not honour more,' I supplied gently. 'Stubborn as ever.'

'He was,' said Cindy in a lighter tone, 'he was, and I ended up accepting it, of course. Then letters stopped entirely and I didn't receive my visiting pass any more. There was complete silence. I rang the prison and they said they couldn't be accountable for the behaviour of inmates towards their families. So I rang the probation officer, and he said Trevor seemed all right and he'd seen him around, but that he was on the censor's list, which meant that he was a security risk for some reason. I was – bewildered. There he was not writing and I didn't know what to think. Well, I knew really, of course. I mean, I knew that he hadn't gone off me or anything, but everyone has their doubts, you know. I was just lost. I couldn't do anything.'

'And nor could he.'

She gulped. 'Then, mid-September, I heard he'd done it. He'd escaped. Absconded, they call it in open prisons. And I thought, Oh God, you know, he'll turn up on the doorstep and he'll have to go back. I was livid with him. We were so near the end, and we'd got through it together and then he had to go and do this. Apparently he'd got a bad letter or something and had just run off in the night. That's what they said, any road.

'I waited and waited. I didn't even dare to leave the house to go shopping or to church or anything. You just never knew when he was going to turn up. Of course, there was no publicity. There never is with absconders. They're two a penny in open prisons, I gather, and they always get caught and brought back.

'It was only last week that we knew how Trevor vanished so

completely. He just never left. He could have lain there forever, and no one would ever have known.'

She stopped her story and looked across the desk at me. For a moment she held my gaze. She gulped, she blinked, her shoulders shook. Suddenly her face crumpled like a burst balloon and she sobbed uncontrollably.

I walked round the desk and put an arm around her. It didn't help. It wasn't meant to. She cried with abandon because she'd been holding it in so long. For dignity's sake, for Trevor's sake, for survival's sake, she had curbed her grief over the past ten days, but now she let it go. Her body shuddered in my arms. She rocked her head from side to side. At last she had acknowledged that her man was dead.

At last, the juddering and whimpering stopped. She gulped for breath like a diver surfacing. 'I'm sorry, love, I'm sorry. I haven't done a thing like this to anyone, ever. I'm being silly.'

'No, you're not. You're doing what nature intended you should do to relax, and you're doing it with a friend. I'm very flattered.'

She looked up at me and gave a nervous little laugh. 'Just wait till them back home hear what I get up to in the smoke. Can I pinch your hanky? Don't know why women have such damned silly little things.'

She sat down again and trumpeted into the handkerchief. 'Eh,' she grinned, 'that's better.'

I walked over to the fireplace. 'Right, Cindy, what do you want me to do?'

'Well, I thought, you know, you being a lawyer, you might be able to make some enquiries, see if we can't get to the bottom of it all. It's only what Trevor would have wanted.'

'Oh, Cindy, Cindy, Cindy,' I sighed, 'if only the advocates and executives of the law had any connection with the law's victims or its consequences, God knows, we'd all retire and become probation officers. The prison service is the skeleton in the Home Office's cupboard, and a well-locked cupboard it is, too. They don't allow anyone, but anyone, to look upon that little world. I don't know much about it myself, but this much I have learned. The officers and executives are all bound by the Official Secrets Act, so only the prisoner is in a position to criticise anything which may occur in that system. And the prisoner loses remission if he complains while he's in and loses credibility when he's left. Anyhow, he cannot produce evidence to support his assertions because he's not allowed back in. Who's going to believe him? It's the sublime Catch 22.'

'Yes, but for God's sake, Sebastian, even the police have not conducted a full investigation. It's a vicious murder we're dealing with!'

'Indeed it is, my love, and the police have looked at Trevor's case and have said, "Here is a man living amongst violent men. He died violently. Since we have so many hundred proven criminals to question, any of whom could have done this thing, we give up." Anyhow, the police can't enter a prison without the governor's permission. A crown warrant cannot overrule the decision of Her Majesty's representative on Her Majesty's land. The governor and the Home Office have decided that further investigation will only mean further unrest, so that's that.'

'And a murder goes uninvestigated? That's not possible, Sebastian!' Cindy stood and walked over to the window. 'And anyhow, not any prisoner could have done it. According to the message I received yesterday, Trevor was leaving sometime after 3 a.m. At that time, although none of the convicts would find it difficult to climb through a window, they all are, or should be, safely in bed. The place is patrolled all night, and this flowerbed is slap bang in the middle of the prison. How long does it take to bury a human body three feet down?'

'Oh, Christ.' I said. 'And there again, why should Trevor be in that state in the first place? Why should he be trying to abscond at all?'

'Exactly,' said Cindy, 'I just can't get any answers. But if it was worth risking death for ...'

'It's worth our investigation. You're right, love. We'll have a go. Oh, dear,' I said suddenly, 'now I'm getting all crusading and ardent and it doesn't suit me at all. What to do, Cindy?'

'I was wondering if the law had no means ...'

'Regina v. Regina? Sorry, love, that won't do. We could try putting pressure on the Home Office, but if their people close ranks, it'll be like that famous flea climbing up the hind leg of an elephant, intent on rape. If they pull the Official Secrets Act on us, we'll just have to retire or end up there ourselves, for a lot longer than two years.'

30

I walked over to the desk and sat. 'Still,' I resolved, 'let's have a go.'

'Of course, it's quite useless.' I said, as I slid behind the table to my seat at The Capital. Bustling waiters pulled out chairs and spread out napkins, smoothed, soothed and smiled.

'It's totally useless. The Home Office will just tell me that any further investigation would be gratuitously harmful, and the Home Office will doubtless be right. So Trevor has given his life for nothing. Oh, hell, I'm getting annoyed about this. The more I think about it, the more frustrated I become. There's something rotten here, something more than a minor squabble between convicts.'

I ordered two negronis, and Verena bowed slightly to the waiter who handed her the menu. He recoiled and retired in blissful confusion. Few things ruffle Capital waiters, but Verena von Kauz, resplendent in Chloe satin breeches and a white lace shirt, just happened to be one of them.

'You mean to tell me,' she said, 'that no one can investigate the conduct of a major public service?'

'That's about it. Silly, isn't it? From what I can see, once a man is a prisoner, he can turn to no one. You know, we rely to an incredible extent on the Sunday newspapers, the law, this court, that court and finally, the sovereign. The convict just hasn't got them. He's totally alone. He may be beaten up, he may witness some gross injustice, and all that he's got with which to defend himself or others is his own body. If he complains, he loses remission. He's not allowed to write to the newspapers or anything, and they in turn aren't allowed to investigate his complaints. The accused is judge and jury and sole witness. What possible chance has the plaintiff?'

'It's absurd. Have you decided, Sebastian?'

'What? Oh, yes. The galantine of duck for me, with those lovely little sorrel things in puff pastry. They're marvellous.'

'Yes, but to start.'

'Oh. I'll have to think about that. Hold on a second. Ah, I'll have this turbot soufflé business. Sounds gorgeous. What about you?'

'First we have to get organised, otherwise you'll end up with nothing. I'm on the turbot, too, and then a partridge.'

'Right.' I raised a hand, but before it was above the table, two waiters were by my side.

'Sir?'

Sir gave his order, added another two negronis, a half bottle of Krug, and a bottle of Haut Batailly. Sir sat back content.

'I suppose, then,' Verena said, when the waiters had evaporated, 'that only another prisoner could possibly find out the facts of the case.'

'Another prisoner?'

'Well, yes. Do you know one?'

'No, no,' I hummed, 'but all the same . . .'

'You're going to do something about this, aren't you?' She was almost accusing.

'My dear, I don't see how I cannot. I mean, Trevor was a friend and he got his head bashed in and obviously thought it was worth risking, which makes it unlikely that this was a trivial matter in itself. I feel almost bounden, if you know what I mean.'

'I know what you mean,' she nodded. She sipped her negroni and sighed, 'I know what you mean. You always were bloody crazy.'

'Nice to see you, Verenchen.'

'Nice to see you.'

Well fed and suffused by a rosy glow, we stood on Chelsea Bridge and looked down the Thames. The lovely raised palazza of Battersea power station arose on our right, and further down, the soft, fleshy glow of the concrete South Bank complex.

Boats and barges cast out squibs of red and white light which cork-screwed in the water. I sighed. Verena, wrapped in fox, looked up at me. 'You're going to do it, aren't you?' she said.

'Damn you. I don't know what I'm going to do.'

'I do,' she said. 'I know, and I think it's mad.'

'There's nothing I can do.'

'We'll see,' she said quietly, 'we'll see.'

4

The Home Office's response was as expected. Enough had been done, and unless any concrete evidence were available, no further investigation would take place.

At El Vino's, I talked to Jack Drake, a tall, tough Australian journalist who had been Trevor's colleague on the *Daily Mail*, and now worked for the *Daily Meteor*. He too didn't understand how or why Trevor could have made a mortal enemy. He too was convinced that something was very wrong. He too could see no means of proceeding. And he, like me, did not like coming up against a brick wall.

'Trevor was such an easy-going bastard,' he frowned. 'And so damned devious. He could charm his way into anything and lie his way out.'

'I know,' I said, 'and he had that chameleon quality that you and I so evidently lack. It doesn't add up, Jack, it doesn't add up.'

Jack gnawed at his pipe stem and puffed heavily for a while. 'He more or less invited you to look into it, didn't he?'

'I can put no other interpretation on that last letter.'

'No. You can't do it, of course. None of us can. You've got your career to think of and, God knows, I'm past such things.'

I looked across at him. The discontented grunts and sighs which punctuated his speech had more to do with the condition of his lungs than with his vision of a world of which he had seen enough to weary a saint. And the steady intake of booze had veined his cheeks and his eyes. It would never kill a man of his size, but he was having a good go at it.

'So what can we do?' he went on. 'I mean it's probably only a matter of some small criminal organisation that the old boy blew up into something larger than it was.'

'They killed him all the same.'

'You know,' Jack spoke with sudden violence and slammed his glass down on the table, 'I have a hell of a lot of respect for the spirit of British law, but this bloody Official Secrets Act is absurd and bloody evil!'

'And so say white-papers and so say high court judges,' I sighed. 'The whole Act passed through all stages of Parliament in just twenty-four hours. A rush job to meet an emergency. The only reason that it remains on the books is that successive governments have found it useful in that they can save money without losing votes by shelving the problem of the prisons. Now things are so bad that no government can afford, in purely economic terms, to put them right. If that Act were now rescinded and the press and public could see our penal institutions, any government must spend several hundred million on reform – or fall.'

Jack shrugged. 'One really ought to go in there and see for oneself.'

'One ought, but who dares?'

'Not I, for one.'

'Nor I.'

Georgie Barnett, just released from Ravenhill, rang at Cindy's instigation. We arranged to meet on Georgie's home ground, the bar of the St James's tavern in Great Windmill Street. I arrived at seven on a rainy evening and stayed until ten, talking to Georgie about Trevor's behaviour in the last days before his attempted escape, about the conditions at Ravenhill, about the persecution to which Trevor had been subjected.

'Oh Christ, yes, they wound him up, all the fucking time. They get like that sometimes, particularly if someone doesn't fit in. You know, if he's had it easy on the out. That was the strange thing. The cons liked Trev. He fitted in, I mean. He adapted. He helped a lot of them, taught them to read and wrote letters for them and all that. They liked him. Of course, there was some who got at him, but he was a quiet guy, and had the right sort of friends – me, for one, and Dick, Dick Cramer. He was the baron in there at the time. We looked after him, I suppose.'

Georgie gulped his beer and licked foam from stubble. 'But then the screws started in on him. No reason. There's one cocky little shit called Forsdyke. He'd nick Trev for anything. Ten cons would walk by with their hands in their pockets and he'd pick out Trev. Fucking little shit. He'd nick him and put him on governor's and shove him in the block just for that. It's a marvel that Trev kept his cool, but he did, somehow. I'd have put an 'ole in the little creep if he'd treated me like that, and I'd have got a fistful – that's five years – for the privilege. That's what they're always hoping for, of course.'

When at last I got up to leave, Georgie said, 'Oh, by the way, kid, you might like to know that Trev mentioned you quite a few times in there. Whenever there was an appeal to be sorted out for someone, he'd say he wished you was around. I offered to get a bent letter out for him that last week. He wanted to get in touch with you. It would've been easy, but he said no, it would be like wiring us both up to a bomb and he couldn't do it.'

'Thank you,' I said softly. 'Thank you very much. I'll see you, Georgie. Good luck.'

'Night.' He got up to order another pint. 'Take care!'

It was raining, and the pavements spat back at the sky. I turned towards Piccadilly. I did not put up the umbrella. The rain refreshed me. I felt hot and worried. I was glad of the cool.

I was running before I was even aware of the cause. A deep, slow roar, all too familiar, had rocked the pavement beneath my feet. I ran towards the source of the sound. Neon tits and price tags flashed by. Tired eyes turned to watch. It was closer than I had thought, and as I swung into the little side street, I saw that it was almost empty.

Wet pavements crackled like tinfoil, and now there was glass crunching too. Smoke poured from an Italian restaurant on my right. It heralded a stream of people who almost ran me down. They felt their way like blind men.

Some of them were.

They sobbed and groaned; people dressed up for the night, men's suits in tatters, women in blood-spattered silk.

I barged past a couple of men who were struggling in the doorway, pulled out my handkerchief and shoved it to my nose. It was like deep-sea diving. Occasional clear images drifted into view and were covered again by a layer of smoke. The smell was of thyme and tomatoes, but there was something else too. A deep, sweet, cloying smell which made a rock barge into my pelvic cavern.

Everywhere tables were overturned, chairs shattered. Sprinkled glass glistened in the half-light like a Hollywood treasure chest. The kitsch reproductions and red gingham table-cloths were now like beggars' rags. On the tiled floor, two people lay.

I knelt. The woman lay still. Her high-collared dress shimmered in the growing light. So did the stuff which now adorned it. I fumbled with the buttons at her neck. They popped off under my clumsy hands. I listened for the sound of breathing, felt for the carotid pulse and sat back with a sigh. She was alive.

My hand ran down her body. I don't know why. Maybe some sort of consolatory caress. My hand stopped.

She was alive, but she wouldn't be kicking again. Both legs were smashed to Osso Bucco just below the hips, and blood pumped out rhythmically.

I gagged. I'm not very good at this sort of thing. Most men say they know a lot about living when they've seen a lot of men die. I can do without it.

Cursing to keep my courage, I raised her hips with their scraggy appendages onto a chair. It was the only thing I could think of.

I turned away and crawled on my knees towards the man so close beside her. For a moment, I considered artificial respiration, took one more look at the wounds which stretched from the stinking, smoking intestines which slopped from a gash in his shirt, to dismembered feet, and decided against it. Nature's got a neat solution for problems like those.

People shouted in the street. Sirens blared. There were others in the room.

Suddenly I saw a pair of legs propping open the door marked 'Cloakrooms'. They were nice legs. They were slim, white legs, splayed like those of a weary whore. I got up and stumbled over.

She was about fifteen. A Laura Ashley print and some cheap grey eyeshadow were still just discernible. She was alive, and I could find no serious injuries. None, save a face peppered and twisted by nails, an eye bubbling almost black blood, and dark hair clogged with blood as thick as syrup.

36

I said, 'Easy, girl, steady now, whoah there,' and cursed my vocabulary. She reached out and grasped my sleeve. 'You'll be OK, girl,' I said, holding her forearm tight. 'You'll be OK, love.'

'What is it? What is it?'

'A bomb, my love.' For some reason I was whispering, which wasn't helping anyone.

'Oh.'

'But you're going to be OK.'

'It's my birthday.'

'Happy birthday.'

'Is Johnny all right?'

If he was, I didn't want to meet him. I said, 'I think so. We'll go and see.'

'What about Mum and Dad?'

'We'll go and see. You should be looking after them.'

'All right, sir, we'll take over,' said a voice behind me. I turned. An ambulance man stood over me. I wanted to hit him. I wanted to hit anyone. Policemen were searching the place now, tipping the tables back up, kicking over debris, swearing. One of them came over, a look of weariness on his face.

'Thank you so much for your help, sir,' he said gently. 'I think you'd better get out now. There may be another. You never know ...'

'OK,' I said. 'You'll need my card. I was just passing by ...'

I walked out into a street which seemed extraordinarily bright. Absently, I wandered through the cordon and the wide-eyed crowd which parted before me as if I were touched by a curse.

Only when I had been walking for five minutes or more did I realise why. My suit was sticky with blood which coloured the puddles at my feet. Usually I'm with T.E.L. The mastery of your sensibilities in the face of death does give you a kick, just as does the mastery of fear. But in London in 1976, or maybe just in the heart of Sebastian Foy, something was wrong. I just felt dirty and sick.

'The bastards,' I kept whispering to myself. 'The dirty, stinking, cowardly bastards. I could kill the lot of them.'

Other people felt the same way.

*　　　　*　　　　*

'Sebastian, my boy,' boomed Sir James, 'I have done everything I know how. There's just no point in continuing. Damn it, I liked Trevor, and I'd like to know what happened, but it could be so many things that he had found out. He might just have discovered the truth about some case in which an innocent man was imprisoned. That would be enough to get him going and, if it were a gang business, they'd have killed him to stop him from revealing it.'

'Then why wouldn't he have gone on the Forty-Threes?'

'On the what?'

'The Forty-Threes. Rule 43 states that any prisoner may place himself under the governor's protection. It means solitary confinement in a closed prison, but Trevor had only a month more to do. He could have coped. The sex-offenders apparently have to serve all their time on the Forty-Threes or else they'd be torn apart.'

'I know, God save us. We're a barbarous race. Maybe Trevor couldn't stand the idea of solitary confinement. One taste of closed prison is enough to put a man off for life. Or maybe he knew that he still wouldn't be safe, if they wanted him badly enough.'

I shook my head. 'It won't do, it won't do at all. Trevor was well aware that men like Charlie Lowe are on the Forty-Threes, and when it says protection it means protection.'

'Lowe? Ah, he was the police informer.'

'The "supergrass". Half the underworld has sworn to kill him, and there are two contracts out for his death, one worth £10,000 and one worth £15,000. More than worthwhile for a man serving life to earn £25,000 for his family. But Lowe is still alive. Trevor knew that.'

'All right, Sebastian, all right. Has it crossed your mind, then, that Trevor might have gone round the twist? It's common enough in prison. God knows, he was already half mad. His obsession with injustice was pathological.'

'True, but—'

'And then he gets sent to prison, is subject to all the violent shocks that accompany a stay in a closed prison, and gradually becomes convinced that he's got another story, that everyone's getting at him, that he has an important secret which must be revealed. According to your account, he displayed all the classic symptoms of paranoia. There was nothing rational about his behaviour, as you have already admitted.'

I acknowledged the possibility. Maybe Trevor had imagined the whole thing. Maybe Georgie Barnett was not sufficiently astute to see when a man was cracking up. Maybe Cindy saw only one aspect of a schizophrenic on those visits – but still the question remained, why had he been killed?

'A mistake?' suggested Sir James. 'Another prisoner might have been where he shouldn't be, heard Trevor coming in the dark, thought he was a warden and cracked him on the head, only to discover that he'd killed Trevor.'

'There were multiple contusions. It's clear that Trevor was in a fight.'

'So they thought that Trevor was a "grass" and that he'd report what he'd seen.'

'Clutching at straws, J.C. No, you may be right. It may be a series of accidents and coincidences that led to Trevor's death, but I just cannot see it. If it was any ordinary threat, Trevor could have gone on the Forty-Threes or got his friends to deal with it. If it was madness, then why did his crazed fantasy come true?'

'Damn you for a fool,' said Sir James. 'I find it difficult enough to work up your enthusiasm for a client's case when we can do something, and as soon as there's a case where nothing can be done, you become obsessed and maudlin about it. Trevor Abbott is dead. For God's sake, man, let him lie.'

But Verena had been right. Trevor had thought it worth his life. It must be worth some effort.

She'd been right on another score too. I needed a purpose. The empty nights of drunkenness and chatter were slowly eating me away. The bitterness and hurt made my brain feel cold and shrunken to the size of a walnut. I longed for peace. But peace was a long way away. Shooting in Scotland perhaps, or dancing at Grosvenor House. Cavorting at cocktail parties – or lying in another man's arms whispering the same lovely liturgy. She was a dream, and I could not sleep.

Maybe Trevor had died for no reason, but it was time that I made a break.

5

Monday: I saw Fiona today. A bit of Fiona. An aspect, that is, which I always admired in the old days; rippling water turned to ice and seeming brilliantly translucent. In fact, you could look in deep and see nothing but your own reflection. I admired it because I knew that I could dive there and find no resistance, could swim and play and splash there, free. It is now the cruellest insult in the world. Mix metaphors. The storm rages at my back and I stand at the door of my own home, without the key.

I knew, of course, that she would be there. I should have been prepared. Damn it, I've spent the last six weeks in telling myself how little I have cause to care, in branding her as every sort of fickle, mindless bitch. I'm a convincing speaker, but you need an open-minded audience.

Because, when she walked into that clinking, purring room in Dolphin Square and sauntered from guest to guest, a firework display of dazzling smiles and flickering eyes and darling, how are yous and humming kisses, my stomach twisted and shrank like plastic in the fire. Every part of her was a relic and was sacred to one purpose. Those lips that parted and pouted as she leaned to greet admiring twits from army or city, the hands that flicked back the black bang of hair above her eyes, the thighs which shifted under rose satin, all were mine, and in seconds I hated her with all the love which my body could muster.

We didn't see one another, of course, for ten minutes or so, but at last I tore myself from a twittering temp with a baby doll ribbon in her hair. Fiona was chattering to a chalk-striped city smoothie with two chins and no chin.

'Darling,' she smiled as I approached, 'how are you? Oh, it *is*

40

lovely to see you. Robin, this is Sebastian Foy, a very old, very dear friend. Sebastian, Robin um.'

Her long left hand rested on my forearm. She offered her cheek for a kiss. It was one of those kisses which, had I been a stranger, would have indicated that I was doing all right. Just enough warmth.

'Darling,' I said, more for Robin Um's benefit than for anyone else's.

She said, 'Now Sebastian, you must tell me what dreadful things you've been up to.'

'Surviving.'

'Not so dreadful. I'm glad, though.'

'How about you?'

'Oh, everything's perfect, darling. Couldn't be better. I've never been so busy.'

'Doing what?'

'Oh, you know, parties and things.'

'Things' reached me. I need no Iago. 'You're better then?' I said.

'Better?'

'You were clearly unwell when I last saw you. A little hysterical, irrational, you know.'

'Sebastian.' Still she smiled, but coldly now. 'Please. There was nothing wrong with me, I can assure you. I was perfectly rational.'

A whole list of resentful adolescent jibes seethed within me, but I just shrugged and forced myself to smile. 'I'm sorry,' I said softly, 'I just . . .'

'Don't, Sebastian. You must have got it together by now.'

'As I said, I survive. That's all. When can I see you, Fiona?'

'You're seeing me now.'

'No, really see you. Without the mob.'

'What's the point, my love? It'll only make things worse.'

'For God's sake, there's every point. We know one another, we love one another. If nothing else, it's such a waste. There isn't a particle of you that I don't know, remember and want.'

'Coward,' she said, unable to resist the old game.

'Same to you.'

'Don't say any more, you're making me cry so dreadfully,' she supplied. In a breezy tone with a brilliant smile.

41

'Meeting like this, full of social propriety, as though we were total strangers ...'

'Do we really know each other, Sebastian?' She was colder now. 'I mean, you don't really know me. We had a lot of fun and talked a lot of nonsense, and it was wonderful while it lasted, but ...'

She knew this dismissive summary to be the most unkindest cut of all and she looked away as she talked. With another attempt at a smile, I tried to draw her back to the game. 'Perdition catch my soul, but I do love thee, and when I love thee not, chaos is come again.'

'A bloody sight more suitable choice of play, but it's nonsense. It's just the green-eyed monster once again.'

'Is there cause?'

'Why ask questions when you don't want to know the answer?'

I drained my glass and shuddered. 'You're right. You're right.'

I looked then into her eyes. She is no coward. She met my gaze. For a second, as through a camera-shutter clicking, I saw, and she knew that I saw and she breathed in deep as though to hold the moment. Her lashes lowered over softer eyes, she said, 'Sebastian', and turned on her heel. I let her go.

It just feels a little bit colder than ever, that's all.

Tuesday:

Late into work because of this girl Belinda who came back with me after the Dolphin Square fiasco. She kept losing things and simpering into her cornflakes.

What strange vanity makes me continue the futile pursuit? I know full well that second-rate substitutes will do nothing to help me forget her. I know that at four o'clock in the morning, their skin will begin to burn me, and the tiny flaws of their flesh will grow before my eyes into gaping cicatrices. Then I have to get up, wrap myself in a dressing-gown and sit at my desk, drinking the passion down. Dirty girls are all right, and those quick tussles which know no *moral* victory. There's no risk of confusion there. But once let her image cross my mind, and the frenzy starts to mount again. Violence is its only natural conclusion, but to whom should I do violence? To her, whom I

42

love? To some man whom she may or may not have in her bed and whom I can scarcely blame? To myself? Take the easy road to Lethe, Foy, and do no harm.

Vile day. Pouring as if they'd been storing the stuff throughout the drought. The Christmas decorations in the shop windows shed light on evening pavements, streets like effervescent treacle. Run for a taxi and home, glowing and panting to tea and whisky and Debussy and the rain on the windows. Tears in a bloodshot eye. Leave it out, Foy. It's past.

Tamasin's party, Chester Terrace this evening. Very late 'sixties, self-conscious decadence. The compulsory black dykes, slinky transvestites, ex-cons, a couple of erstwhile rock stars etc., and a dark girl who told me she was Ava Gardner but I'm told she's some sort of singer. She had a sherbert fountain full of coke with which to keep up my stamina. And her's. Thanks. Can hardly walk and have frozen scampi for tonsils.

Wednesday:
I found an extraordinary note on the kitchen jotter this morning. Suppose I scribbled it smashed last night. 'The mute could not tell her that he loved her, so he carved it in her too-white skin.' Must mean something.

Verena telephoned to know what was happening about Trevor. Bloody good question.

Dined Imogen tonight. Imo gorgeous as always. Far too good and bright and beautiful to have a place in this diary. Went on alone to a seamy Soho dive so as not to have to return home sober and alone. Groped a few hostesses and got rooked for a fortune.

Thursday;
This Trevor business is really haunting me. Did he really expect me to follow him? All responses to my enquiries have been identical. 'What do you expect *us* to do?' Prison is as hush-hush as the Intelligence Services. Too bad. Forget it. No chance.

I'd be frustrated enough by it in any case, but why did the old fool have to make things worse by involving me? There's one hell of a riddle to be solved here, but playing amateur detective isn't as easy as I thought.

A quiet dinner at home, then down to the club for a game of pool. No energy. Early bed.

Friday:
A good day at work. J.C. wasn't there, so I had to appear for him. Catkin and I talked about Trevor at lunch.

I went to the opening of a pretty ghastly exhibition of West Coast 'sculpture'. Lots of velvet-voiced culture-mongers and actresses who want to be valued for their minds. Lots of champagne. There was this slim, bronzed, blonde girl in white called Toni and she's got long, long legs and green eyes and a lovely smile. She's Californian and owns her own gallery in Geneva. She's good news. We went out to dinner and I told her about Trevor. Poor thing, she'd never heard of the man until 8 o'clock in the evening and now she knows everything – or, at any rate, as little as I.

Saturday;
Sandown races. Toni came with me. It was good to see the old clan again. Saw Jack Drake who said he should have been covering a story miles away for the *Meteor*. We talked about Trevor. Edward was there. Haven't seen him for months, but that never seems to make any difference with old friends. Back to Lambourn for drinks afterwards. Ended up having a bloody silly row with Edward about nothing, abusing him and storming out. I suppose that means more apologetic postcards. Why is it always my best friends?

A nice peaceful evening with Toni. We discussed Trevor, hypothesised as to what might have happened. No joy. Toni goes back tomorrow morning. She's great.

Sunday;
Lie-in till eleven, then packed Toni off. Up to the Scarsdale for Sunday lunch, and got involved in an impassioned political discussion. They just cannot see beyond the ordained terms and values of the time. Got fed up with the lot of them and came back home. Thought. Sort of. No prizes for guessing the subject. There cannot be, there must not be, a citizen beyond the guardianship of the law. Damn the positivists. No politician can have a mandate to enact statutes which transgress the very

natural law whereby he is elected. He is democratically entrusted with power *within the limits* of a democratic system.

> *Let not tomorrow then ensue today;*
> *Be not thyself; for how art thou a king,*
> *But by fair sequence and succession?*

I wanted to sort it all out with someone, so rang Catkin in the hope that she might come round. No reply. She's gallivanting. Everyone's gallivanting. Momentary bout of self-pity. A moment long enough for a hell of a lot of whisky to find its way from the bottle to the region of my complaining guts. My health's going fast. Woke up on the sofa feeling impotent. In all respects.

Someone's got to do it. I suppose it might as well be me.

6

Keep thinking, keep talking, keep pacing. Don't stop for an instant, for that way madness lies. *King Lear*. William Shakespeare, 1614? Can't remember. Poor naked wretches wheresoe'r you are. No. I'd done that one. I'd also recited 'To His Coy Mistress', ten Shakespeare sonnets and 'Harmonie du Soir' six times. 'The Owl and the Pussycat'. Good idea. Funny accent for the owl and the pig. 'Dear pig, are you willing to sell for one shilling your ring?' Said the piggy, 'I will' . . . So this is sensory deprivation. Plain white walls. Shining white. No window, no furniture save a board on one wall and a loo in the corner. No seat and it doesn't flush. They can only keep me here for twenty-four hours. Habeas Corpus. Magna Carta, 1215. Nonsense. They've already held you for thirty and they couldn't give a damn. If any questions were asked, they could always plead the Prevention of Terrorists Act. That gives them carte blanche for seventy-two hours. Oh, Christ! Let them come soon.

Nobody knows where you are. Fool, why didn't you tell someone first? Statutory right to a solicitor. 'Balls,' said the policeman. Statutory right to a doctor. 'Balls,' said the policeman. So much for Judges' Rules. How often have you rung that bell? All yesterday, most of last night, demanding, demanding, demanding.

'I demand a solicitor.'

'Fuck off!'

'I demand to see my doctor. I've been receiving therapy and am endangered—'

'Fuck off, I told you.'

46

'You're not entitled to hold me any longer without charging me.'

'Are you making trouble son? Are you? We'll tell you what you're entitled to – and I don't see your friends around the place, do you?' Now they'd switched off the bell at the mains. I was, to all intents and purposes, buried alive. I might stay here forever, and on one would know. No cigarettes, no matches, no belt, no tie, no shoes. You might do yourself an injury. Foy, you're crazy. I know, I know.

And last night when I'd tried to sleep, it had been their turn. Every half hour or so the light had come on, the door had rattled. 'Yes?' A numb, nagging pain at the back of the brain.

'Just making sure you're all right.' You could scream and yell and cry and curse and still there would be no response. I knew. I'd tried it. So you just kept pacing and forcing the mind to work, giving it something to do, because if you didn't, it invented something for itself. It invented pictures on the white walls and other people in the tiny cell. It invented policemen with sweet smiles on their faces and knives in their hands. And men with white hair lay on the bench beside you, their dry white hair caked with blood and their heads beaten to a pulp.

Fiona.

For Christ's sake, where was she? 'I wonder who's kissing her now. I wonder who's showing her how ...' No, no, don't. The thought is a sheer white streak of flame. Something else. Quickly, before the horror gains control. Translate Ad Pyrrham into good modern English. 'What slender youth soused in scent is making love to you amidst the roses?' Damn, damn, damn!

Sit down, think. Laugh a little. After all, it is funny. Sebastian Foy, MA – educated Eton and Trinity, Cambridge, man about town and latterly barrister – is sitting in the police cells in a suburb of Birmingham and is shortly to be charged with a variety of crimes ranging from deception to behaviour liable to cause a breach of the peace. That'll go down a wow in Dolphin Square et al. Will I be banned from the Royal Enclosure? Or the Pitt? Hope not.

It was funny. And it had been fun while it lasted. Writing out an Inland Revenue Giro for £5,350 rather then £53.50, cashing it and distributing the money in the streets. I shouldn't have ridden my motor-bike through the Bull Ring, scattering ten pound notes the while, but it had been fun. And the faces of the young lovers in the Bull Ring. They had been worth it. 'Good morning, my dears. Have £500 and for heaven's sake, don't go round confessing. Yes, of course it's stolen, but then it was stolen back, so that's all right.' Marvellous what Clicquot can do for you. And that girl in New Street. 'Good morning, and thank you for smiling so beautifully. Have £200.' She had shrieked with delight and run for her life. I grinned. I should do that sort of thing more often.

A bang and a clatter of keys. My door. Thank God. I wondered if they'd yet connected me with Mr. Foy of the false Giro. So far as this lot were concerned, I was Simon Smith of Scarborough, with a coarse Yorkshire accent to match.

'All right. Come on. We'll have a word with you now.'

The officer was tall and slender and no more than thirty. He wore a sharp grey suit, a pink shirt and a pinkish patterned tie. He also wore a complacent smirk which made me feel sick. He knew that no one could touch him. For the time being.

I was led down the corridor of cells to another barred door. Again keys clanged and scraped in the keyhole, then we were through. Along one white corridor, then another, seemingly endless, we walked. 'Right. In there,' said the officer. 'Sit down.'

I sat. Another plain white room. A desk, a chair, a filing cabinet. How did the police avoid hallucinations? Maybe they didn't.

'Right, Mr. Smith. We're going to have to wait a moment until – ah, here he is. This is Detective Constable Thompson. My name is Chadwick, Detective Constable.'

The new policeman's image was rather different. He wore the uniform smirk, but his checked shirt and tweed suit denoted that he was more interested in becoming chief constable than in imitating Starsky or Hutch for the benefit of admiring cadets. A precise black moustache jerked over his lips.

'Right, Mr. Smith,' said Chadwick, 'we've given you the standard warning. We want to discuss exactly what you thought you were doing yesterday morning. You can either co-operate, in which case we will co-operate and you'll be able to go home tonight, or else you can be difficult, in which case we become difficult and you have to stay for the weekend. It's all the same to us.'

'Oh, I'll co-operate,' I said, 'provided of course that I have my solicitor.' My assumed Yorkshire accent tended to come and go a bit.

A deep sigh, a nod, a grin exchanged by the two policemen. 'We cannot get hold of a solicitor on a Friday afternoon,' said Chadwick softly. 'We would like to be able to release you on bail tonight but of course, if you want to wait till Monday ...'

So this was how it was done. A hundred times I had instructed clients not to make a statement in any circumstances. Ninety times they had done so. It was all very well telling a man that he could not be held forever, but when he is totally alone and his mind is numbed by the cold white of the walls, by sleeplessness, by filth, by the stench of the police cells, he only hears one voice in his brain. It's whispering, 'Get out!'

I considered the situation. They were entitled to hold me over the weekend without reference to Habeas Corpus if I was arrested on a Friday. I had been arrested on a Thursday, but I somehow fancied that that might not appear in the police records. Three more days and nights in that hell-hole and still no means of getting in touch with the world outside. I could not, I must not make a statement. I was committed now.

'I find your methods curious, not to say pernicious, and it is evident that you have never heard of Judges' Rules,' I said at last, 'but, very well, we will discuss the situation. What do you want to know?'

'Why did you do it, Mr Smith?'

'Why did I do what, Mr Chadwick?'

'Why did you steal a motor-bike from London, ride it to Birmingham, distribute money all over the town and throw a brick through the Council Office's windows?'

'For fun. I was drunk.'

'Are you aware that you endangered life by so doing?'

'Scarcely. I never drove faster than twenty-five miles per hour.'

'That we will leave for the judge to decide. About the money, Mr Smith ...?'

'Yes?'

'Where did it come from, Mr Smith?'

'I can't remember,' I said.

'How much was there?'

'Just over five thousand pounds.'

'And you can't remember where it came from.'

'No. Have you got any of it back?'

'Fifteen pounds so far, Mr Smith.'

'Good on 'em,' I murmured.

'What?'

'Nothing.'

'If you don't remember where that money came from, fairly soon, Mr Smith,' said Thompson, 'we might just lose our tempers, and that's something we don't want to do.'

'That's something you're not allowed to do.'

'I wouldn't try telling us what we're not allowed to do, Mr Smith. We get a lot of clever boys in here, Mr Smith. None of them wins.'

'I'm not very surprised,' I said, 'if you can keep them for as long as you like contrary to the fundamental tenets of British law.'

'What about that money, Mr Smith?'

'What about it?'

'Where did it come from?'

'The Post Office. That's right, I remember. The Post Office!'

'You have an account at The Post Office?' snapped pink-shirt.

'No.'

Pink-shirt nodded to Thompson. Thompson nodded to pink-shirt. Pink-shirt got up and walked behind me. 'We've got to get to the bottom of this, Mr Smith, and we haven't much time.' He leaned over the back of the chair. A whiff of some scent the same colour as his shirt came to my nostrils. 'People just don't give away money like that, do they, Mr Thompson?'

'Not unless it's stolen' said Thompson.

'Stolen,' the voice went on softly at my ear. 'Ah yes, stolen, from the Inland revenue, perhaps, by means of a forged Giro cheque addressed to someone else. A Giro cheque addressed to the same person from whom you stole the motorbike, one Mr Foy of Montpelier Square.'

Thompson leaned back with an assured smile. He crossed his legs and his hands. Clearly he expected some reaction. I smiled back. 'Sebastian Foy? Good friend of mine actually.'

50

'You wouldn't like us to check on that, would you?'

'Yes, please do. Have you got his number? 01-235-2—'

Suddenly there was a rush of air and I dropped. Chadwick had kicked the chair out from under me. As I landed, I saw the foot rise again. I ducked and rolled. The shoe caught me on the right shoulder. Caught me a hard, jarring blow. Then I was being pulled up by my shirtfront. With one movement, Chadwick propelled me across the room and slammed my body against the wall. The air was forced out of me and my hair fell before my eyes.

But, confusedly, I saw the grey shoulder drop and Chadwick's fist went hard and fast into my solar plexus, low down. I retched up the last gob of air and had to go down.

I twisted and fell sideways. I was damned if I was going to give the constable the pleasure of placing a knee in the way of my jaw as I doubled up.

I hit the floor again and jackknifed, clutching my stomach and gasping for breath. The air came back in heavy gulps like water. I had better play my only ace.

'I am ...I *am* Sebastian Foy,' I said, resuming my usual accent.

'Oh, sure,' said Chadwick, breathing heavily through gritted teeth. 'Sure, that's why you're here.' Again he grabbed a handful of my shirt and pulled me up against the wall. He shoved his face towards me. 'Look here, clever boy,' he said, 'we get enough shit poured on us, and we haven't got much patience left. You can say what you like about police brutality, but if that's the way we can protect the public, then that's the way they're going to be protected, and I'll whip the clever shit out of you if I have to. Got it?' This time the smell of his after-shave was mixed with sweat. It didn't improve it.

'Hold it!' said Thompson. 'Hold hard, Bill. You are Sebastian Foy, you say? Would you care to prove it to us?'

'Would you tell me how I can?' I panted. 'I disposed of all means of identification ...'

'What about your clothes, shoes—?'

'Hold on,' I said. I reached down and pulled down my socks. I thanked God for the diligence of old nannies. A Cash's name-tape still bore my name and school-number, 'Foy, S.B., 103'.

'There you are,' I pointed, triumphant, 'satisfied?'

'Bloody hell,' said Thompson. 'Check it out, Bill.'

Chadwick snarled and stormed from the room. I picked up the chair again and sat. Thompson and I looked away from one another like Englishmen on a train.

Chadwick returned after five minutes. He slammed the door behind him and said 'Fuck!'

'We're in the shit, Bill.'

'Well, it's not my fucking fault, is it? If the little sod plays games ...'

'That's enough, Bill, for Christ's sake. Sit down.' He turned to me. 'Look, Mr. Foy, I hope you'll realise that for certain sorts of professional criminal, these are the only efficacious methods and that at certain times our patience runs, shall we say, a little thin?'

'Shall we say,' I answered pleasantly, 'that you are paid public servants for just one purpose, which is to keep your patience, and that, good money or no, you occupy a position of trust and considerable privilege which you choose to abuse. Shall we say that, even if I were to have raped your daughter, it would be your business, your duty, not only to retain control, but to protect me, or that otherwise you have no place in the police force?'

'That's going a little too far,' said Thompson.

'Is it? I don't think so. Furthermore, I deplore the way in which you kow-tow to me because of what I represent. At least if you're going to be savage and moronic, be consistently and sincerely so. Anyhow, I *am* Sebastian Foy. Sir James Crashaw will be informed of your interrogation methods and he will inform such members of the establishment as he sees fit. All right? Now, you have a job to do. I am prepared to make a short statement. Are we ready?'

'Hold it, Mr. Foy,' said Thompson, 'if we did as you say, we'd never get statements from half the murderers, thieves and rapists that we get in here, and they'd probably never even get convicted. It's all very well saying that the end doesn't justify the means, but our end is the protection of society ...'

'Of one aspect of society.'

'Maybe,' he stood, 'maybe. But that aspect is the peace of society as a whole. From there on, provided that peace is assured, society can sort out its own ideological problems. Yes, we should be "nice", but the criminal shows no mercy to his victims and will show none if we let him go. Is it the letter or the principle of the law that we uphold? You want us to be good village bobbies, symbols of all things bright and beautiful, never harming a soul? I wish to God we could be. But we protect a country's peace by war, so how in hell are we going to protect the security of the fictional man in the street save by using terms that he understands?' He stopped and hit his thigh with a sheaf of papers. 'Well,' he sighed, 'I suppose you know the procedure.'

'I think so,' I said wearily. 'Just give me a cigarette, a match, a statement form and a pen in that order.'

It was done, faster than the cigarette lighters had been produced at The Capital just three weeks before. I lit the cigarette and drew deep upon it. The world spun deliciously, vertiginously, as the smoke curled around my brain. I sat back, irresolute. This was the moment of truth.

Thus far, I had been playing a game, the sort of game for which soldiers get medals. I had been playing an heroic part, for the sake of something to do. I tried to separate my motives, the desire for self-respect and the genuine concern as to the cause of Trevor's death. It was impossible.

All that I need do now was to write a full confession and then plead guilty in court, and in the circumstances, I'd still get off Scot free. 'Strain began to tell. Mr. Foy was drunk. Years of treatment for manic depression. Temporary insanity.'

Conditional discharge, and my career finished.

Maybe it was vanity. I sometimes think that all acts of courage are inspired by nothing more. I'd sooner die than admit to anyone that I'd taken an overdose and changed my mind. I had started this absurd quixotic business, and I reckoned there was no going back. I was going for a holiday.

Very carefully, I wrote:

'I, Sebastian Barclay Foy, of 139 Montpelier Square, only son of the late Major Roderick Foy and Lady Caroline Foy of Redway Park, Cirencester, Glos., refuse to make any statement to the police as to my activities on December 9, 1976. Any further statement which may be offered in evidence, be it in question and answer form or in that of supposed dictation, will be a police fabrication, for henceforth I claim my right to remain silent.'

This I signed, dated, and handed to Chadwick. He read it, coloured and sneered, 'I suppose you think you can push us around just because you're some kind of toffee-nosed, high-class poofter.'

'It was not my decision that you should stop hitting me, my dear,' I said, 'and if you wish to continue to do so, I can see nothing which could possibly prevent you. So who's class-conscious, Mr. Chadwick? You can either keep me here against the law and face the consequences, or you can charge me and release me. Well?'

'We could oppose bail.'

'On what grounds? You'd scarcely satisfy a magistrate that I was likely to commit further offences since my record is totally clean, and as for prejudicing the course of my trial, I don't very well see how I could do that, since you caught me red-handed and I'd have to bribe half the anonymous people of Birmingham who witnessed my offences.'

'Release him, Bill. We're not going to get any further here.'

'All bloody right,' drawled Chadwick, his Brummy accent absurdly exaggerated in a bid to identify himself with a class. 'We let him go.'

They led me down further corridors and up the stairs to the charge-room. It was a gloomy room, well suited to its purpose. There was a floor of dark-red pocked linoleum and a high desk above which there hung a solitary light, an uncovered bulb. It cast a dome of light in the middle of the gloom. In the dome stood a sergeant who read an interminable list of charges, first to a group of young football enthusiasts, then to me. Fraud, deception, dangerous driving, driving whilst under the influence, malicious damage, criminal trespass and one or two more. I stood still before my accuser and said nothing. I heard the voice of Dr. Loring at law-school: 'Remember, the police are omnipotent, for in almost every action of your life, you are guilty of a technical trespass. Think of any set of circumstances in which you might be charged with a criminal offence, and I will find you another ten charges, to all of which you will have to plead guilty and all of which carry prison sentences. I challenge you ...'

The sergeant concluded his monologue, and Chadwick led me into a little back room. He started rolling black ink onto a tray. 'Right,' he said, 'we've got to get two perfect sets of prints of each finger in their proper places on this sheet. Here, give me your hand.'

I shuddered, removed my coat, and rolled up the sleeves of my much-abused shirt. Dawlish sighed and waited. I held out my hand.

'Right. Don't move, just relax and let the fingers roll as I push them.' He flattened my pads on the ink and rolled my fingers.

'Right thumb,' he sang, and rolled the thumb in the suitable square on the paper. 'Don't worry about your lily-white hands, Mr. Foy. It comes off with a bit of scrubbing.'

'Thank you so much, Mr. Chadwick,' I said.

My belt, tie and shoes were returned to me, then my wallet, my keys, my cigarette case and lighter. I flicked the lighter a couple of times. Fiona. Damn you, Foy, for a soft-hearted, dedicated fool.

'Well, then, Mr Foy, you're free to go now. I think you know the procedure. You'll have to be at the magistrates' court at ten o' clock on Wednesday for extension of bail.'

'Very well, I will be there.' I straightened my tie and turned to leave. Suddenly a thought crossed my mind. I turned back to Chadwick and spoke softly: 'Mr. Chadwick, I do not like to use undue influence, but in the circumstances I feel compelled to do so. I do not wish to spend several months on bail just waiting, and my case is not a complex one. Now, I could inform some important people of your behaviour in the course of our conversation today. Most of the people that you thrash in there cannot complain because no one will believe them and it only harms their case. I can promise you, however, that my word, despite all this, yet inspires some credence. Wait, Mr. Chadwick,' I raised my hand, 'wait until I have finished. Now, little as I like such deals, and much as I would like to see you suspended from the force, I am prepared to overlook the incident if you and Mr. Thompson will expedite my case. And don't say you can't because you damned well can. It's up to you how long you keep us sweating.'

'Bloody upper-class fuckers,' said Chadwick, weary rebel.

'All bloody right, I'll see it's done quickly. You'll get time, you know.'

'Yes,' I smiled, 'of course I know. That's why I did it, actually. Goodbye, Mr. Chadwick.'

Chadwick gaped at me as I moved towards the door. 'Well, fuck me sideways!' he said. I waved.

Outside in the street, I looked at my watch. I could still be back in London in time for dinner. But where, oh where, in this stinking suburb with its pollarded mock cherries and Swiss-style des. gent's reses would I find a taxi to bear me to New Street?

'Excuse me,' I said to a wild, dirty-looking character who had just left the police station behind me, 'can you tell me where I'll find a taxi or a telephone box?'

'Sure,' said the man, whose black hair, beard and teeth stuck out in all directions, 'I'm walking along that way myself. Saw you get charged. Nice little lot. Well done.'

I smiled. 'Thank you,' I said, faintly astonished, 'And what about you?'

'Oh, I'm Mick Murphy, anarchist,' he mumbled. 'I'm an old friend of theirs. They couldn't land me with anything this time. They tried, poor bastards. Who dealt with you?'

'A fellow called Chadwick.'

'Oh, Bill the Pill. Fancies his chances, he does. Suffers from penis envy, I reckon.'

I grinned. Murphy rambled on. 'He always kicks me about and seems to feel better for it, poor little creature. Suppose he's got to get his thrills somehow. I sent him a copy of *Mutual Aid* last Christmas. I don't think he read it.'

I snorted. 'You think Kropotkin should be standard reading for officers of the law?'

'Sure, and then there wouldn't be any officers or any law and we'd all police ourselves and we could be like little flowers.'

'Hmmmm,' I pursed my lips. 'Tell me, do they always beat suspects up in there?'

'Not always. There are a couple that are OK. You almost prefer it if they do, though. At least you understand the terms they're using, you know that you're on top. They didn't try it on you, did they?'

'Chadwick did, as a matter of fact.'

'Jesus, he must be losing his marbles. Or maybe you weren't

56

being yourself then.'

'No. I was under an assumed name.'

'Ah, that explains it. 'D'ye know—' Mick Murphy started to laugh, a breathless, rasping laugh, 'd'ye know, the first time I was arrested here, I didn't quite look like this. I'd just left the LSE and I had a suit, and despite my beard and all, I looked reasonably respectable, ye know? And I got thoroughly pissed one night and they picked me up and took me to that station. And I happened to say, "Jes' had a very convivial evening at the lodge. Very congenial evening at the lodge." Pissed as a fart, I was. You should have seen them. They escorted me down to the cells, and in the morning they were in with coffee and breakfast and all that.

'Sure, they're meant to do that for anyone, but they don't. You're damned lucky if you get anything to eat for a day, then suddenly along come lunch and dinner within an hour. It's one of their nice little ways of making sure you lose your mind. Mid-day they turn out the lights so you think the day's gone short, then they serve you breakfast at four o'clock and give you twenty hours of light. Lovely people.

'Anyhow, along came my breakfast. "Mornin', Mr. Murphy. Hope you're feeling better, Mr. Murphy. Kiss your arse, Mr. Murphy. Come an' get yourself released, Mr. Murphy. Sure it won't happen again, Mr. Murphy. Ite missa est and bugger off."

'Just as I'd been released officially, like, along comes one of them an' says, "Excuse me Mr. Murphy, but the Chief Superintendent wants to see you." So I thinks, "Jesus, what've I done? Knowing this lot, they'll verbal me up on a murder."

'Anyhow, I go along. Chief Superintendent Boylan it was, all brogues and jolly good show and I'd-be-a-gentleman-if-only-I-knew-where-to-start. He greets me, gives me another cup of coffee an' says to me, "I hear yer went to see mother last night?" I says "Yer what?" He says', "I hear yer went to see mother." Nudge nudge, wink wink.

'I must have looked pretty fucking silly, so he leans forward and says, "My officers tell me you had a convivial evening at the lodge. Which lodge would that be?"

' "Wine lodge in Barton Road, yer silly fucker," I says.

' "Get out!" he screams. "Get out of here this instant." ' '

Murphy doubled up with laughter and the sawing noise started again in his throat, ' "Get out!" he screams, Oh, Jesus, it was funny!'

I laughed immoderately, whether because of the tension of the last few days or just because of this extraordinary man, who accepted everything in a spirit of humorous resignation. He had nothing, no friends, no roots, no relations. Prison and freedom were much the same to him. A line from Kris Kristofferson ran through my head, 'Freedom's just another word for nothing left to lose' – and Murphy had freedom, if nothing else. Nothing bound him save such obligations as he acknowledged by his nature.

'Now, and there's your taxi-rank. And I wish you joy and peace. If you're going to nick, arrange it well in advance. Get plenty of burn – tobacco, that is – whether you smoke or not. Burn is money, remember. You're not allowed more than three ounces officially, but you can arrange it. And, remember, when the socks are in with the cabbage, all it takes is a little fucking love and hope. There endeth the gospel.'

And dragging his soft-shod feet, Mick Murphy strolled off. Heading nowhere, like a malodorous little flower.

7

I breakfasted well from the usual array of silver on the sideboard, and strolled out onto the steps before the portico. I gazed down the lime avenue and stretched. It was good to be home.

It was a cold morning, and the columns on either side of me glistened in the lemon light. The air was rock hard and fissile as mica, and my breath bounced back at me. I crunched across the gravel to the stable-yard.

Christmas was coming, and I had returned, as usual, to my mother's home. I was glad to escape the rush of traffic, society's curious prodding, and the constant threat of sudden annihilation by some improvident terrorist's bomb.

What with the restaurant, the attack on the Old Bailey, and two narrow misses as I had dined out, I was beginning to feel that I was marked out as a special target. It is strain enough to live on bail pending irradiation without the addition of sordid little bombs.

Reactions to my Midlands adventure had been mixed. Verena had sent a visiting card bearing the message, 'I told you so. Bonne chance – et bonne vacance!' One or two friends teased me with the prospect of balls and chains and suits decorated with arrows. One or two others expressed vicarious and unrealistic envy. Some acquaintances were heard to say that they'd always known that I was a wrong 'un, and looked the other way. Nothing so well sorts wheat from chaff as an attack on one of the poppies.

Catkin, cool and amused as ever, sat down to prepare a dossier on prisons. No one dared to tell Sir James.

As yet, I had not told my mother either. I did not anticipate any great distress on her part, but she simply had not given me a chance. She had greeted me warmly, gabbled out her news, had masses of things to attend to in the village, and would I decorate the tree, and had disappeared again.

She was to go to the Rendcombe meet in the trailer. I had elected to hack. Tonight there was to be a dinner party. Maybe when all the guests had left, I would have time to inform her that her son and heir was about to become a con.

Jim Coverdale, the old groom, came out to meet me as I crossed the cobbled yard. 'Fine day we've got for it, sir.'

'It looks it, indeed,' I said, 'And how's my old Trafalgar?'

'Pretty well, sir, pretty well. Bit gassy, mind. You'll have a handful for the first hour or so.'

He returned to his saddle soaping.

'How's Gwen these days?' I asked.

'Oh, none too bad, sir,' Jim said. 'Doctor says she's got to take it easy, but she says what the hell. You know what she's like.'

I nodded, 'Heart, is it?'

'Yes, so they say. I see no signs of it myself, sir. Bright as a button, she is, I reckon. Not enough to do now the children are gone, that's her trouble.'

'Well, send her my love, will you, and tell her I'll be down to see her, and if she hasn't got a Dundee cake ready now that I'm down here, I'll shoot her.'

'Oh, she knows that, sir. I think she's had one ready nigh on a year.'

'What about the boys?'

'Oh, so so. Young Jim as worked here for a while, now as he's married and all, has gone off to Harwell. He's cleaning offices at the atom thing up there. Good job, I'm told, and plenty of money in it, and he's got ever such a good home and car and that, but I get the feeling that he'd like to be back. There's plenty of future in it, but it strikes me, like I was saying to Gwen, that there's never going to be any now, if you see what I mean.'

'I do,' I said.

'He saved and saved and saved, you know, for one of those life insurance things like they advertise everywhere, then he

60

rang me not so long ago and he says, "Dad, what's money, I mean, what is it worth and who decides?" I thought he'd gone loopy. I says to him, "I don't know. Why?"

'And he says, "Well, I've just worked it out. If we keep going at this rate, this bloody nest-egg thing is going to be worth the equivalent of about five hundred pounds by the time I get it, and that won't buy a damned thing." "Yes," says I. "And they're taking in the interest, and my share of the profit isn't as great as what I'm losing in inflation and all that, so I'll never get free." "No," I says. "So I decided to sell out," he says, "and take the kids on a damned good holiday." So he did. A whole month in Torremolinos and he came back flat broke, and good for him, says I.'

'Amen,' I said.

'But what I think is, he's doing the same thing with his working, too, doing what he doesn't want to do to get things he doesn't really need and which he'll have to get more of pretty soon.'

'It is ridiculous, Jim,' I agreed. 'The propaganda gets us all, I'm afraid, and comfort is success as far as the propagandists are concerned.'

'Haven't much use for comfort myself,' said Jim. 'Kills you, just the same as starving, only you can't do much about it.'

Redway, my family's home for three generations, is a large Palladian mansion of stuccoed Cotswold stone. It's got a mile-long lime avenue and two wings and a Thomas Archer Tuscan barn-style chapel and it stands on top of a hill in the middle of some five hundred acres of sporting land. I call the land 'sporting' because it has never been used for much else. There were a few hundred head of cattle about the place, a few crops and a farm manager. The rest of the estate's revenue was derived from a shooting syndicate and two banks of the Windrush.

My mother found no difficulty in reconciling our relative wealth with her convictions. She was a prominent member of the old Socialist aristocracy. Her visitors' book was crammed with the signatures of Shaws, Webbs, Cripps, Carpenters, Russells and Morrells. She was witty, fond, hugely energetic and barmy.

As a child, I was subject to a hundred volatile changes of atmosphere every day. One moment she was casting her hands up to heaven in a gesture worthy of Bernhardt at some imagined disaster in the kitchen; the next, she was snatching me up to smother me with kisses, only to drop me again in order to harangue the gardener's boy about his politics. Her absent-minded air, at first assumed, had since gelled as an essential constituent of her personality. My friends loved her, but then they only had to cope with her for a weekend at a time.

No one, I suppose, was terribly surprised when my father took to drink and womanising in early middle age. My mother was wonderful and had not a malicious thought in her head, but she was totally exhausting.

He had married her because he admired her. She had married him because he was charming and aggressive and totally unlike either the keen young Crispians and Quentins who stood on one leg and stuttered, or the intense young 'activists' whom her father cultivated. He always adored her but, at the last, he was afraid of emasculation and he ran. He spent the last years of his life on the yacht, indulging his every desire for dusky maidens and exotic booze and returning only at Christmas. If this indication of her failure as a wife ever distressed her, she gave little sign of it. My father died of a heart attack in Nassau when I was just fourteen. He left Redway to me, but I, like him, was happy to leave my mother to take charge. I missed her when I was away from her, was always happy to see her again, but could stand the constant chaos for no more than a week at a time.

Trafalgar was a handful, all right. He flapped when fertiliser bags flapped and flew when pigeons flew. When we arrived at the drive of the house where the meet was being held, the sight and smell of a hundred horses proved too much for him, and I proceeded inelegantly up the drive with his head twisted round in the vague direction of his off hind. Matters were not improved by a sudden shriek of 'Sebastian' from the lawn above us.

'Hello, Sebastian!' cried a girl's voice, and I looked up to see Sylvie Howard pulling her grey up from a hack canter as though she'd taken the nursery hobby horse out for some fresh air.

'Hi, Sylvie,' I grinned, glad to see her. 'Kiss me ere I die.'

She drew up beside me, leaned over and did so. Loyal Trafalgar didn't understand the mechanics of kissing and, concluding that war had been declared, took a chunk out of her mount's neck. There was a deal of squealing then, and prancing around on tiptoe. At last, we disentangled ourselves and rode side by side towards the gathering on the lawn.

Sylvie, the younger daughter of our local peer, was one of those girls whom my mother pushed at me. For this reason, I would probably have disliked her, were it not for the fact that Sylvie was funny, eccentric and attractive. She had a fine little face with bright grey eyes and a turned up nose which inspired all sorts of protective impulses.

The stately home had long since been stocked with moth-eaten lions and hocked to the public, and Sylvie had been brought up in a little Georgian rectory on the edge of the estate. She had, to my certain knowledge, worked as a model and as a waitress, lived in a self-sufficient hippy community, and had now taken over part of an old warehouse in Covent Garden where she worked a loom and ran a craft studio. She was an eclectic, gentle critic, and the best debunker that I knew.

We were greeted at the meet by the usual 'my dear, how are yous' and other sporting salutations. Sylvie stayed at my side and we bitched and traded news and chat with the assembled 'aunts', vicars and 'friends of the family'.

'For God's sake, Sylvie,' I said as we moved off, 'stick by me, or I'll get trapped by one of those inquisitive harridans who think that thigh muscles were made for equestrianism.'

'And I'll be told that I've got a lovely seat and a jolly good mount by twits with gobstoppers in their giblets. Fear not, Sebastian, whither thou goest . . .'

'Talking of which, will you come to dinner tonight? My mother's having a party to which she's invited four party political broadcasts and a gaggle of women who regard mindlessness as a marital duty.'

'I'd love to,' she said, and we had a great day.

I left the field at half past three, tired and elated. I hacked back home, settled Trafalgar down, soaked in a bath for an hour and then watched 'Dr Who' before changing. At half past six, Sylvie arrived in a romantic creation of flame-coloured crêpe de chine. We sat in the morning-room playing racing demon until the first of my mother's guests arrived at eight.

My mother's idea of a successful dinner party was to have as controversial a mix of guests as possible. This one promised to be no exception. It started as soon as the first two couples had arrived, when my mother quite intentionally revealed that we'd spent the day in the hunting field. Mrs Arbuthnott, the dutiful wife of our local Labour candidate, had achieved the full lotus position for the first time just before she had set out. She gave a little 'involuntary' shudder at the mention of hunting, and said, 'I don't know how you can!'

'How I can what?' I asked.

'Oh, nothing. It doesn't matter.'

'No, come on, Judith,' said my mother, 'are you talking about hunting?'

'It doesn't matter,' she said, and shook her head, pitying.

'We are both opposed to blood sports,' announced her husband. He was a fat, ginger-haired man who had made his money out of golfing umbrellas or something.

'Why's that, sir?' I asked him.

'Because they're cruel, of course.'

'Rubbish,' said Lady Jasmine McDonaugh, a jovial trencher-woman, who had also been out that day.

'Rubbish,' echoed her mild moustachioed husband.

'That poor little fox ...' said Mrs Arbuthnott.

'My poor little chickens,' bellowed Lady Jasmine.

I said, 'No, Jasmine, of course it's cruel. It's totally savage. What of it?'

'Oh, Sebastian, cruelty's always wrong!'

'Why?'

'Well, because ...'

'Well, by definition ...'

'I just want to know how you would like to be torn to pieces by a ravening pack of hounds,' said Mr Arbuthnott.

With which startlingly irrelevant question, battle was joined. They told me that anything which caused pain was wrong. I asked why. They said for heaven's sake, well, of course it was. Everyone knew that. Of course, they accepted that foxes had to be kept down and that, in theory, it was healthier for the fox to be culled by its natural predator whom man had domesticated than by impartial means. But really, Sebastian, we aren't just animals, you know. Man has developed beyond the stage of such passions. We're meant to be civilised.

And so it went on. I grew annoyed at the woman's condescension and, like a fool, I started playing to the gallery. I wanted to know what we were if we were not animals. I wanted to know why the Grand Boulder Dam or the nuclear bomb was essentially less 'natural' than the digging paws of the mole or the longer beak of the mainland Darwin finch. They said because. Why can't I let such idiots go? Some damned fool, self-destructive urge makes me bully them simply because they presume.

I ended up asking Mrs Arbuthnott, terribly politely, of course, whether she was really so far above the animals when she got her nightly shot of adrenalin from television violence or when she gnawed on bullocks' flesh.

My mother was giggling contentedly. Mrs Arbuthnott was scratching herself and trying to look liberal. Just when her husband was trying to decide whether he was on the side of liberal sympathy or whether he wanted to knock my head off, other guests arrived. Julius George, a portrait painter who wasn't quite sure whether he was a country gentleman or an outrageous Bohemian, and his wife, all chiffon and bangles and hyper-thyroid eyes; David Lardiner, MP, our member, and his pretty second wife, Valerie, who had been his secretary at the Commons and who had raped me in the morning-room last New Year's Eve.

At eight-thirty, I went out to the kitchen to find out when dinner would be ready and to bring the wine into the dining-room. I came into the hall again to find Sylvie standing between the fire-place and the huge Christmas tree which reached into the darkness of the cupola.

'Sylvie?' I said.

She looked up from the fire-dogs. 'Hi, Sebastian.'

'Absconded from the merry throng? What's the matter?'

'Oh, I don't know,' she said, and slumped down into a chair.

'Come on, Sylvie, what's up?'

'Oh, I just get so frustrated by all that crap.' She flicked back her hair and the underside of her forearm flashed in the

65

fire-light.

'Not generation gap blind intolerance from you, of all people?' I put the bottles down and unconsciously adopted the classic paterfamilias stance before the fire.

'Of course not. It's not that.'

'Well, what then?'

'It doesn't matter.' She shrugged and stood again.

'Now you're behaving like the Arbuthnott biddy. There's nothing crueller than "It doesn't matter". It keeps you wondering just what doesn't matter so much for the rest of the evening. Dirty fighting.'

She grinned, but didn't look up. 'I know,' she said, 'I really don't believe in sulking. It really doesn't matter, though. It's just me. I get so bloody annoyed with you sometimes. If we hadn't been surrounded by people, I'd have thrown some of that Delft at you rather than standing here moaning.'

'Why so?'

'Because I really like you nine times out of ten, and then you start being all arrogant and I just can't stand it. You change completely. In your own way, you become violent, using your gifts impersonally, just as a heavyweight mugger might. You're different then, totally different from the Sebastian that I know, who can be gentle and witty and sensitive and all sorts of nice things. I really hate you when you become like that. I feel it almost – almost as an insult – an insult to me.'

I nodded. I'd heard it before.

'I know,' I sighed, 'I become intolerable at times, but I'm never aware of it as I'm doing it. I'm so damned intolerant of fools, and whenever anyone takes reason, or one of my friends, or anything that I care about in vain, I just freeze over and let them have it. Especially when someone dares to condescend to me.'

'Surely you've more confidence in your abilities than that?'

'In my abilities, sure. That's why. When I get angry or feel attacked, I snatch up the most accessible weapon. The permanent underdog does the same, but he just snarls like a cornered rat and gets pity, which I can do without. I use the arrogance that I learned as a child to protect me. Locked up there with my talents, I'm unassailable. What do you use? Your tits?'

'Suppose so. Or sexual coldness. It's just that . . . I wish you'd try to stop it. It's so hateful. It's like molten steel suddenly chilled. I mean, if there's going to be a fire, let it burn, let it really burn.'

'OK, little one,' I smiled and offered my arm. She looked up at me and squeezed my forearm, so I scraped an invisible strand of hair from her eyes and looked down at her lips and I kissed her. A vague sense of guilt touched me as we stood there breathing tangled words under the Christmas tree in my own home. I could imagine nothing more delightful than to wake up beside Sylvie every morning, to cuddle her close every night. We shared interests, we shared a sense of humour, we shared friends. We wanted one another. She would keep me up to the mark with her wit and her energy. She would bring hope and sense of purpose back into my life. But she knew nothing of those nights on which I'd shadowbox with memories, of the Lebanese woman who, two nights before, had said, 'Take me to Tramp and I'll do anything you like', of the quest for cheap kicks with which to justify self-hatred, a quest that I was not yet ready to abandon. Sylvie needed a man, and I suppose I was still a child, sucking oblivion from quart bottles.

8

The letter arrived only two days before the trial. It summoned me to attend at Birmingham Crown Court at 10 o'clock on 4th February, to face trial.

On my last evening, I sat in the window seat facing the square. My white shirt shone blue in the liquid lamplight. There was a single spotlight on the desk. Otherwise the room was completely dark. The telephone stood with a glass of whisky by its side. Three times I picked up the receiver and dialled the first five numbers, only to pause, and slam it down again. No. Fiona would come if I called, but I would never be sure whether it was from pity or from love. She must come to me freely, or not at all.

Tomorrow would be interesting. I told myself that, as a lawyer, I would see the system from the other side. The soulless machine would turn once, and I would be spewed out in a different form, no longer a worker or a director, but the product itself, analysed, categorised, packed and consigned. How often had I taken part in the process without allowing myself to consider that other consciousness which was thus disposed of, without allowing myself to see behind the glinting eye of the hardest man the sorrow of a child rejected? Yes, tomorrow would be interesting.

I kept up that analytical line of thought for a minute or so, then I saw a fur-wrapped couple wandering in the square, nodding to the bobby, wishing him good night, and suddenly I hit my forehead, swigged at my whisky, and told myself that I was mad.

But the die was cast. To fight the Erinyes is a waste of

energy. Had I not written a thesis at Cambridge in which I identified the distinguishing moment of tragedy as that at which the inevitable was accepted and welcomed? The sleigh rider has dragged his feet until the downward drag is irresistible, and he lets go with a cry of joy. The lover had delayed ejaculation until at last the wind is in his hair and he bids the ego, 'Go!' The Indian chief, the rebel, knows that he must die, yet dons his paint and rides with the irresponsible laughter of one who resigns his fortunes to the gods. There is an assertion in such laughter, and to complain is to blaspheme.

I got up and walked over to the record player. It could only be Bach, the master problem solver. The double violin concerto. Beauty which resolves itself, free of associations. Not the sublime terror of the untamed, but that formal loveliness which empties the mind and reassures. Everything works out in the end.

I leaned back and sighed. The violins dipped and swirled and wound about each other like swallows, skidding on the ice-slopes of the air. I closed my eyes.

'Darling?' A dream. Don't move. 'Darling ...' The voice was gentle, the whisper of material soft. For an instant, my heart did all the standard things that hearts do when they are about to find their peace. But it was another voice, another smell. Down, boy, down.

I opened my eyes.

A girl leaned on the door frame, her body silhouetted against the light. I blinked. Long hair which gleamed at the edges like an aura, a preposterously thin crêpe dress.

I stretched out a hand in silent gratitude and a moment later she was there, curled up warm against my shirt front, sipping my whisky, resting her cheek against mine.

Sylvie.

'Darling, how in God's name did you get in here?'

'Fellow in the ground floor flat let me in the main door, and you left the front door open.'

'And what if I hadn't been here?'

'Then I'd have gone away again.' She shrugged. 'Anyhow, I knew you were here. I had this feeling. Hold me very tight, darling, or something might fall off. It's freezing outside.'

I pulled her close. She sighed. With one hand I enclosed her cheek, drawing her head onto my chest. With the other, I raised the glass. She sipped. I freed my mouth from her hair, drained the glass, and threw it down. Then I kissed her.

'Pleased I came?' she said in a little voice.

'Very, very, very.'

'Thought you would be.' She kissed my nose. Unbuttoning my shirt, she laid her head against my bare chest. 'I just had dinner in Beauchamp Place with an insufferable bore from Chile, and then I got signals from you. Or, at least, I thought I did ...'

'You probably did, my love,' I said. The whisky had made my voice deeper. 'Sylvie, you know—'

'I know. I know. Don't worry about it. Whatever the complications of this life, we have two young, appreciative minds and two young, appreciative bodies and . . . Well. That's it, isn't it?'

'I rather felt like saying I love you tonight, but it would probably be taken all wrong.'

'Don't insult me. Say it. Say I love you.'

'I love you.'

'I love you, too. I really do. Ghosts need not prevent that. Let's exorcise them, at least for tonight.'

I kissed her neck, and suddenly felt absurdly happy. My right hand ran over the front of the dress. The nipples stood out firmly, 'Still cold?' I said. 'Amazing.'

She screwed her nose up at me and buried her head under my shirt-front.

'Darling,' I said softly, 'we're going to have to be up very early tomorrow. It's the trial.'

She did not stop. Her tongue was still slicing patterns on my skin as she undid my belt. She simply murmured as my head caressed her neck. 'Then we'd better make the most of it.'

We made the most of it, slowly, languorously, appreciatively. We chatted and joked and afterwards I slept with Sylvie curled up in my arms. The sleep of the just.

'I'm coming with you,' Sylvie announced as we drank coffee in the kitchen.

'No, you're not. I want no one there.'

'Ashamed?'

70

'I suppose . . . In a strange way, yes.'

'Oh my darling,' she stirred her coffee noisily, 'are you really prepared to sacrifice companionship for the sake of appearances to me? Me? You seem to forget. We abandoned appearances a few hours ago. I don't see why it should be any different because silly old men are saying unpleasant things about you.'

I stood. 'I love you, *querida*, but the answer is still no.'

She shrugged. 'OK. I'll just clean up the flat and settle down to wait for five years like the good little woman.'

The buzzer sounded. I walked over and talked into it. 'All right. Hold on for one minute. I'll be right down.'

I pulled on my overcoat, picked up my briefcase and stretched. 'I feel brave as a lion,' I said, 'thanks to you. That's the taxi outside. I've . . . I've got to be, sort of, going.'

I bent and kissed her, gently ruffling the hair behind her ears. Standing, I half-turned, and grinned at her. 'Oh damn you for a rational bitch. Haven't you got anything warmer to wear?'

'I left my hold-all downstairs in the hall,' she laughed, taking my hand. 'Come on. I can be a gangster's moll at last!'

The lobby of the Birmingham courtroom was crowded. On either side of the corridor, on low benches, there sat a motley crew reminiscent of the Rake's Progress. Whole families of gypsies, unshaven dypsomaniacs who had not abstained on their last morning of freedom, and professional-looking villains dressed up to the nines in patterned shirts, sharp-edged trousers and clogs. They all argued with counsel and themselves, as officials of the court trotted to and fro.

No one noticed Sylvie and me. I briefly studied the charge sheet and sat. A mood of strained apprehension swallowed me up. Each snapped remark, each tapping foot, each rustle and fidget echoed as if in a public lavatory. A pair of concerned parents paced back and forth, rehearsing their son's case as though they might uncover some undiscovered point of law.

Two counsel, wigged and gowned, rustled by. One turned and curtly nodded.

'Know him?' asked Sylvie.

'Know them both,' I replied. 'I have an idea that they were envious of my ill-deserved riches in student days and are now, understandably, crowing.'

71

'Bastards.'

'Humans.'

She took my hand. 'How long do you think you'll get?'

'I don't know. One of the things that you very rapidly learn about criminal law is that its execution is well-nigh totally arbitary. First it depends on the judge – how well he has slept, what he ate for breakfast and so on. There was one judge at this court who went barmy and started sentencing people by the clock. Seriously. At twelve forty-five, you couldn't get a prisoner up the stairs. They'd be fainting, feeling sick, foaming at the mouth, anything rather than face sentence then. At one o'clock, they'd make a concerted rush for the dock. The villains recognised it long before the law did, but finally some bright young barrister pointed it out and it was proven. The judge retired rather rapidly, and a few prisoners had their sentences drastically commuted.'

'Help!' said Sylvie.

'Help indeed. The other thing is that the prosecution makes deals with the defence. Plea bargaining, it is called. Doubtless someone will be along to make some sort of deal with me in the next half hour. You know. "You plead guilty to such and such and we won't bring up so and so." That sort of thing. It saves the court's time, of course, and it helps the police to clear their books, and it's all very well with someone like me. What's not so good is that they are inclined to do it to youngsters and illiterate idiots, who find themselves pleading guilty of far more serious crimes than they have ever committed.'

'Help!' said Sylvie.

'The important thing to remember is that I deliberately chose the Inland Revenue for a good reason. I might otherwise have got off Scot free. The list of things which may not be taken in this country runs, roughly, first, Inland Revenue or Excise Revenue; second, private property; third, life, and fourth, virtue and self-respect.'

'You're kidding!?'

'Alas, no. Sentences for stealing five pounds from private individuals are minimal. Sentences for stealing five pounds from the tax man or the customs man are almost always custodial, even for first offenders. Very few murderers and still fewer rapists ever receive a sentence as great as that of train robbers.

72

The average murderer is eligible for parole after seven years and is released after eleven. The train robbers were given thirty years which means they weren't even eligible for parole until they'd been inside for ten. As for rapists, four is about average. So which is more valuable, life, or paper consigned to the scrap heap?'

'Jesus,' said Sylvie, 'and I thought we were civilised.'

'So I would make a guess,' I continued, 'that, if I play my cards right, I should get eighteen months, which means twelve, in effect, or twelve, which means eight.'

'You mean you automatically get remission?'

'Yup. One third remission is automatic. You don't earn remission by good behaviour, but you can lose it by bad behaviour. Common misconception.' Suddenly I stiffened. 'Oh dear,' I said softly.

Across the tiles, striding easily on rubber soles, came Chadwick. This time he wore a magenta shirt and tie. He ran his fingers through his polished hair and smiled.

'Hullo, Mr Foy,' he said.

'Good morning, Mr Chadwick.'

'Fast enough for you, was it?'

'Yes, thank you, Mr Chadwick.'

'This your young lady, then?'

'This is a friend of mine. You will forgive me if I do not introduce you, but I am rather anxious to spend my last hours of freedom in the company of my choice.'

'Hair out of curl a bit, is it?' Chadwick smirked and preened, invulnerable. 'Well, well. I'll introduce myself. Detective Constable Chadwick, miss.'

'Go to the devil,' said Sylvie quietly.

'Well, well. The manners of the gentry aren't all that I was told.' Chadwick smiled. 'I was wondering if you would spare the time to answer a few questions, Mr Foy. Help clear up a few things, you know.'

'No,' I said, 'and there is no means whereby you may insist upon that privilege. I would remind you, Mr Chadwick, that I am on magistrate's bail, not police bail. I am therefore a free man and you cannot revoke that freedom save by lawful arrest or by the court's warrant. As a free man, I demand that I be left alone. Now. Otherwise I will be forced to call a policeman and

73

to inform him that you are making a nuisance of yourself and behaving in a manner liable to cause a breach of the peace ...'

'Are you threatening a police officer in the execution of his duty?'

I raised my voice. 'Fool, begone!' Heads turned. Chadwick looked about him and shifted from foot to foot.

'Cocky bastard,' he said between gritted teeth. 'We'll see.'

'And that,' I said as Chadwick padded away, 'is the other problem. The police can and do communicate their suspicions and prejudices to the judge. They are not meant to, but it's common practice. They may arrest you for petty pilfering, but if they know or suspect you of being involved in other crimes, they can inform the judge of their opinions. A crime which merits six months can therefore suddenly earn two years.'

Sylvie's hand tightened around mine. 'Sebastian,' she said, 'I'm frightened.'

'Join the club.' I smiled. 'I'm bloody terrified. Did you say that you had a hip-flask in that shapeless cornucopia?'

At last the time came. At half-past eleven, I stepped up into the dock and gave my name and address to the clerk of the court. Journalists with hungry eyes scribbled in the pew to the right. On my left, in the ranked wooden seats of the public gallery, Sylvie sat very still, her face serene, encouraging.

It had all been arranged with the prosecutor. I would plead guilty to the forgery, theft, malicious damage and breach of the peace charges. The driving charges had been dropped and would remain on the files *sine die*.

As each of the charges was read out, the question was asked, 'How do you plead?' Clearly and quietly I said, 'Guilty, your honour.'

'You may sit,' said the judge. I sat. A police constable sat beside me, smelling of stale tobacco. The sun was just breaking through the clouds, and the soft light streamed through the window in dusty streaks. The walls were of pale cold blue. The sunlight didn't warm them. But for the scarlet flash of the judge's gown and the old gold gleam of the coat of arms, there was no touch of warmth in the room. I wondered whether one could rig up the heavy wooden shield to fall on to the judge's head. Nice idea for a murder story.

I leaned back, watching the judge through half-closed eyes.

There was a movement in the corner of the courtroom. A door swung open and someone walked in. I grinned. Catkin, in dark blue, looking far from efficient and wagging her finger at me.

Sylvie turned round and waved. Catkin waved back and skipped down the steps to join her.

'Have we now finished the floor show?' the judge asked. Catkin bowed and smiled. Sylvie crossed her legs.

Papers were rustled. Chairs scraped on the floor. Chadwick came to the stand.

'I assailed the defendent, whereupon he said to me, and I quote, "Hullo, ossifer. I have had fun." At this I said, "You are making a nuisance of yourself, sir, and I have reason to believe that that vehicle upon which you are riding is a stolen vehicle." I then gave him the usual warning and took him into custody.'

'How much of the money has been recovered?' asked the judge.

'Only twenty-four pounds and thirty-two pence,' Chadwick answered, running his thumb along his collar. 'I have been instructed to seek a compensation order.'

'I scarcely think that this is the sort of case in which a compensation order will be sufficient,' chewed the judge. 'Mr Foy, have you anything to say?'

I stood and looked about me slowly, rhetorically. 'I have little to say, your honour, save that I enjoyed myself thoroughly in redressing, admittedly in a somewhat chance fashion, the wrongs committed by a crippling, corporate state.'

'I see that you have declined to have a social report compiled.'

'Yes, your honour. I regard such an invasion as an impertinence. Nor am I anxious to excuse or extenuate. I acknowledge my guilt within the terms of this court, and I consider that the whole business was well worth the trouble that it might cause.'

The judge eyed me curiously, almost sympathetically, then blurted, 'Do you not want a psychiatric report? It could make all the difference, you know.'

'I am aware of that, your honour, but I do not consider myself to be deranged. One of the strange features of the law, as you are aware, is that a man may only be deemed insane if he himself is prepared to plead insanity. Thus, if his insanity takes the form of paranoia or delusions of grandeur, he cannot be given the treatment suitable for such a man. Witty, isn't it?'

Catkin frowned. Sylvie looked confused. The judge sighed.

'Very well, Mr Foy. Mr Foy ...'

'Stand up,' said the policeman by my side.

'Mr Foy, I have considered this case with great care, recognising that, in passing sentence, I am further punishing a man who has already been gravely punished for this irresponsible crime. You have destroyed for ever a promising career at the bar for, in all executive branches of the law, law-abiding and honesty are the first, the most important qualifications. The public cannot maintain respect for the law if those who enforce it and represent it are not above reproach.'

The clerk of the court was already tying up his papers and snapping elastic. A shadow passed over the sun, sliding obliquely about the room like a magic lantern image. I stood still. Out of the corner of my eye, I saw Sylvie's hand moving to take Catkin's.

'Inevitably, therefore, it is a painful task for me to inflict further penalties upon a man who has already suffered. You seem, however, bent on self-destruction. Despite your profession, you have shown nothing but contempt for the law and for this court. You have mocked the court and are clearly totally unrepentant of your dangerous, irresponsible and dishonest behaviour. I see no reason why, merely because you have brains, you should be treated differently from others.'

He sighed once more and leaned forward, clasping his hands upon the desk. I closed my eyes. 'On the first count, you will go to prison for twelve months. On the second count, you will go to prison for twelve months. On the third and fourth counts you will go to prison for six months apiece. These sentences to be served concurrently.'

'Thank you, your honour.' I bowed my head briskly and turned to the girls. Sylvie was holding Catkin's hand tightly. Again I bowed.

'Come on,' said the tobaccoo-reeking officer, 'downstairs.'

I turned. A hand gripped my upper arm. The stairs ran down below me into the shadows. I could not see the bottom for it was deep in darkness.

The door clanged shut and I found myself in a cell of bars, like those in Western films.

'Bad luck,' said the prison officer who turned the keys. 'I thought you'd get off with a bender.'

'A bender?'

'Suspended sentence.'

'Oh, yes. Oh.' I sat on the little bench. Suddenly I felt very tired. 'How long do I stay here? I mean – here?'

'Just a couple of hours,' smiled the officer. 'Then you'll be moved to the Cliff – Clifton – with the rest of 'em. Don't worry though. You'll end up at Ravenhill. No previous, have you?'

'No. No previous.

'Well, it'll be Ravenhill then. Not too bad there, so I'm told.'

'Thanks.' I felt a hard core within me, like the stone within a soft fruit. My body seemed no longer my own, but merely an unfeeling instrument temporarily at my command. I was now a convict. For ever more, I would be Sebastian Foy, ex-con. I was very cold.

An absurd fancy suddenly occured to me. I would return to the court and tell then I had changed my mind. I had been temporarily deranged by strain. They would listen . . .

But no. The law struck but once. There was no redress. And a little man who had already been through this had had his brain smeared across the earth. He too had been so totally alone in a world disassociated from any other, and for him too, there was no redress.

Sylvie and Catkin came down, still hand in hand. 'Hi, Foy,' said Catkin, 'anything you need?'

'No. Well, perhaps you could get me a book, a big book that'll keep me happy for a while. Would that be all right, officer?'

'Oh, I should think so,' he said.

I patted my crown and shook my head as if trying to awake. 'I'm wondering when it's going to sink in.'

'Well, don't worry,' said Catkin.

'No, don't worry,' Sylvie echoed, 'all will be well.' She paused. 'Hey!' she cried, 'do they allow private visits *à deux* like in Sweden?'

'Don't think so, little one. Still, I'll be back in eight months' time, all things being equal, and we'll blow the town sky high in celebration. OK?'

'OK.' She kissed my hand. 'Oh damn you, Sebastian, there's nothing more captivating than a distant unattainable lover, fighting a war.'

'Hey, hey,' I said gently, 'there's no point in both of us being captive, you know. I got myself into this.'

'And so did I.'

'Who was it who said that occidental education gives women one perennial fantasy – to be fucked by the unknown soldier? Maybe it was me.'

'Shut up.'

Catkin winked at me. 'Foy, darling,' she said, taking my other hand, 'do you want any messages taken?'

'Yes, Tell the monster I'm sorry and I'll see him soon. See Jack Drake and tell him what's happened. I'll let him know if he can help.'

'Yes, and—?'

'Tell my mother the news and send her my love. And . . .'

'And?'

'Yup. Ring her and tell her, will you?'

'I will.'

Both hands tightened around mine. 'Idiot,' said Catkin, and blinked. 'Bloody, intolerable, bumptious, stupid idiot.' She rested her head against the bars. I kissed her. She turned and walked out in silence.

'Well, Sylvie,' I said quietly.

'Well – I agree with her. Look after yourself.'

'I will, and thanks for coming.'

She stuck out her tongue and kissed me quickly, spun on her toes, and she too was gone.

I was more alone that I had ever been before.

9

The minibus bore me and four others through the endless suburbs of Birmingham to Clifton prison. Numb and unheeding, I sat in the corner, cocooned. I was handcuffed to a warder.

A black burglar, two young men who had just received seven-year sentences for Grievous Bodily Harm and a sad middle-aged company secretary were my companions. The G.B.H. merchants prattled contentedly, chiding the warders and reflecting on their own good fortune. They were going home. The negro glared, contemptuous and taciturn. The sandy-haired company secretary fidgeted and muttered. He wanted to feel superior, but kept glancing suspiciously at me.

Of present company, I felt kinship only with the bad boys, unbound by rules and unashamed. They had no axe to grind.

When we finally reached Clifton, I scarcely saw the wooden gates swing open to let the van pass through, scarcely saw the high grey walls or the towering brick building to which they reversed. Another warder appeared from nowhere and unlocked the van's back door. A moment of painful jostling, a second of fresh air and the evening chill, and we were inside. Up flaking yellow stairs. Through barred doors which were locked again as soon as we passed. And again.

Still handcuffed to the warder, I was led down a low-ceilinged corridor. I walked, as I always did, with my head high, and was shocked when, suddenly, my uniformed companion turned sharply right, painfully jerking my arm. We were in a dusty bare room. It would always be dusty.

An officer in a white shirt sat at a desk under the high window. He did not look up until the prisoners and warders were all drawn up before him.

'Today's lot, sir,' said my Siamese twin.

'How many?' asked the reception orderly wearily.

'Five. Taylor and Dean are back with sevens. The coon's got a fistful, the old lady's got two, and junior here is twelve months.'

The senior officer looked us up and down. He raised his eyebrows, and smiled at his colleague.

'Right,' he said, 'has all their property been taken into charge?'

'Yes.'

'OK. Take 'em next door. Strip off in there. Put your clothes in the boxes provided. Then take a shower. It's the last wash you'll get for a week, so make the most of it.'

Make the most of it. They'd be back in London by now.

The handcuffs were unlocked, and five new convicts were bundled into a plain room of pocked stone. It was almost dark outside. We stripped, and I shuddered for my tailor as his handiwork was folded and then stuffed into a flat cardboard box. We stood cold and nervous until the warders returned.

'Right, showers. You've got three minutes. Get moving.'

We were led through into the washing arcade. I climbed in under the shower and scrubbed myself down as best I could with carbolic soap and lukewarm water.

I was the first to be sent back to the reception room, still naked.

'Name?'

'Sebastian Barclay Foy.'

'Sentence?'

'Twelve months.'

'Any previous criminal record?'

'None.'

'Right. You're a star. Looks like a Ravenhill case. Collar size and waist?'

'Er, I don't know. That is – I'm not trying to be difficult, you know, but I've really no idea.'

'Jesus!' The warder slammed down his pen. 'How the fucking hell can you go through life without knowing your own size?'

I thought it better not to explain, so I said meekly, 'I'm sorry.'

'All right. Make a guess. Waist 30, 15½ collar. Shoes?'

I sighed with relief. That much I knew. 'Nine and a half.'

'Right. There are your clothes. Get dressed. Your number is D71107. Remember it.'

'Do I get any of my property back?'

'No, we look after it until your discharge.'

'I was wondering about the two books that were brought to me today to the cells. The officer there said that I could have them.'

'Did he indeed? Those them?' he pointed.

'Yes.'

'Hmmm. John Donne, *Complete Works*.' He flicked it open. ' "Hope I hit the mark, I love you. Sylvie." Huh! And what's this one? Fuck me. *After Babel* by George Steiner. What fucking language is that? "Good hunting, darling. Catkin." ' He shrugged. 'Well, I'll see. They'll have to be censored. If they're all right, you can have them.'

'Thank you.'

'Right. Sign for your property here.'

I signed.

'Get dressed and wait till we come to fetch you.'

I returned to the pocked stone room, where the others joined me, one by one. I pulled on the grey trousers which stopped two inches above my ankles, blue and white striped shirt, a pair of thick grey socks and black elastic-sided shoes. A knitted blue nylon tie and a rough grey woollen jacket completed the miserable outfit.

'What's the routine now, then?' I asked.

'Get put in yer peter. Might get some tea if you're lucky,' said one of the G.B.H. men. He was small but moved with an easy grace which spoke of instant reactions, violent reactions. 'What you in for?'

I told him, and he laughed. 'Hey, you're fucking crazy!'

'Yes,' I said, 'I'm beginning to think so.'

'Bloody hell!' The fighter giggled, wiping his mouth with his sleeve. 'I've always wanted to ride round that fucking Bull Ring!'

'Mmmm. It was quite fun. What about you?'

'Ah, some bastards tried to pick a fight in a Bierkeller. I happened to have a baseball bat and Pete here got a bottle and eight of them sort of got in our way. Did us for Gobblin Behind 'Edges.'

'So who's crazy?'

'Yeah. S'pose so.'

'And you got seven?'

'Not bad, eh? Thought we'd get more. We've been on remand here for nine months already.'

'What's this place like?'

'One of the worst nicks in the country. It was built to hold six hundred and something people, and I've seen fourteen hundred in here. Even the fucking Victorians intended each peter – each cell – for just one con, but now we're all three'd and four'd up. It's filthy, but you'll be OK. Just keep your head down and don't let 'em give you any shit.'

'Who, the cons or the warders?'

'Either. The screws will try. Just remember, in here it's number one that counts. You may have been an easy touch on the out, but forget it in here. Don't give burn to anyone. It's fucking priceless and you'll only get paid sixty-five pence a week. The cons will try to tap it. Don't listen. They wouldn't give you the drippings from their noses. And the screws, they'll try to wind you up. Laugh. It doesn't matter what they do, just laugh. And keep fit. Doesn't matter what the cons you're with may say. Do sit ups, press ups, trunk curls, anything. Just keep that body working. You've got to. You gotta missus?'

'Yes, but she's not so sure.'

'Oh. 'Nother man?'

'No, no. Don't worry about it. What else?'

'Anything else, Pete?' He turned to his blond accomplice, a broad-shouldered youth with more tattoos than skin.

'Dunno, Billy. Oh yeah, watch their heads. You probably think you still fight with fists like they do in the ring and the flicks. All you get for that is bruised knuckles and a broken arm. You go in with the nut and then the knee or a snap kick. Queensberry rules will kill you in the nick. The nut's harder and faster than anything else. One sharp butt and he's sliding down the wall with his nose splattered.'

'Yeah!' said the negro. It was the first thing that he had said.

'Who asked you?' Billy glowered. He strolled easily across the little room. His shoulders rolled as he walked. He looked down on the negro. 'You want a demonstration, Sambo?'

Sambo did not want a demonstration. 'Oh, man!' he whined.

'I wouldn't get violent,' said the company secretary as if he were sucking a gobstopper. His jowls shuddered as he spoke.

'Eh up, lad,' said Billy. He grinned. 'You're in nick now, not in East Cheam. If you can't do the time, don't do the crime. And don't lecture us, OK? We keep this place in order, and no one gets hurt if everything runs smoothly. Right?'

'Well . . .'

'Good, good. Hey, Sebastian, kid. You might need some help at some time before you get moved out to the funny farm. They won't take to you too easy. You're the real thing, I know, so you should cope. It's the fakes around here that make you puke. There are a hundred fucking millionaires in here, and none of them have two pennies to rub together. You're OK. If you get any sort of trouble, say see Billy Turner.'

'I will,' I smiled. 'Thanks.'

Two screws appeared at the door. 'Pick up your kit,' one of them commanded, 'and come with us.'

We filed out of the cell. On the floor outside lay a blanket roll, a transparent plastic receptacle which looked like a squashed teapot, a plastic mug and a plastic knife and fork, for each man. We picked them up. More doors were opened and slammed shut.

And then it began. We were in a huge, dry drum round which landings snaked on five levels, connected by iron spiral staircases. It echoed like a cathedral and smelt like a geriatric ward.

And all around there were doors, hundreds and hundreds of doors, with little cards hanging outside. Doors with no windows. Plain green studded doors, like a Piranesi nightmare.

Warders and prisoners clattered up the spiral stairs and I heard for the first time those sounds which were to become as inevitable to me as that of the sea or the London traffic. Day and night, feet thud on iron landings. Keys jangle on warders' belts, grate in locks. Doors swing firmly, finally shut with a clunk.

Otherwise, everything is silent.

I found myself in an unpainted cell, about six by eight feet. There was one single bed and a bunk, a table and a chair. A thick smell of urine and carbolic soap instantly closed about my senses and pressed down.

'Hi,' said the boy on the top bunk.

He could not have been more than eighteen. He grinned on one side of his face, which was encrusted with acne of the same honey colour as his hair.

'Hi,' I responded, and unrolled my blankets onto the bottom bunk. 'My name's Sebastian, Sebastian Foy. Who are you?'

'Mullins,' said the boy. 'Tony.'

'Tell me all about it,' I sat on the chair and crossed my legs, ever so casual, and scared shitless.

'Nothing to tell. You a star, then?'

'Yes.'

'You'll learn quick enough. Got a fag?'

'Yes.' I handed up my tin. Mullins rolled a cigarette which looked more like a match. The heavy man on the single bed rolled over and put down his newspaper.

'Give us one,' he grunted.

'No,' I answered amicably. 'Not until you wake up and tell me what the routine is in here.'

'Fuck off!' said the other. He was dark and middle-aged. He had heavy blue jowls and a huge gut. Black hair bristled from the nape of his neck and the back of his hands. Despite his age, he could have made chips of me simply by pushing me through the barred window. 'Routine's simple. Slop out, shave, breakfast, banged up, dinner, banged up, exercise, banged up, tea, banged up, slop out, lights out, bye-byes.'

'What's slop out exactly?'

'When you empty your slops, of course. Empty the piss out of that jerry, have a piss if you can get a place, collect some water for a shave in that bowl there. Five minutes.'

'Right. Now have a cigarette.'

'Oh thank you, kind sir.' He heaved himself over. A paunch flopped out.

'What about work, then,' I asked, picturing stone-breaking parties and petit point in hemp. The boy snorted. Neither man replied.

'Well, don't we have to work?' I persisted.

'Look, kid,' the older man leaned forward and addressed me pityingly, 'we've got a big 'ouse here. Lots of naughty people,

84

you know? Sure, there are shops here. There's the mailbag shop and the shop where you put the red blobs on the cheeks of garden gnomes and the shop where you assemble caravan television aerials. There's the kitchen and there's a few orderly jobs. Reception orderly, medical orderly, and so on. With your tarty way of speakin', you could probably get one of those, if you like the taste of screws' arses. Enough jobs to keep a proper nick working fine. But this isn't a proper nick. About twenty percent of the cons, if that, actually get out of their cells for more than an hour every day.'

'You mean that we just sit in here?'

'That's just what I mean. It's called overcrowding. The Victorians built these cells for one man. There are three in 'em now, if not four. No one does anything about it, of course. There's a guy next door, now. He's doing a fifteen. He's been here five years, and he don't work. He'll just sit there, twenty-three hours a day, until his sentence is up.'

'Just stewing?' I gulped.

'Just stewing. Maybe have a J. Arthur if he's got the energy. that's all there is.'

'Christ.' I said. 'You'd go mad.'

'Yup. Plenty of headbangers in here. They go stair-crazy, but not for long.'

'Why? What happens to them?'

'Nothin'. They stay here, but they either get ECT or they get pumped full of stellazene or somethin' so they don't feel like bein' troublesome any more. You see them coming back from the infirmary after the treatment ...'

'Straight back into the cells without supervision?'

'You think the screws are going to sit over them, singing lullabies? Of course, straight back into their peters. You'll see 'em tomorrow. They got the shakes, like the 'paraffin lamps' only worse. That's how you know 'em.'

'Stellazene ...' I searched my memory. That department wasn't overfull, but there were dregs, and they stank.

'It's the best thing. Oh, sure, there are side-effects; they get so they can't concentrate and all that, but at least they leave able to talk and to find their way down to the boozer.'

'But—'

'Do your bird, kid.'

'What?'

'Do your bird. It's the only thing anyone in here'll tell you if you start complaining. The oldest of all nick expressions, that. Just do your bird.' The big man rolled over on the bed and sighed. 'Fuck it,' he said. 'It's all there is to do.'

He lay silent for a moment, then, 'You're going to see a lot of things to complain about, a lot of things which don't correspond with your high-falutin' ideas about how things ought to be. You'll learn the language, you'll learn how to survive, you'll be as happy or as unhappy as you choose to be. But keep a low profile. Don't spit into the wind. We've got it pretty well sussed in here. If you fight, you'll die. If you complain, you'll lose ninety days and be victimised from there on by the screws. Lie low, do your bird, and remember, you're a con now, like the rest of us.'

'You lose time even if the complaint is justified?'

'It's never fuckin' justified,' the spotty lad broke in. ''Ow can it be? You'll lose ninety days. You've only got cons for witnesses, and they won't open their mouths because they'll get ninety days, too. When I were at Walton, the governor told me, "If one of my officers tells me you was ridin' a motorbike along the landings, I'll want to know where you got the petrol." You're a con now. There's no one you can scream "Mummy!" to. You're on your own. 'Ow long you got?'

'Twelve months,' I told him.

'A stretch!' Tony laughed. 'You'll do it on your 'ead! A doddle!' He saw my raised eyebrows and patiently explained. 'Twelve months is a stretch, three years is a laggin' – that's what I've got – a five is a fistful – that's what Benny's got – three months is a tramp's laggin', and so on.'

'Tony's right,' said Benny, 'you'll do it on your head. You don't believe it now, but it's true. Those eight months will fly so fast you won't know which way to look. One day runs into another like in a dream. Just keep your head together, think a bit, try not to lose what you got and these poor fuckers haven't, and don't get all bitter and twisted.'

'You're lucky really,' Tony said, climbing onto the table to look out into the dusk, 'you'll go to Ravenhill.'

'Yeah. Open prison's a bit slower, but at least you can keep fit, and there ain't that many doorbangers around,' said fat Benny.

'I'll tell you, I've done plenty of bird, mostly for blagging – armed robbery, right? – so I never got to open nick because of the violent aspect, you know? But anyhow, once I did a lagging here at the Cliff, and when I got discharged, I just stood outside those fucking gates, and I couldn't move. My missus was sitting in a car right opposite, but I couldn't cross the road because there was no one to tell me to. I couldn't walk into a boozer, because there was no one to lock the door behind me. I just wanted to come back in here. Couldn't stand the great open spaces.' He shrugged, smiled. 'You won't get that at a place like Ravenhill.'

I did not expect to sleep that night. As I made up my little bed and climbed inside, there swept back into my brain the disquieting, inevitable memory of first nights of term at my old prep. school.

There had been confident, vigorous boys who had known their way about. They had shown no signs of home-sickness. They displayed their new acquisitions and exchanged their new jokes. I would lie still, scornful of the snivellers, pretending to read Russian novels and imagining how it would be at home. Crisp linen sheets would become warm in a moment when the lights went out, and I would bury my head in the pillow and cry for my absolute solitude.

I heard the echoing footsteps outside my cell as once I used to hear the matrons about their business, and again I felt, as then, the shattering loneliness of Copernican revelation. The world was not made for me. I stood at the centre of nobody's universe. I was but a transitory incidental. One of many, to be dealt with.

But you know the gloom of the first days, after a lost love? It was like that. I didn't know what would happen, but I was full of excited apprehension at the doom that I'd incurred. My stomach muscles bunched taut. My scrotal sac stuck to my thigh and I shifted it from side to side, aware of it as never before. My brain throbbed.

The lights went out suddenly. For a while my two cell-mates exchanged elliptical, incomprehensible growls. Nick gossip. I was grateful for their acceptance.

I laid my head on a rolled up blanket which smelt of buses and irritated my cheek. There were no sheets in here. The moonlight just slipped through the high slit-window and splashed on the table beneath.

The courtroom seemed many miles and many days away. I thought of Fiona. The boy above me rolled and grunted like a pig in sleep.

Soon the darkness itself began to roll rhythmically. A womb with a view. This is bloody terrible, I thought, and fell into a deep, fearless sleep.

10

There was a bang, a bustling, a glaring bright light in my eyes.

'Slop out!' bellowed a voice an inch away. I rolled over. The others were already up, pulling on their trousers and their vests.

Wearily, dutifully, I laid my feet on the cold stone floor and followed suit.

'Come on, your lordship,' said Benny, squeezing his paunch into his trousers, 'Grab a bowl and head for the fucking tap.'

'Then what?' I asked obtusely. The floor was freezing, and I was shifting from foot to foot like a circus elephant.

'Fill the bloody thing, of course. We've got to shave. And see the PO on your way back. Tell him you want to see the education, the welfare, the padre, and anyone else you can think of. It's your last chance.'

'Who – where's the PO?'

'He's the screw in the white shirt at the end of the landin'. Come on.'

We stepped out onto a landing filled with identically dressed convicts rushing back and forth. The ironwork throbbed and hummed. If Knightsbridge at nine o'clock in the morning had seemed to me purgatory, then this was its carbon copy in hell. Unshaven cons with skin like Brillo pads jostled with puckered old men and beardless boys for places at the solitary basin.

I blinked in the unexpected light. Just thus must a bull feel as he charges from the dark pen into the spinning red and gold of the arena.

The prison was cruciform. Each of the four sections had four landings running along its sides, and each of the three sides was about seventy yards long and contained twenty cells per landing.

They gaped now like aged eyes, unaccustomed to the light. The whole place seethed. I felt like an atom with ears.

From the landing below, my van companion of the previous day, Billy Turner, waved, exuberant. I nodded and grinned. As I bent to fill my bowl, my shoulder bumped that of another man who turned sharply, and hissed. His snub face was twisted as though permanently pressed against a window-pane.

'Who the fuck do you think you are?' the leer asked, apparently without moving his mouth.

'Sebastian Barclay Foy. Good morning, dear boy.' I smiled on him benignly. Someone behind me laughed.

'Oh yeah?' The leather leer bent a little. With a vocabulary and a face like that, he should have had a tail with which to elucidate his emotions. 'Well, just fuck off, will you, fancy cunt, unless you want your fucking nose the other side of your head.'

A hand grasped the sinewy shoulder. 'Lay off, little shit-pile,' said a deep Irish voice. 'Where you can't grovel, you've got to spit, haven't yer?' A dark man built in Gothick style and proportions gripped the leer's arm and smiled sweetly. His eyes twinkled. A nice guy. Somewhere between Mickey Rooney and King Kong.

His left hand must have moved, but I didn't see it. There was a thud as it struck the base of the plastic pot. Urine sprayed up to splash in the leer's face.

'You . . . you . . . you fucker!' spat the leer from under dripping hair.

The Irishman grinned, ignoring him, and turned to me. 'Hello there,' he said. 'The name's Johnny, Johnny Nash. Don't pay any attention to that little divvy. He's cracked. He'd sell his baby for jam-roll.'

'Whoah there!' I held up my hand. 'Translate.'

'Jam-roll? Parole,' Johnny explained. 'Billy told me you'd arrived and were on this landing.'

'He *told* you?'

'Yeah. Oh, don't worry. There's a signals system. You're a barrister, aren't you?'

'How in God's name . . .? Even Billy didn't know that!'

'No, but his pet screw did. You'll be useful.'

'Well, um, I gather I've got to see that screw over there.'

'Pike? Oh, he's all right. Send him my love. See you at

90

exercise, eh?'

'Yes. Yes. That's fine. I will,' I said. 'Thank you, John.'

'Good morning,' I said to the fat screw. Convicts bustled by. Doors slammed. I had already decided that the clown is the safest man in a strange environment, and I wanted to be safe. 'My name is Sebastian Foy – at your service.' And I bowed.

'Are you taking the piss?' said Pike, thrusting out his chest like a courting pigeon.

'Ah, God forfend!' I cried. 'Or rather, no.'

'What d'ye want then?'

'I want to see the doctor, the catholic priest, the education officer, the probation officer, and anyone else who might alleviate the constant *ennui* engendered by my cell-companions.'

'Like the governor, for instance?'

'Yes, I'd love to meet him. That's very nice of you.'

'Watch it, Foy!' the officer bellowed as he swelled, 'or you'll see the governor soon enough and lose time for yer pains! What's yer number?'

'Er. Oh. D something or other. I forget.'

'You do not forget your number.'

'Oh, sorry. I thought I . . . Silly of me. I'll go back to my bedroom and find out. I've got it all written down on this little pink card, you see.' I turned.

'Foy! Come here!'

Foy went there. 'You think you're fucking clever, don't you?'

'Yes,' I said quietly.

'Oh!' Pike grinned. 'Well just remember, Foy, you're not arsing about at fucking Eton now.'

'No, thought not.'

'I wonder, I wonder just how long you think you can keep this up. By the time you leave here, there'll be none of this shit left in you. It'll have been squeezed, fucked and beaten out of you. Your number is D71107. Never forget it. You're down for padre, welfare, doctor and education. Now, get yourself back to your 'bedroom' fucking quick!'

I was the last to get the cell razor-blade, which was passed from prisoner to prisoner. I shaved as fast as I could, but had only just started on my neck when the door was unlocked and a screw stretched out his hand for the blade. I unscrewed the

91

razor, cursing in the vernacular.

The door was left open. Benny and Tony sauntered out onto the landing. I followed.

We leaned on the railings above the centre, awaiting the call for breakfast. The inhabitants of the ground floor were first summoned, then those of the first, and so on.

A small grey-haired man with a face like a dried up apple wandered over to where we stood. ' 'Ere, Benny!' he said.

'Yeah?'

'Need some burn?'

'What's the rate?'

'Cash or interest?'

'Interest. Got no bread.'

'One and a half for half next Thursday.'

'Christ! Ah well, I've got a visit Saturday. OK, damn you.'

'And also with you, my son,' said the little man. 'I'll see you on the way back up.'

He turned to walk on up the landing, saw me, and stopped. 'Who are you?'

'Who are you?'

'Name's Fred. Fred de Villiers Adam.'

I spluttered, incredulous, and had difficulty in introducing myself.

Fred eyed me slowly and suspiciously. 'If you want some burn, I'm the man to see. It'll cost you.'

'No, thanks,' I said. 'I don't smoke much, and I've got a few ounces myself.'

'Come prepared, did you?' snarled Fred. 'Well. You'll need some soon enough. Come and see me.' He smiled. His eyes were like dying bluebottles. I didn't like him.

'Who the hell was that?' I asked as he swaggered away.

'The Baron,' Tony replied.

'*He's* the Baron?'

'Yup. Runs a porno outfit on the out. Live shows and things. He'll be makin' about a hundred quid a week in here.'

'Just with tobacco?'

'Yeah, for the most part. It's all we got, isn't it? And if we can smuggle in some cash, 'e's got it to sell. Sometimes it's as much as five pounds for an 'alf ounce.'

'Who's that with him down there?' I pointed at the landing

92

below, where Fred was now leaning against the wall with a
chubby blond boy at his side.

'That's 'is missus.'

'His missus?'

'Yeah. He's only a YP – a young prisoner, right? – so 'e
should go to a special nick. But Fred's got it all worked out.
Shares a peter with 'im, and seems to have arranged that the kid
don't get transferred.'

'He occupies the position from choice?'

'Now 'e does, yes. They raped 'im first, when 'e come in.
You should've seen 'is face the mornin' after.' Tony giggled.
'Since then, 'e chooses to be Fred's missus. Got a taste for it.
It's the burn, an' the protection 'e gets, an' a few other things.'

Benny guffawed. 'Yeah, a few other things. Mind, don't get
the wrong idea. Fred's no turd-burglar. He can just afford what
we can't, that's all.

'Oh,' I said, and shrugged, amazed.

We filed down the landing when summoned, past screws who
stood wide-legged, watching. Each convict picked up a tin tray
divided into three sections. A spoon tapped a disc of margarine
into one section, a fried egg slithered into another. Into the
remaining large section, a ladle dumped a lump of porridge
which very slowly sank and spread to fill the tray.

Two tea-urns stood at the end of the row of hatches. You
filled your mug and returned directly to your cell.

I started up the stairs, gazing in awed fascination at the slow
contortions of the grey-brown mass in my tray. Suddenly, I
heard Billy's voice on the landing immediately above me.

'So I've got two eggs. So what do you intend to do about it,
cock?'

A young screw, his hair bubbling out from under his cap, his
chubby cheeks burning, stood before Billy. He was asserting
himself, trusting to the uniform. He'd picked the wrong man.

'Turner, you do not speak to officers like that. Do what you're
fucking well told and take that egg back immediately!'

Billy's easy stance suddenly changed. His head went down.
He advanced towards the young screw like a cat towards a
hobbled bird.

'Turner ...' the young screw murmured. His hand fluttered

at his belt.

'*What* did you say to me?' Billy said slowly.

'I said ...'

'Do you want the fucking egg yourself, then?' Billy picked up the offending sliver of greasy white and weighed it in his hand.

'Turner ...'

Two older screws marched quickly towards the scene of the confrontation. They grabbed the young officer and pulled him back. I just shook my head, bemused. Billy leaned back and smiled.

'How come nobody stopped Billy, then?' I asked when I returned to the cell.

' 'Cos, like we told you, we few got this place sussed,' Benny said through his porridge. 'Billy couldn't give a monkey's about losing time. This is his home. It's just a matter of who he kills, really, not whether he does, and they know that, don't they? So unlike you or me, who want to get out, Billy and the screws are on an equal footing. He's stronger and fitter and faster than they are, so they're shit-scared. You can't pull rank with a guy like Billy.'

'Hey, Seb, you didn't finish shavin',' said Tony.

'No. They took the blade away.'

' 'Ere.' Tony reached under the bed-frame and pulled out a razor-blade. 'We always keep an extra blade 'idden in the cell. You need it to split matches. You get four for every one that way.'

'Oh, yes, of course,' I said daftly.

'Gotta suicide kit in here, too.'

'A what?'

'A suicide kit. Make it out of a coil of wire from the bed-springs. It 'eats water, see?'

'What happens if we get caught with these things?'

'Go to the block, I suppose. Lose two or three days.'

'Where is the block?'

'Down in the basement. Plain cell, no paint, no furniture, no heat. Just a dead plain cell. Not much fun, and you always fall down the stairs.'

'Yup!' Benny sat up and set his tray aside, 'Unless you're someone like Billy, you fall down the stairs every time. The screws have got to get it out of their systems somehow.

Remember when we had the Birmingham bombings last year? They put all the Micks in the nick in the block 'for their own protection'. There wasn't a single fucking Irishman in the place hadn't fallen down the stairs when they got back. Black eyes, smashed noses, broken ribs, the lot. They'd made 'em run the gauntlet between truncheons. Bastards. They keep the nonces and the grasses down there in the basement, too, but they've got it really cushy. Carpets in the peters, television, it's bloody incredible.'

'Nonces?'

'Sexual offenders. Sometimes the cons manage to get at them, but the nick works hard to keep 'em safe. They're on the forty-threes, so they're the governor's responsibility. The cons would kill 'em if they could, poor bastards.'

Tony was tougher. 'I reckon the shits deserve it,' he said.

Benny turned a heavy gaze on the boy. 'Do you?'

This was the most exciting day I was to spend in closed prison. Full of treats. I talked to the education officer, who told me that there was no point in talking to him. I tried to engage the padre in a conversation about Tillich, but his correspondence course hadn't got that far. The welfare officer tried to explain his function, and had difficulty.

The medical examination was the most frightening and depressing experience of the day. The doctor was clearly contemptuous and had little time for the convicts who so largely contributed to his livelihood. The consequences of his disregard, after all, were invisible both to the public and to the BMA.

I sat on a little bench outside the doctor's room. On both sides of the corridor sat other men with various parts of their bodies already exposed. Each examination had to take up as little of the doctor's time as possible.

A long thin man sat opposite me. He was full of that belligerent cockiness which marks a man who's done a lot of bird. His shoes and socks were in his hand. I wished that he'd kept them where they belonged. The feet were alternately black and red, and large flakes of dead skin hung between his toes like charred wallpaper. The nail on the left big toe was coal black and twisted. This was particularly interesting because the other nails had dropped off completely.

'Trying to get a change of socks every day,' he told me. 'Won't succeed, of course.'

'How often do you get them changed now?'

'Same as anyone, twice a week. It's taken me three weeks to get past the medical screw and as far as the doctor.'

The man was summoned into the doctor's room. He came out again two minutes later, swearing and smiling.

'No luck?' I asked.

'No luck. Regulations, see?'

I didn't see. I didn't see what prison regulations had to do with a doctor. I couldn't remember a clause of exemption relating to criminals in the Hippocratic oath. Maybe I hadn't read it closely enough.

'Foy!' called the officer at the door. I entered the room obediently.

The doctor sat behind a desk in the centre of the room. He was a small, rotund man, with a white military moustache and a pin-striped suit which he wore like principles.

'Give your name to the doctor,' said the screw who stood by the desk.

'Sebastian Barclay Foy.' The doctor flinched as he heard my voice, but he did not look up.

'Any medical problems, Foy?' he sighed.

'Yes. Manic depressive psychosis.'

The screw snorted.

'What treatment have you recieved?'

'Therapy and, of late, a course of Monoamine-oxidase inhibitors.' I'd practiced that on many a drunken night. I was rather proud of it, really. No one here seemed impressed.

'Yes, well,' said the doctor, 'you won't be getting anything of that sort in here. You'll just have to cope. No pills.'

'What if I were to become depressed? Is there any treatment available?'

'No. No psychotherapists here. Take down your trousers and underpants.'

I took them down.

'Cough.'

I coughed. The doctor raised an eyebrow to check the reaction. 'Right. Back to your cell.'

He had not once looked at my face, and I didn't think he

would recognise me again by my genitalia. There's nothing like the personal approach in medicine. This was just the sort of man you'd feel free to approach if you were worried about your nightmares, your breathing, a lump on your chest, a sore on your penis, or a foul canker gnawing away at your brain.

In the lunchtime queue, a boy who could have modelled for Cow and Gate lobbed a hunk of bread at a colleague. A screw was crossing the centre. The missile narrowly missed the peak of his cap. He stopped. For a moment his expression of astonishment was that of a comic cartoon character. The convicts laughed. A few scurrilous jibes were shouted.

Three more officers stepped rapidly into the centre. They were being mocked, and they were frightened. One of them, a Welshman, shouted, 'Who threw that?'

No one spoke.

'Who threw that?'

Still there was no reply. A few giggles trickled through the queue.

'All right, then,' the Welshman said petulantly, 'if you're going to behave like stupid fucking babbies ...'

He strode away amidst a roar of mockery. He left the sentence unfinished, but Benny sighed behind me. 'Oh bugger,' he said, 'that's not the last we've heard of that. Petty little sods.'

'Exercise is depressing when the weather is gloomy, a lot worse when it's fine. Grey figures wander alone or pace in pairs, round and round the high-walled yard, heads bowed, like Dante's damned souls. Already the sky and the smell of the air seemed unfamiliar to me, and the clouds reflected the slow circling grey whorl below.

Johnny Nash and Billy Turner joined me for a few circuits of the yard, thus giving me a degree of security and 'respectability' at which I could only guess.

I knew, of course, that they intended to use me, but I preferred their company to that of the petty thieves and yobboes who snarled or toadied to me so soon as they heard my voice.

These men had chosen to be villains, in so far as free choice exists for any man. They made no attempt to pretend to be

97

anything else. Their talk was friendly and witty, their relationships founded upon mutual respect and a shared code of morals to which they loyally adhered. They appeared to know all the other members of their distinguished profession, and to be familiar with most of Britain's prisons.

As they talked, I began to understand their motivation. They were, in a sense, free spirits, free to create their own ethics and their own obligations, for they acknowledged no debt to anyone save to their friends and their families.

So far as they were concerned, the demands of the social morality as enforced by law and church were meaningless. They regarded themselves neither as beneficiaries nor as components of the social unit. It was too large and nebulous to make any sense. Where its demands proved irreconcilable with those of self-interest and with their fundamental morality, whose touchstones were sentiment and survival, they scorned society's demands, and served their broods alone.

If a Bangladeshi child is starving and our own children have a mild bout of 'flu, we will spend our last few pounds on relieving the discomfort of those nearest to us. No doubt the liberal universal sympathy-mongers will tell us that this is immoral, but sympathy is, of its nature, restricted to those with whom we can afford to sympathise. A soldier cannot feel the agonies of his enemy, nor a warder with his charges. His brain would boil over. These men had merely extended that natural morality just one degree further. They did not see society as a survival mechanism, but merely as something which deprived them and theirs of that which they could naturally take. They took.

Such men, I discovered, would thieve for a living and fight just to test their right to survive, but they would weep for a child subjected to cruelty or neglect and would take it on themselves to punish those responsible. They regarded self-seeking (under which heading came loyalty to friends and families) as a duty. They were intelligent, canny, powerful men, but someone had failed to explain to them the cause and nature of a society's genesis. Or again, maybe they were right, and the relation between social law and survival no longer exists.

It was half-past four, and again we lined up to be fed. The first cons took their tea. A murmur arose. A message was passed down the line.

'Don't touch the tea.'

'Thank you,' I said, and passed the message on.

I looked up at the tea-urns. None of the convicts filled his mug. The big Welsh screw stood there with his hands linked behind his back. He smirked. His colleagues' expressions were echoes of his own.

'What the hell was that about?' I asked.

'Owen. He's pissed in the tea. Remember dinner-time? They got to get their own back somehow. That's one of their little ways. Doesn't matter much now but in summer, it's no joke.'

That night was restless, Tony had no tobacco, and neither Benny nor I would give him more than one cigarette. He pined and whined and coughed and gathered up Benny's dog-ends like a dog at a picnic.

As soon as the lights went out, a man in the next cell began to whimper. Then he howled like a wolf and rattled the cell door. Occasionally he fell silent, then there came a high, soft whine which rose to end on a little flick like a whip-crack, and the sobbing and screaming would start again.

Other voices joined in the howling. Some started by bellowing at the original voice to shut up and ended by screaming in inarticulate fury and frustration. Others merely joined in the chorus.

At last, there was a hideous, amorphous cacophony of deep throated shouts and falsetto squeals, punctuated by the rattling of bars and the sound of feet stomping. It went on and on, swelling and ringing through the cavernous centre.

There was a click of keys. Feet thudded on the landing. Metal grated and rattled. The noise subsided like something punctured, and only the original singer, impervious, still whimpered and cried.

We heard feet, six or seven pairs, clattering assertively about the landing. We heard in the darkness the door swing open, and the whining grow in volume, to die on a squeal like a piglet's. The door slammed again. The footsteps receded. Something dragged on the iron. There was silence.

'Thank Christ for that,' sighed Benny.

'What happened?'

'They took him to the block.'

'Who was it?'

'Dunno. Junkie, I should think. They usually make a lot of row on their first few nights. Withdrawal symptoms.'

'Oh!' For the first time since the court case, I felt a longing for oblivion.

'There'll be trouble tonight, though,' muttered Benny. 'Get one, and they all start getting gloomy.'

'Yeah. New Year's Eve, eh, Ben?'

'That's right, kid. Should've heard it then, when the bells started at midnight. The whole nick howled like a knacker's yard. Ten cells smashed to bits.'

'Oh,' I said again. I lay still for a while, listening to the huffing and sighing. 'Look, how do we shit in here?'

'Press the bell.' Benny grunted.

I stumbled to the bell-push and pressed it hard. Tony sniggered.

'Leastways, that's what it says in the rule-book,' Benny went on. 'Of course, you can keep pressing all night, and no one's going to come. Two days before you come, this nigger topped himself. The other cons in his cell pressed that bloody bell from ten thirty in the evening till six thirty in the morning when one of the screws came and cut 'im down. We had an epileptic the other day, too. Had a fit. The cons didn't know what to do, did they? They pressed that bell forever. Chap choked on his own vomit.'

'Thanks for the bedtime stories, Benny. So how do we shit?'

'Here.'

I stretched out my hand. A sheet of newspaper was thrust into it. 'Just throw it out of the window when you've done,' said Benny. 'Create labour for cons. The barmy army goes round every morning, clearing up the yards.'

I looked down on the paper in my hand, and wondered about the mechanics of the process. I sighed, shook my head, reflected on the sudden decline in my fortunes, squatted in the corner and did as I was instructed.

11

Nothing happened on the second day. By evening, I felt as though I had been in that prison all my life. This dismal routine was familiar now, and inevitable as the movement of the sun.

The third day, however, started with what passed for 'an event'.

After breakfast, I heard my name spoken by voices outside the cell. I moved to the door to listen.

'Sebastian Foy, Esquire, yet! See how long he'll remain an esquire, eh? Right now, what have we here? "My darling Sebastian" – Ooooh, my darling Sebastian, is it? Someone likes the little poofter!'

'Cool it,' said Benny from the table. 'It's Cooper. Gets his kicks this way. Pay no attention.'

I wondered from whom the letter might have come. 'My darling Sebastian . . .' Probably Sylvie.

' "How can such a horrible, terrifying thing have happened to you of all people?" ' the rough voice read on. ' "Oh, darling, if I could only tell you of the cold, shattering wave of sheer terror which swept over me when Catkin rang to tell me. I just sat and howled for hours and hours. I still haven't sorted myself out. In fact, you've made me bloody ill . . ." Ah, poor diddums. Did we howl when we were told that our naughty little poofter had been nicked?'

I just leaned my head against the door, closed my eyes, and smiled for simple joy. Tears burned in my eyes. At last, at last, at last!

' "Everything I do is filled with thoughts of you. I cannot sleep at night and I am totally useless by day. Everything

101

reminds me of you, and I just crack up without warning. Oh, darling why you? I keep listening to 'Hide in Your Shell', which is very silly, because it only makes things worse. I know you will survive, my love. You have the courage. I feel that you must be thinking of me, too, for you are constantly with me and sometimes I feel that I can just reach out to touch you. Oh, darling, darling, darling ..." Oh, Jesus! I can't go on with this crap. She needs a good fuck, and that's all there is to it. Sure as hell she won't get it from this creep, eh? Here, Foy, it's all yours.'

The door swung open and the letters were thrust through. I caught the screw's eye. He looked at me triumphantly. I looked back, pitying. 'Mr Cooper,' I said, 'whilst I understand that you must find some substitutes for the free and natural pleasures enjoyed by others, I would yet ask you to be very careful.'

Cooper opened his mouth to speak, but I cut him short. 'Just be very careful, Mr Cooper. I understand your problem. I sympathise, but others in positions of considerably greater authority might not. Good morning.' I slammed the door in his face.

Benny laughed. 'Good on you, kid. He's a stupid little shit. Can't cope with guys like you.'

'Shut up, Benny. I want to read this letter very slowly, two hundred and thirty-two times.'

'Right.' Benny grinned amiably and turned back to his Western.

I sat on the bunk and read. I felt vertiginous, I felt happy, I felt that I must explode, though whether I would laugh or cry, I had no idea.

'Everywhere I go, everything I do makes me think of you. You are inside me. Oh, God, I suppose you always have been. I will never forgive myself for not being there when you needed me most. I'll devote myself forever to making up for it when at last this is over.

'I keep thinking back. Back to that night when we walked up to Leicester Square and you sang all those crazy, lovely songs, and we watched the dawn come up as we lay in bed after. Damn it, the stones of this town ring with echoes of you. Oh boy, will we have a celebration when you get out at last!

'Anyhow, darling, just remember that, no matter what may

happen, I'm right there beside you, and every bad thing that happens to you hurts me too. I know you're strong enough to surmount it all. Just hold on, my love, it'll be all right. Oh, how could I have been such a fool as to waste so much time! I always knew, really, that it had to be you. I love you.

'Write to me as soon as you can. Dream with me, as we always did. I'll write again when I'm a little more together. All my love, always, always, always, your F.'

All right, so I'm a grown man, but a sob bubbled up and burst from my lips. I turned to the grey wall, rocking in a kind of ecstasy. 'Oh, you wonderful, fickle bitch,' I whispered, and read the whole letter over again.

It is not surprising that I could never justify this passion for Fiona Gunn to Catkin or to any of those others who bade me forget. She was inconsistent, though never an inconstant friend. She was vain, proud, romantic, provocative and totally impossible. She moved like a thoroughbred, bitched like Saki, giggled like a schoolgirl and suddenly clung like a lost soul to the secret of the darkness. She was brilliant, but she might spend four hours of a day in making herself look beautiful, two to buying clothes and Diet-Pepsis, one to the *Evening Standard* junior crossword, and the rest to making me happy. All right. I can't justify it to myself. She was a one-woman harem, tone-deaf Pellegrina Leoni, and I was bound to her. I suppose I still am.

Physical attraction and common arrogance had drawn us together, but as I breathed too familiar words on that first night, as my hands performed too familiar motions of self-seeking selflessness, she stretched out her hand to check mine.

I looked down on her, questioning. The traffic in the little sleepy square seemed very far off. Her eyes were so deep in darkness as to be scarcely visible, but I looked into them very deep, and very slowly I found myself smiling. Her cheeks were smooth and cool in the lamplight, and the shadow of her long lashes curled into an arabesque over her cheekbones, just dipping into the little scar; flesh, then skull, then flesh, as the headlight beams swung through the room and receded.

A flash from the headlights, and her eyes were *her* eyes, flecked with lust and the need for laughter, with every still-present childhood dream, with greed and cunning and the memories that had made her.

I held her head and looked down on her. The smell of her body changed just slightly from that of the cool sweat on her arms and breasts to that of animal rut. Sudden and smooth as a duck-dive, I slipped into her arms as if into deep, cool water.

Words were no longer necessary. I belonged. Together we shed and shared the accumulated knowledge and experience which constituted ourselves. All was accepted. To complain or to define were to blaspheme. For once, ideal and animal were reconciled.

Human and full of worship, wild yet warm, her golden body flashed on the deep red coverlet. Like the quick flash of a fish, her shoulder stood out and was doused in darkness as she reached out to clasp. Her neck stretched as I kissed her. She croaked, and her breastbone hummed.

Tumbling buffeted and blinded down, 'Oh, so that's it', one of us said, though neither of us could remember which.

That night when we walked up to Leicester Square ...

White silk jersey gloved her. We had dinner at the Savoy and walked up to the square in not very serious pursuit of a taxi. London sweltered. The heat came in waves which struck your face and shook the shadows, climbed the walls and overflowed like wine.

We sat on a bench, and I sang 'London Pride' and 'Just the Way You Look Tonight' for sheer exuberance. For the first time since infancy, I knew what it was to belong. A group of Scottish drunkards, all rosettes and tartan, thick oaths and whisky breaths, gathered round.

Fiona sat there in my arms as they laughed and sang and danced around us.

I looked down at her there in the crook of my arm. Her eyes shone in the lamplight. Her black hair whispered about my mouth. She was smiling, excited and happy.

The whole bloody world melted, and she seemed to glow, the real still centre about which the shouting red-faced men circled as if in a magic lantern show. She alone was real. I suddenly clasped her very tight and squeezed her to me with an upsurge of possessive pride and defensiveness for which I had to apologise to myself later.

When she ran away, she became churlish and frenetic,

defending herself from what we had discovered. She came back, she ran off again, but always I believed that she must at last return.

I lay still, clutching that letter to me. It was half an hour before I realised that I had two other letters. One was from my mother. It was full of ill-disguised maternal concern and inconsequential gossip. The other came from Catkin.

'How are you, darling? The monster knew all along and is growling and bellowing and swearing that you'll never be allowed to the bar again and that he'll never talk to you again etc., etc. I suppose that comes to the same thing as sending his love and wishing you well. Beastly, dirty, odious little censor-grockle, keep your nose out of my Foy's letter. Nothing could deprave or corrupt him. Your nice friend Sylvie and I got very tight and tearful on the train and still more so when we got back here. Ended up collapsed on my floor (enjoying yourself, Mr Censor?) and we're to see *Equus* tonight. Now *she's far* more suitable than whatsit, But I suppose you know best. Good hunting, darling. I've got a crim. dam. to sort out, (v. gory), so must go. Tell me what you want and how I can get it to you. What about books?'

We emerged from the cells, and once more rubbed our eyes at the sudden light and the frenetic activity of the central hive. Exercise time.

Suddenly there was a shout from the landing above. A grey thing shot by. I ducked, although it was some yards off. It hurtled down the central well, buffeted by the corners of steel 'safety' netting. At the end of its fall, it was no more than a little lump, crumpled in unfamiliar grey and stippled with bright red and the white of splintered bone.

'Oh, bugger,' said Benny. 'That's fucked exercise for today.'

Tough kid Tony gazed out, fascinated and awed by first death. ''E kept 'is 'ands linked all the way down,' he gulped. ''E kept 'is 'ands together all the way down. Jesus!'

Fred de Villiers Adam strolled by, his hands in his pockets. His 'missus' simpered by his side.

'Who was that, Fred?' Benny asked.

'Polish chap. Name of Wasinsky or something. In for handling swollen goods, but his wife was bringing further charges against him.'

'His missus was?'

'Yup. Been messing about with their kid, so she said. She'd never have made it stick, but it don't really matter now, does it?'

'Did he owe you burn?'

'That crime he did not have on his conscience, my son. No, he's not one of mine. See you.'

I looked down the landing for Johnny Nash, but saw him nowhere. I walked along to his cell and asked where he was.

'He's in the block,' said a deep, cultured voice. 'I'm afraid he got nicked for having contraband. Bottle of Scotch. He was grassed up.'

A slender, middle-aged man stepped forward. His milk-white hair was swept back over his ears. He held out his hand. 'My name's Dennis, Dennis Blake. You must be the barrister fellow. Delighted to meet you.'

I shook the hand. Dennis practised the twinkle which, I guessed, constituted his livelihood. 'I think, dear boy, that we will be going to Ravenhill together.'

'Oh yes? I'm glad. When do we go?'

'The next draft is about ten days from now, I understand. A delightful spot, so I am given to believe, and so far better than that we should suffocate in this malodorous inferno. It is reminiscent, is it not, of Joyce's sermon on hell?'

'It is.' I grinned at the affected grandiloquence of this elegant man in bristling grey.

'And so, we shall be together. I have some experience of incarceration, whereas you, I believe, are, or were, that is, *virgo intacta*. You will probably be glad of some guidance and instruction. Horrible business, that fellow taking a dive, eh?'

'Beastly.'

'Happens quite often, you know. Totally unnecessary, mind. I mean, stone walls do not a prison make, what? All a state of mind.'

'Quite so. Absolutely,' I said, feeling rather guilty at my own happiness.

'By the way,' continued Dennis, 'tell the fellows in your cell that Maurice Boyes will be here tomorrow. That'll cheer them up. I say, you'd better get back to your peter, old chap. I'll see

106

you anon.'

'Maurice Boyes will be here tomorrow,' I told my cellmates.

'Jesus,' said Benny.

'Cor,' said Tony.

'Well, who *is* M. Boyes?'

'The gaffer of half the cons in here, that's all,' said Benny. 'You find me a pie in Brum and I'll find you Maurice Boyes' finger in it. Not up to Kray standard, perhaps, but big, very big. It's the strongest firm in the Midlands by a long way.'

'What sort of firm?'

'You name it. Fencing, tarts, drugs, porn, land deals, local government, the whole shooting match. He's got himself done for trying to pervert the course of justice. Some big white chief in the Old Bill got ideas about stopping corruption, see, and he got Maurice for bribing a few cops. Only trouble is, so soon as they did that, Maurie got sort of chagrined, didn't he? So he revealed a few things about the Old Bill, like how they sold him back confiscated porn and that. So he got twelve months and they lost ten top officers. That'll teach 'em to fart in church.'

'Yeah, he did the bastards properly,' said Tony, still shocked and subdued, 'but Fred's going to be shittin' 'imself.'

'Oh, why so?'

''E mentioned Mr Boyes in evidence. Nothin' too serious, but still, 'e mentioned 'im.

'Don't be daft,' said Benny, 'if Maurie Boyes had wanted to get Fred, he'd 'ave got him months ago. He's got as much pull in here as anywhere. No, he's perfectly happy to have Fred sweat a bit. He'll have uses for him.'

'S'pose so.'

'Mind, someone else is going to get hit pretty soon if he don't get on the forty-threes.'

'Who's that, then?' said Tony.

'Joe Christian – you had a bit of a barney with him your first morning didn't you, Seb?'

'Did I? Who was that?' I asked, tearing myself from the twentieth re-reading of my letter.

'Christian. Little shit who tried to wind you up at slop-out.'

'Oh, the leer! What about him?'

'They're out to get him. Seems he took offence when Johnny Nash came in on your behalf. Grassed him and Tim Bates

107

up for having a bottle of Scotch.'

'What'll they do to him?'

'Dunno, but it won't be nice. He's a fool to grass up Johnny, of all people. Someone'll hit him; your mate Billy, I should think. We'll see.'

They hit the leer all right.

I was bearing my tea-tray up the stairs when two swarthy characters hailed me. They were smiling broadly.

'Come on,' they said.

'Hadn't I better lock myself up or something?'

'Nah. Don't bother. The screws know about this. We gotta treat for yer.'

Apprehensive, I followed them to a cell just along the landing from my own.

Six or seven inmates were already gathered there, so it was a full minute before I distinguished the form of a man stretched out on his stomach on the bottom bunk. The body was shaking. Little whimpers of terror were the only sounds but for the rustling of the convicts' clothes as we stood and waited.

It was the leer. His trousers were pulled down to his ankles, and the scrawny naked buttocks twitched.

'Right, you little shit-pile,' said a bald man crouched almost astride the leer's head. 'So you grassed up Johnny. We can't have grasses in this nick, can we?'

'I didn't. For God's sake, I didn't! I wouldn't . . .' the little man whimpered. His usually twisted face was screwed up as tightly as his buttocks.

'Ah, come on, Christian. Don't try bullshitting us. Leave that for the judge and the Boy Scouts. We don't like grasses. Do you know what we're going to do to you?'

'No . . . no.'

'We're going to uncork you.'

'Oh Christ!' moaned the leer, his buttocks contracting still further. 'Oh, Christ, no. I didn't do anything! On my baby's life I didn't.' He made a sudden twist and plunge, but was quickly restrained and held down. His buttocks arose like a wave. He kicked and twisted vainly. The smell of sweat and of old grey jackets was now pervaded by the stench of animal fear.

Suddenly I saw the glint of metal. Here, where all metal

objects were forbidden, it drew the eye at once. It would draw the eye anywhere. A carving knife, with a thick tapering blade and a cutting edge nicked by use, gleamed dully in the hand of the man at the bed's foot.

The screams and whimpers of the thrashing leer were redoubled. A raucous male voice broke through, 'Go on!'

The point of the blade was shoved between the buttocks of the man on the bed.

'Oh Jesus,' whined the leer, and lay still.

With a sudden heave of my stomach, I saw the knife driven home, up to the hilt in the rectum.

The leer surged up in the bed like a whale. He hissed. A deep groan erupted from his stomach. He lay still again. His shoulders juddered, his buttocks twitched. Watery blood squirted out in little spurts with a gulping sound.

I swallowed a lump of nothing. My mouth was rasping dry.

The man holding the knife twisted it once, then again, until it had turned a full circle in the anus. With each twist, the leer's arms flapped as though he were floundering in water. His whole body shuddered.

Slowly, smoothly, excruciatingly, the blade was drawn out. I closed my eyes.

Then from behind the darkness of my eyelids, I heard a scream, a high, broken shriek of agony, which escaped the cell and ran ringing through the ironwork. Again and again the leer screamed, until the air seemed a thick-textured mass of grey shoddy and male sweat through which there was threaded a scarlet shaft of steel. I could move neither to left nor to right. On all sides spectators pressed in.

'Give us that burn!' The voice of the executioner quavered.

I opened my eyes. The leer was still struggling. His head was now on the stone floor. The cons held him down with expressions neither pitiful nor vindictive. They just looked businesslike. One handed over a small wad of brown stuff. It was raw tobacco.

The man at the foot of the bed knelt with his legs apart to avoid the spurting of the blood. He took the tobacco and forced it with his fingers into the inflamed, pumping orifice.

'Right,' he shouted. He wiped his hands on the bed with an expression of disgust. 'Let's go!'

The cons turned and pushed towards the door, bearing me with them. I breathed the air on the landing like a diver surfacing. Bemused and almost drunk, I reeled back to my own cell. The screams pursued me.

A screw stood at the door of the cell, impervious to the noise. He grinned, bowed as I passed, and shut the door behind me.

No more was seen of the leer. Two days later, Johnny Nash was in the exercise yard with Billy and friends. Again they hailed me as I walked around the yard with Benny.

'Hi, Seb,' said Johnny.

'Hi, Johnny. What did you get?'

'Lost sixty days.'

'Damn!'

'Yeah. Look, Seb, can you do us a favour? I'll pay you.'

'What do you want?'

'Well, you're a good guy with the verbals, aren't you? I was wondering, can you write poems?'

'Yes, I suppose I could. What sort of poem?'

'It's for my missus. She's going to be a bit wound up by this fucking business, you know, two extra months and that, and I thought it would be a good idea, you know, just a little poem. They like that sort of thing.'

'Sure.' I smiled at his embarassment. 'What's her name?'

'Carol.'

'Any children?'

'No. Only been married a year. Got a dog, though.'

'What's it called?'

'Ah, some silly fucking foreign name. Bianca ...' he spoke the name softly. 'Yeah, that's it, Bianca.'

'When did you get sent down?'

'Last September.'

'OK, that's all I need to know. I'll do it by tonight.'

'Great. I'll give you a half for it.'

'Thanks.'

Billy broke in, 'Fucking poems, I don't know!' He laughed. 'But listen, Seb, if you can help with a letter or two . . .'

'Sure, Billy.'

I was in the money.

Back in my cell, I sat at the table and wrote Johnny's poem

110

on the *After Babel* dust-jacket. I introduced as much artificial sentiment as I dared, and still found myself affected by the sheer banality of my own plagiaristic composition.

In the sweltering heat of last summer,
Your trusting head on my arm,
You lay pressed close in the darkness,
Your body soft and warm.

I could feel your breath on my shoulder,
Your hair splashed out on my chest,
As bathed in a quicksilver sweat we lay,
'I love you,' I said, but you were at rest.

There's Carol with her silly jokes,
Nose turned up in laughter,
Carol stoned when friends come round,
Music and wine when we're all alone after.

Carol crying in my arms,
Her crazy, trusting dreams,
Carol when she comes in late,
Her hair's all wet, her body gleams.

Carol running in the fields
And playing with Bianca,
God, how I wish I knew a way
In which to truly thank her.

For without these thoughts there were no hope
As I sit in this cold grey cell.
Stay with me, darling, stay in my dreams,
Only you can make heaven for me of this hell.

I presented this embarrassing hotch-potch to Johnny as we waited to go down for tea. He glanced over his shoulder, then slowly read it. 'Fuck it,' he said at last, 'fuck it that's really . . . well, fuck! Read it for me, Seb.'

I read it slowly. Johnny stood still. His great hands hung loose at his sides. At the end, he shook his head as though

111

trying to dislodge an insect, said, 'Great, thanks, Seb,' and walked rapidly away, clinging to the shiny black dust-jacket.

When I returned to the cell with my tea, I found Dennis Blake waiting for me. 'For you, old boy, from Johnny,' he said. He held out his hand, palm downward, and thrust two half-ounce packs of Old Holborn into mine. Already I knew the pleasure of power contained in those crackling packets. Benny whistled. Tony said, 'Fuck me, an ounce!'

I smiled and shoved them in my pocket. 'Thank Johnny very much,' I said.

'I will.' said Dennis. 'Transfer soon. Good news, eh?'

'Excellent.'

'Maurice Boyes will be coming with us.'

'You what?' Benny turned and stared. 'Maurice Boyes going to open nick? How the fuck did he manage that?'

'Well, Benny, old boy, he's only in for impeding the course of justice, you know, and he's got almost no form, even though he is one of the nation's biggest villains, so the powers that be have no choice. Silly, isn't it?'

'Bloody hell, that's a joke!'

'It is rather amusing, is it not?' and Dennis wandered off.

The news soon spread about Johnny Nash's poem. A stream of cons came to me seeking my help with letters, petitions for transfer to prisons nearer their homes, and love poems. One young dope dealer wanted a letter translated into French. I accomplished this easily, having problems only with the curious sentence, 'I want to fuck you sideways,' which, after some thought, I translated as, *'Je veux te baiser comme un crabe.'*

Another old lag gave me a scrap of newspaper on which he had scrawled a summary of that which he wished to tell his wife: 'My dearest wife I miss you very much and I love you I hope you are well Im OK Look I trust you but just rember I got someone watching you all day and if you mess around hell put a blade in you so watch it I love you as I have said. Your husband.'

12

At last the day for transfer came. I had only just finished breakfast when the screws arrived and told me to make up my bed-roll and to follow them to 'reception'. We were bundled into a van again but, this time, without handcuffs. Already this demonstration of trust seemed an honour.

For the first half hour of the journey, as we passed through industrial suburbs and the country grey in their shadows, I stayed silent. I just gazed out of the window at people unlocking shop doors, at cars which bumped out of little terraced gardens, at a world going about its morning business unaware of D71107 Foy, a con with seven months and two weeks yet to serve. Even road-signs could crack you up after a couple of weeks in the big house.

The fields of Leicestershire are somehow greener than those of Warwickshire where the dead elms line the roads like beggars leaning, watching, and as the van dipped into valleys and mounted little hills, my spirits rose.

So soon as Dennis saw me looking about me, he smiled. 'Ah, good, our advocate has aroused himself from the doldrums. My dear boy, you must meet Maurice Boyes. Maurice, this is Sebastian Foy.'

Boyes was a huge, heavy, bald man with a high domed forehead. His paunch was massive, his hands soft and thick. As he held out a hand to engulf mine, his flabby lower lip curled humorously, snagged with saliva, and his eyes twinkled. Since Boyes had arrived, I had hesitated to approach him because he was always surrounded by his acolytes.

'I'm very glad you're going to be with us, Sebastian.' His

113

voice was deep and resonant. 'Billy tells me you've got a sense of humour. You can do your bird. That's good news. We need intelligent cons around. There are plenty of clever people around, but bloody few intelligent ones. People are always asking me what the difference is and it's bloody hard to explain. Do you play the piano? You have done? Well, I think intelligence is like sympathetic harmonies; each note finds its own relations and starts a whole chain of harmonious reactions. With the clever, you have to strike every damned note, and still it doesn't make a chord, because there is always that dissonant factor, the awareness of his own cleverness.'

'Yes,' I agreed. 'Wilde says somewhere that in the minds of the ignorant there is always room for a great idea, but that in the minds of the clever there is room for nothing save their own self-esteem.'

Boyes smiled slowly. 'He's right, of course. Clever fellow, Wilde.'

'Pity, wasn't it?'

'*Wasn't* it just?'

Boyes, I felt, could never have been a normal working man, with his air of slow wisdom and his great bulk. He could have been a great priest or a great impresario. Come to think of it, I suppose that his profession was a bit of both.

'You two should cause quite a sensation at Ravenhill,' said Dennis. 'You're quite the most illustrious cons around at the moment, other than Stonehouse, of course, but he's not there.'

'What it is to be famous, eh, Seb?' Maurice laughed.

We chatted on the journey, and I felt, as I had rarely felt before, that I was being appraised by that slow, heavy, ironic gaze. I found myself absurdly anxious to win approval.

At last, the van turned off the road. It stopped immediately at a little white shed. The driver got out and exchanged a few words with another discipline officer.

I crouched down to see through the windscreen. Straight in front of us there lay a large tarmac parade ground. White-painted, one-storey buildings ran all along the right-hand side. Immediately on our left there stood a larger wooden hut with a barn roof and a cross on top. Flower baskets hung from the eaves.

Over the roof, you could see a three-storey, brick building

114

with large plate windows. That, I knew, was 'D' block, the last home of Trevor Abbott.

Straight across the parade ground from us stood a long, wide windowed barn. Beyond that, open fields stretched out for half a mile or more. Around all these buildings, there were neat herbaceous borders and small trees. Trevor had seen all this as he arrived, just as I saw it now.

Just as I saw it, but for one thing. Trevor had left a sad mass of brown dead heads in the big bed in front of the church. The bed was packed with old-fashioned, thick-stemmed moss roses – Trevor's monument.

The driver climbed back in again. 'You're in luck,' he said, 'we made good time. Should have you all sorted out in time for dinner.'

'Good,' Maurice grunted. 'For the first time in weeks, I'm famished. What's for dinner, then?' He addressed himself to the prison officer who had climbed in beside the driver.

'Shit, of course,' said the screw, 'what did you expect?'

'I'll tell you what I expect in a week or so, Mr. Leach,' said Maurice with a charming smile, 'so will Mr. Foy here.'

Leach turned. 'Oh, so you're Foy, are you?' He eyed me with interest. He had tried to conceal his chubby baby-face with a limp red moustache which made him appear perpetually lugubrious.

'I'm Foy,' I said, returning his stare.

'Ah, well! He hummed in the enigmatic tone of a Brummy Sybil.

'I don't care what's for dinner,' said a little Irishman who had not spoken throughout the journey. 'I'd eat two tons of best nick duff if I had to. Ravenhill goulash isn't bad, actually.'

I turned to him. 'You've been here before, then?'

Leach guffawed. 'Mickey? It seems as if he was only here yesterday. Go on, Mickey, tell him how often. Five times isn't it?'

'No,' he pouted resentfully, 'four.'

'Lord save us, you've been out of luck,' I said.

'That's what I always say.' He shook his dark head sadly. 'Bad luck is all I got.'

The van chugged past the low white buildings and turned right down another tarmac road. On the left there was a bowling green, on the right a gymnasium on which 'GYMNASIUM' was writ large.

The van doors were opened and we were summoned out – unaccompanied. I inhaled a load of fresh air. A light wind fanned the hair back off my brow. It was as startling and invigorating as first frost.

We were escorted into a large shack and told to sit on the bench. Leach rang a small bell as though in a hotel lobby. He leaned on the counter and made a few jokes. Again I noted with what greater ease screws move and talk when they are safely in their own environment.

A tall, thin, middle-aged man with a bouncing Adam's apple emerged from the back room. 'A new lot, eh?' he keened in a high-pitched voice. 'Well now, who've we got?'

'Me, turkey-neck,' said Maurice.

'What?' The tall man jumped and squeaked.

'That's right, my son. I am here, Officer Forsdyke.'

'Fucking hell. You! I never thought I'd see you here.'

'Bad luck.'

Turkey-neck looked at the rest of the batch. His gaze stopped on Mickey. 'Oh, Jesus! Moaning minnie's back again,' he sneered.

'What?' said Mickey.

'You like this place, don't you, Rourke?'

'I don't,' Mickey said petulantly, 'I don't like it. I always get sent here, that's all.'

'Ah, come on.' Forsdyke was anxious to assert himself after his put-down with Maurice. 'Talk about institutionalised, you can't even live two days on the out like an adult, you only left three weeks ago.'

'Lay off, turkey-neck,' said Maurice.

'Shut up, Boyes.'

Maurice cleared his throat. Forsdyke gulped. 'Which one of you is Foy?'

'I am Sebastian Foy.'

'The governor wants to see you as soon as we've finished with you.'

I felt rather than heard the jeers of the others, who must have believed that I was already the object of special treatment. I could have done without this. 'Very well,' I said, 'the governor

116

shall have his will.'

We had travelled up in our own, very creased clothes which were now confiscated again. We were then issued with regulation uniform and reminded of our positions of trust, and then, amazingly, we were released and instructed to go to our billets without supervision. It was almost frightening to step out of that reception shed alone, to see no cells, no walls, but only a community territory bound in by a waist-high fence.

Forsdyke had directed me to the governor's office, on the left of the parade ground. I duly knocked on the door marked 'Governor'.

'Stay out!' cried a voice from within.

I stayed out. In closed prison, my uniform had merely been standard. Here, in the open air, I felt ridiculous.

After five minutes, an attractive fair con swaggered out, confident, like a man who's had a beating. 'All right,' he said, 'it's all yours.'

I knocked again. Someone called, 'Come in!' and I entered, shutting the door behind me.

'Give your name and number to the governor,' said a West Country voice. It was a senior screw who stood at the governor's right hand. An ordinary discipline officer stood at ease with difficulty on my left.

I looked at the governor. A red-faced man with a white moustache, he looked, in his tweeds, like Polonius cast as Tamburlaine in a court play.

'D71107 Foy,' I pronounced, well-trained.

'Er, yes. Foy.' The governor hummed and scanned his papers. 'I just wanted to say a couple of things to you. Um, now, it may seem to you that you're pretty special and everything, you know, but while you're here, you're not. You'll be treated just like everyone else. I wanted to speak to you because I felt that you ought to know that no one gets special treatment in here, whoever it might be. All right?'

'Yes, sir.'

'You could be Prince Charles himself, but you wouldn't be treated any different from the rest of the inmates. Is that clear?'

'Clear in conceptu, inexact in re, sir.'

'What?'

'Quite clear, sir.'

The officer on my left grasped my arm as if he feared that I might bolt. The senior officer shouted. 'Don't answer the governor back, Foy!'

'No, sir, of course not.'

'As I say, you will absolutely not get any special treatment,' resumed the governor. 'That is all.'

'Just one question, sir,' I said.

'The governor said that is all!' squawked the senior officer.

I raised an eyebrow. 'Just one question, sir?'

'Look, Foy ...' The screw moved forward, all bombast, but the governor raised a hand.

'Um, what is it, Foy?'

'I am, as no doubt you know, sir, reasonably highly qualified academically. I believe that there are several men here who are anxious to learn and have never before had an opportunity to do so. I have already met men who blame their present misfortunes on their lack of skills or qualifications and who are anxious to study for 'A' levels and 'O' levels. Is there anywhere in the prison where, in our free time, I may conduct classes in some degree of peace and privacy?'

'No!'

'Have you no empty rooms?'

'Foy, we have many empty rooms, but we are not going to encourage inmates to consort in this way. It creates unrest, and you could unduly influence other convicts. And that reminds me, Foy, you are not to use your expertise to help inmates in the writing of petitions and so on.'

'I will give no such undertaking, sir,' I said. 'While the articulacy and literacy of the plaintiff cannot be the measure of his cause's rightness, they are the measure of his success or failure. I have every intention of redressing the balance wherever I can, in accordance with the precepts of law.'

'If I find that you have been composing petitions, I will have you transferred to a closed prison immediately. Do you understand?'

'I understand.'

'Very well. You may go.'

I walked across the parade ground to the long shed which, I had been told, was to be my billet. There were three such sheds, each in turn divided into three sections.

Entering 'B' block, I saw that it was constructed in the form of two capital Es, connected back to back by narrow corridors. Each of the prongs of the Es was a long dormitory containing some thirty beds.

At the head of each bed there stood a chest of drawers and, above that, a board on which a few surprisingly modest photographs were pinned. Everything was meticulously clean.

My dormitory was empty. I unrolled my blankets onto the only free bed and slumped down on it with a sigh, relishing my first taste of solitude in two weeks.

It was short-lived. Two cons came in, wearing ill-fitting overalls on top of their grey uniforms. They chattered, and opened and slammed their locker doors. 'You the new one, then?' asked one of them.

'Yes. Yes, I am.'

'Where you from?'

'London.'

'No. Nick.'

'Oh, the Cliff.'

'Oh!'

'Is there anything I've got to do now?'

'Nah, you're OK. You're a new boy. There's nothing for you till tally and dinner. I've got to get back to my fucking shop. I'm on the skive.'

'What do you do?'

'Fucking bricklaying course. Don't touch it.'

'I won't.'

'What do you do on the out, then?'

'I'm a lawyer.'

'Jeesus H. Christ! We got a bent brief in the billet, Eddie. Fuck me, have fun in here!'

The two cons left, and I changed into the gym shoes and the shorts with which I had been issued.

I trotted out onto the playing fields and started to run.

I had never seen the purpose of running for running's sake. To pass weeks in puffing, sweating and suffering in order to save a few days of hypothetical life always seemed to me to be singularly silly. At school, I concocted a particularly convenient brand of petit mal and thus contrived to be 'off games' whenever such nastiness was proposed. Even at Cambridge, though I managed to acquire a fencing half-blue, I exerted myself only in those activities which I enjoyed, rather than in those which were 'good for me'.

But that day, I enjoyed running for running's sake. I ran as I had never wanted to run before, round and round the field, my feet pounding, jarring on the grass, until my lungs felt like buffed leather flapping. I ran up to the top of the fields, where I could see the Vale of Belvoir in the distance, down the track towards the prison and round by the huge dining-hall. I ran until all the weighty grime which had coated my body and my mind in closed prison had been scraped off by the abrasive air, and then, my temple throbbing and my stomach heaving, I threw myself down on my back and just worshipped the earth which spun beneath me, the sky which spun above.

And afterwards, the greatest luxury; a bath. There was no door to the bathroom, so I was still as apprehensive as I had been since my conviction, but I was damned near happy as I sat in that steaming bath, putting off the moment when I would lie back, and the water would cleave the skin of my back and shoulders.

I heard another tap running across the room, heard a rough male voice softly say, 'Mmmmm, fuck!' heard someone splashing and humming in his bath. Then the someone started to sing. 'There's a place for us, somewhere a place for us, peace and quiet and open air wait for us somewhere . . . Somehow, somewhere, we'll find a new way of living, we'll find a way of forgiving . . . somewhere.'

It was then, after two weeks of tension, discomfort and ill-repressed horror, that everything suddenly gave at once, and I let myself cry my heart out.

At lunch I shared a table with Maurice, Dennis and two of their colleagues, and received another wonderful letter from Fiona in which she informed me, at some length, that she loved me. The new cons were conducted around the prison workshops and encouraged to decide how we would spend our days in the service of Her Majesty.

Her Majesty, in fact, was prepared to serve us. We could undertake a sixteen-week course, we were told, learning to be bricklayers, painters and decorators, plumbers or electricians. We could work in the kitchen or the gardens or occupy ourselves with maintenance of the buildings in the prison. The alternative, commonly regarded as preferable only to hell itself, was 'textiles'. Those who worked in 'textiles' spent their days in a room full of sewing machines with which they assembled shopping bags by numbers. Radio One blared from speakers at each end of the room. The sound of the machines was incessant, the temperature unalterable, the atmosphere impenetrable.

I elected to be a gardener, reasoning that it would give me a chance to be alone for, amusing as I sometimes found the company, few cons shared my interests, and solitude now seemed the greatest of luxuries. There, too, I would best be able to observe the comings and goings of inmates and staff. Trevor had worked on the gardens. It might have been there that he first saw that which occasioned his death. I wanted to inspect those roses.

The labour board accepted my application. I was told to report to the garden shed at eight o'clock on the Monday morning. Mickey, too, was returning to the gardens. Maurice somehow acquired a singularly cushy job as cleaner of the Roman Catholic church, which assured him absolute privacy and no duties. Dennis chose to join the electricians' course. 'My dear, my good lady cannot forever be responsible for the fuses.'

I wandered about the camp that evening when it got dark. The cons watched television, played snooker, or sat in their billets talking and writing letters.

I was intrigued by the delicacy and care with which prisoners adorned their letter home. Apart from the inevitable SWALK in copper plate, Gothic and whole series of imaginative scripts, they lovingly chalked flowers, hearts and quotations on the envelopes, and traced 'Love Is' cartoons on the letters themselves.

At nine, the tally bell summoned all inmates to their billets. I sat at the end of my bed, trying to look interested in a week-old edition of the *Sun*, while the others flung questions and taunts at me.

'Who're you?'

'Sebastian.'

'Fucking hell! Sebastian!'

'Yeah, he's a bent brief.'

121

'Did you go to a good public school, Sebastian?'

'An excellent one.'

'Does your mummy love you, Sebastian?'

'Intensely.'

'Jesus, what's 'e in for?'

'Bribes, I should think.'

'Picking daisies contrary to park regulations, more likely.'

'What you in for?'

'Dishonestly appropriating money from the Inland Revenue.'

'Well, that's not too bad. It's thick, but it's not too bad.'

A voice from the doorway yelled, 'By your beds!' The cons wearily pulled themselves to their feet, and three screws entered. One, a senior officer with a pear-shaped torso, carried a tally-board. Another, a young discipline officer with a cocky air, swaggered down the aisle between the beds, counting.

'Evening, Mr Carter,' said one con who looked like a genial prop forward.

'Good evening, Lea,' the screw smirked.

'Good evening, Mr Carter,' said every con in turn, so that Carter lost count and had to start again.

'Gosh, I do admire you, Mr Carter.'

'Yeah, can I have your autograph?'

'Wish I could walk like that.'

'Shut up!' called the senior officer with a smile. 'Mr Carter is having difficulty.'

The cons laughed. 'Have you met our new boy, Mr Farrell?' asked the con who had talked to me that afternoon.

'Yeah, he's a bent lawyer, ever so smart. This billet is going up in the world.'

'He's called Sebastian.'

Farrell flicked a glance at me. I bowed. His smile did not change.

Carter finally concluded that there were twenty-eight prisoners in the billet, and the screws left. After tally, the social life of an open prison begins. Backgammon boards and playing cards are whipped out. Cons start strenuous variations on the push-up and the press-up on their beds. Conversations of a sort, some semi-private, some general, begin. That night the conversation was general. I was its subject.

From the start, I knew from whom I could expect trouble.

122

Charlie Lea was OK. He had the slow gentleness of so many giants. His best friend, Bill, another huge man with legs like saplings, a silly smile, and a liking for practical jokes, was easy so long as no one pushed him too far.

Three Glaswegians from Corby were not so funny. They were loud-mouthed yobs who liked no one on earth. The others seemed to tolerate them, and laughed at their occasional flashes of coarse wit, but one or two followed them, and egged them on, vicariously enjoying the consequences of their wildness. They were called Jock, Jimmy and Scooby.

Jock start the ball rolling. 'I hate you focking public school fockers.'

'Yes, pretty useless, most of us.'

'Ye're fockers.'

'I bet ye've taken it up the arse, haven't ye?'

'Sorry?'

'I bet ye've had it. All you public school nonces, ye're all stoat the balls. Ye've had it up your little red ring, haven't ye?'

'I haven't actually, no.'

'Ye're a focking liar!'

'Shut up, Jock,' said Bill, 'I'm trying to write a letter, and so far, all I've written is, Darling wife, how's your little red ring?'

The Scots snorted, but Jock had not done. 'I'm going to give it to yer, fancy-pants,' he said, coming close and thrusting his broad, stubble-covered jaw in my face. 'Just ye wait. Ye'll get seven and a half inches of quivering gristle up your rectum tonight. I desire your body, you public school focker.'

'Here, Mr Sebastian?' shouted Jimmy.

'Yes?'

'Do you play snooker?'

'I have played a little, yes.'

'Well, come and put a bit of bottom on this, then!'

I was centre of attention now, and did not know how to cope with this brand of cross-questioning. Silent scorn, I knew from bitter experience at school, would only aggravate them. I could only play the game as well as I could.

I could not gauge the seriousness of their sexual threats. These men undoubtedly hated homosexuals and, if questioned, they would be affronted by the imputation that they were serious. I knew better. I had seen sexual needs disguised as horseplay before, but that was amongst schoolboys, and reflected mutual desires. These men were violent, and would not respect my feelings.

The banter continued for the next hour, some friendly, some menacing. One man came from another dormitory to ask my advice on his appeal, a complex *autrefois acquis*. He had heard about me from Dennis. I took the papers, and promised to read them through. We washed, and everyone climbed into bed. The duty screw came round for the last time, the lights went out, and the new sort of conversation, the conversation of the darkness, began.

They talked of getting their legs over, of screws and cons whom they particularly disliked, of fights and of sexual encounters years before.

Then the trouble started. Jock crept over to my bed and sat down beside me. 'Och, darling little poofter, I want to give you a nice meat sandwich. Come on, now, you don't mind. Och, what a smooth little body ye've got.'

The others giggled nervously.

'Can't we get some fucking sleep?' shouted someone from the other end of the dormitory.

'Fock off,' said Jock. 'I'm making focking love. Don't interrupt me.'

I laughed nervously. 'Bugger off, Jock.'

'Och, bugger, bugger, bugger!' Jock sighed. 'Now, come on, Sebastian. I'm going to give it yer up your arse. You'd like that, wouldn't ye?'

He slipped his hand under the sheet and grabbed my thigh. My muscles tautened. I could smell the man's sweat. His tobacco thick breath touched my face. 'Go to hell, Jock,' I said, and pushed away his hand.

'Och, no,' said the Scotsman cajoling. 'Ye want it, don't ye?' He put his hand back and started squeezing.

'To be brutally honest, I can think of nothing I would like less. Nothing personal, you understand.' I swept the hand away again. The other cons laughed, uncertain.

Jock leaned forward and rubbed his cheek against mine. I shuddered away. My whole body was shaking. 'Come on, give us a gobble,' he said. 'Ye'd give us a gobble, wouldn't ye?'

'Go on, get it up the little poofter!' called Jimmy from the other end of the room.

'Come and give us a hand, then, Jimmy!'

'Oh, Christ, can't we get some fucking sleep?' groaned Charlie Lea.

'Scoobie, come here!' called Jock.

'Oh, get back to bed, you idiots,' I said.

'Fock off,' said Jock.

Then three of them were there. I was very frightened.

Three pairs of hands held me down in the darkness, rough hands grasping and stroking. I squirmed away from them, but they were relentless. These men might hate homosexuals, but I could smell that their prejudices would not deny desire.

A pair of hands now grasped the back of my neck, turned me over and pushed me down. A bare leg straddled my back. The Scots sniggered, excited, and Jock spoke his pet obscenities. 'Ye want to feel it up yer, don't yer? Filthy public school poofter!' On the word 'poofter', he thrust forward, and something hard hit me just above the rectum.

'You sod!' I gasped.

Forcing my head back, I could just see the edge of my locker. I had to feel for the blade that I'd put there at lights out. I fumbled, cut myself, drew the blade back, reached behind me and slashed as hard as I could.

I struck the Scotsman's upper thigh, and felt the blood warm on the backs of my knees before Jock realised, reared and squealed, 'Fock you, you focking bastard, he's got a blade!'

'The little fucker. You OK, Jock?'

Jock leaped off the bed and crouched. 'The focker! Christ, he could've focking killed me! The bastard! I'll do you!'

'Yeah, we'll do you,' said Jimmy. He grasped my arm and tried to tug me from the bed. 'We'll fucking do you!'

There were two other figures suddenly by the bed. Bare feet slapped on the linoleum floor. I clung onto the frame and thought that it was all over. They were going to kill me. I had misinterpreted their intentions, had broken the rules. Affronted, they would now kill me.

I heard skin hissing on skin, and cotton rustling. 'Serves you fucking right, you filthy Glaswegian bastard.' The calm voice was Charlie Lea's. 'Your joke went kinda wrong, didn't it?'

'Yeah,' laughed Bill, pulling Jimmy back and tossing him over

125

the next bed as though he were a sack of coal. 'Now perhaps we can get to sleep.'

'The focker, the filthy cowardly focker!' Jock growled, clutching at his leg.

'Ah, poor diddums,' Bill laughed. 'Did you get a little surprise? Fuck off, Jock, and get back in yer pit.'

Charlie looked down on me. 'OK, Seb, fair enough. But no blades in future, right?'

'OK,' I said, still trembling, 'someone should have taught me the rules before they started.'

'Night.'

'Night.'

'Now perhaps we can get some sleep,' said the man at the end. I got none.

13

The next day was a Saturday. There were games of football up in the fields, but most inmates either slept or watched racing on the television. The prison bookie and his runners sat in the BBC 1 room, taking bets. A quarter of an ounce was the minimum stake. All bets were at starting price. Prison bookmakers, I was told, operate illicitly, but the authorities turn a blind eye, reasoning that betting is inevitable and that it was better that one acknowledged bookie with capital should organise it than that there should be small personal bets and resultant quarrels about settlement.

At some time during the evening, Jock, Jimmy and Scooby were assailed by three unidentified convicts. By the judicious application of knees to elbows, the strangers broke the right arm of each of the Scots.

Quietly, resignedly, like stags usurped, the wounded men went to the PO's office and asked to be transferred to closed prison under the governor's protection.

Nobody spoke to me of the incident. Maurice and his friends just smiled and said that someone had to keep the yobboes where they belonged.

I duly reported for work at eight o'clock on Monday morning. Within a week, the routine of prison life seemed natural and inevitable.

I awoke at seven, eschewed the eminently eschewable, unchewable breakfast, went back to sleep and, at five to eight, dressed, made my bed, panicked and ran flat out to the first tally of the morning at my place of work.

I spent the first half-hour tending the plants and shrubs or digging, and the rest of the time in dodging my gaffer, an aged, cantankerous civilian who circled the camp on a bicycle, checking on those in his charge. Skiving became a full-time job, for a convict leaves his place of work at the risk of three days lost remission, and my first concerns were reading, writing letters, and cautious detective work.

There was another tally at half-past eleven. After lunch, inmates kipped for half an hour, returned to work and skived until half-past four, tea-time. Thereafter, we were free to do what we would – what we could, for most of the prison was then out of bounds.

I soon found myself the object of much curiosity and much animosity from both screws and convicts. A few liked me, others toadied, most snarled at me. And I, happy because of Fiona's letters and happy because I had to be, disconcerted resentful screws by smiling courtesy.

I came to like those senior officers who played it by the book. Officer Vallance, for example, a red-faced ex-Naval commander, blustered and bellowed at all men. Some cringed and growled at him like cornered beasts, and he, a natural bully and macho snob, pounced on them and worried them. I smiled at him, answered him back, and coaxed a reluctant twinkle from him. But Vallance had no favourites, and treated his officers in exactly the same way as that in which he treated the cons. He would avert his eyes from a trivial trespass, but only for so long as he could pretend not to have seen it.

Officer Loveday was a short, quiet, squat man who really wanted to do good in his chosen profession. He was confused to find that no good could be done. He readily admitted that he was afraid of life outside this secure and ordered system, and he asked no more for his contentment than his state-supplied home, his scraggy, spiky, neurotic wife (whom he thought to be beautiful) and the odd day spent fishing or golfing. Loveday often came up to me to say, 'Everything OK, old lad? Keep your pecker up!' and to ask me who was the muse of lyric poetry or what did 'encensoir' mean.

Such men were fair and used their absolute, arbitrary power responsibly. I met the administrative staff only rarely. The governor of a prison, and his deputies, live in comfortable houses some miles from the prison, and come in only to perform occasional inspections and to try wrongdoers.

The prejudice which I feared soon manifested itself in the great daffodil scandal.

The daffodils were blooming in impudent defiance of the skies. I was turning the earth in a large flowerbed when I accidently struck down one bold flower. I apologised to it, and then to my gaffer, and stuck the yellow head into the buttonhole of my donkey-jacket.

The bell rang just at that moment, and I gratefully stopped pretending to be doing something, slung my spade over my shoulder, and set off towards the garden shed for lunchtime tally.

I passed groups of convicts on my way. They were all reassuring screws as to their presence. One such screw was Carter, 'Superscrew', as everyone called him. He saw me, strutted forward, snatched the daffodil from my buttonhole and, throwing it to the ground, pulverised it to a dull orange paste on the tarmac.

'Hello,' I said, 'what's all this about, then?'

'You're not allowed to wear daffodils,' said Superscrew, feigning assurance.

'Oh, I see,' I said, 'and where will I find this extraordinarily sensible rule in the book? Under 'D' for daffodils, 'F' for flowers, or 'C' for Carter, special rules of?'

'Don't be fucking impertinent, Foy. Flowers are not allowed.'

'The shamrock is forbid by law to grow on Irish ground,' I smiled.

'Look, Lord Foy,' Superscrew sneered, aware of the eyes and ears of the convicts standing round us, 'when an officer tells you something, you obey him and don't ask questions, unless, that is, you want to get nicked. You're a convict now, remember? You're an ordinary, common, nasty little convict. Right?'

'And you, sir, excellent young officer though you may be, are technically guilty of an assault. I think we'd better see a senior officer about this daffodil rule, don't you?'

Superscrew bridled. He must either back down before the cons or he must make a fool of himself before a senior officer. Alternatively, he could lie to a senior officer and thus have me

129

sent to a closed prison with two or three months extra to serve. 'Senior officers make no difference,' he said at last. 'I am an officer, and what I say goes.'

'Absolutely,' I said. 'I'd just like to find out more about this whole daffodil business from a senior officer who knows his business thoroughly. Not that you don't, of course; I'd just like to know.'

'I've told you the rule, and that's that.'

'Yes, yes, my dear sir, of course, but you are a junior officer and I must know the ramifications of this rule. Are daisies permissible, for example? Is clover forbidden? Am I allowed to wear a daffodil behind my left ear? Or, again, are you entitled to pull my coat off my back, my hair off my head, my head off my neck? Let's just see a senior officer and sort the whole business out. All right?''

The cons around us were now laughing and jeering. Superscrew turned round to see whether he or I were the object of their derision. He turned back to me. His cheeks were red. 'You'll see a senior officer, all right, mister high and mighty Foy. You'll go on governor's immediately!'

At this, one man bellowed with laughter. 'You'll go on governor's and face the consequences! You've been impertinent. You've been disobedient. You'll go on governor's!'

'With much pleasure.' I made a theatrical bow, dropped my spade and my boots at the garden shed and walked straight to the central offices.

The governor was not in that day, so I faced the officer who had stood at the governor's right hand on that first day, Senior Officer Glaser.

I knew that Superscrew would soon arrive, hoping to give evidence to my crimes. That would mean a pseudo-formal trial, in which I could call two witnesses who would be disbelieved, in which Superscrew would give his own account, and in which I would be sentenced to the loss of anything from three days to one hundred and twenty days, depending on Superscrew's story and on the Senior Officer's mood.

I decided to forestall my accuser.

I knocked on the door and walked in. Glaser looked up at me. He snarled. 'What d'ye want, Foy?'

'I want to ask you about the daffodil rule, sir. Mr Carter

instructed me to do so.'

'What?'

'I was wearing a daffodil in my buttonhole, sir, with my gaffer's permission. Mr Carter, however, declared that to do so was contrary to prison rules and, assailing me, destroyed the flower. I am anxious to know exactly what the position is on this score.'

'Are you making a complaint against Mr Carter?' Glaser asked hopefully, but I knew that ruse. 'No, no, far from it. Excellent young fellow, and well within his rights. No, I am merely anxious to elucidate this rule so that I do not unwittingly transgress.'

Glaser stood. 'I'm going to do you, Foy,' he said. 'I'm warning you, I'm going to do you. I can't do you on this one, but you'll give me reason in time. You've had it too fucking easy all your life, Foy. I'm going to see to it you don't have it easy in here. One slip from you, and I'll nick you and have you shanghaied to a closed nick before your feet can touch the ground. And you just won't survive eight months of that, you won't survive it, Foy. Do you understand?'

'I understand you perfectly, sir.'

'Don't be fucking impertinent, Foy.'

'I would not so far demean myself, sir.'

'What?'

'I would never so far demean myself as to be impertinent to you, sir.'

Glaser's brow furrowed as he tried to work this out. I wasn't too sure what I meant myself.

'I suppose that's meant to be clever,' he said at last.

'Not particularly, sir.'

'You get out of my office!' he shouted.

'Certainly, sir.'

I turned to go.

'Foy, come back here!'

'Yes, sir?'

'Don't answer back!'

'Very well, sir.'

'Now, get out and stay well out of my way!'

Once more, I turned to leave, this time in silence.

'And, Foy!' I looked at him, silently questioning. 'I won't

131

tolerate fucking dumb insolence either.'

'Very well, sir, what should I do?'

'Just don't be fucking insolent.'

'I'll try, sir.'

'You're no better than anyone else, you fucker. Just remember, I'm going to do you.'

He tried.

Despite my unpopularity with some of the cons, I found my services greatly in demand. I wrote letters, poems and petitions, and earned a healthy living by drawing portraits from photographs. Not only are prisoners sentimental, they are also prolific, so there was a constant supply of commissions. I drew wives and children by the thousand. I used sanguine conte, always a flattering medium and the easiest for covering up mistakes.

I charged half an ounce for each portrait, and was thus able to 'buy' such illicit luxuries as an extra change of clothes each week, a cheese sandwich or two smuggled from the kitchen, and 'bent' letters, that is, letters which some fast runner would post for me in the village post-box, thus avoiding censorship.

The prisoner's life exists from visit to visit, and soon I too came to depend on that one Saturday afternoon every three weeks, an afternoon spent in holding Fiona close, smelling her scent and feeling the softness of her skin as the rarest and finest things on earth, an afternoon spent in planning what we were going to do when it was all over, in whispering assurances and reassurances, in forgetting everything which we had reminded ourselves to tell one another. Although I was in prison, those were the happiest, most carefree moments of my life.

Desire is infuriatingly unpredictable. When a relationship is dying, you can sleep beside your woman for months and feel no stirrings. All creativity has been exhausted. You have nothing left to express to her. Yet no sooner are you free and alone than you feel your gifts to be wasted and long to make love again.

I had expected to suffer appalling frustration in prison, but I scarcely noticed the lack of plen. and coit. abs. I suppose that I have no cause to be surprised. There is nothing in prison to stimulate sexual yearning, and so much did I long for the warmth of a woman's body enclosing me that I found the

132

pornography which circled the dormitories even less of a turn-on than usual.

The constant tension to which a prisoner is subjected is also destructive of all outgoing vigour. It is impossible for the convict to be alone. His back and neck muscles are taut by day and night. Abrasive maleness surrounds him. He can only dream of the peace engendered by love, rather than of the act itself.

So did I dream, of and with Fiona. The extent of our telepathic communion was astonishing. Letters telling of the previous night's fantasies crossed in the post, but told of identical images. Fiona knew when I had a bad day, when I was happy, when I could not sleep, and at night, when all the lights were out and the ragged conversations had subsided into snores, she came to me as surely as she had come to me on that first night in London. The smell of her crept to me through the carbolic and stale sweat smells of the prison. Her hands gripped me and ruffled my hair as I kissed her. The taste of her swirled on my tongue and she sighed with the breezes which slipped through the windows. Two days later, the letter would arrive, telling me everything that I already knew.

I came, too, to be dominated by those fears which dominate every prisoner's life. Tobacco is the greatest motivation. Parcels packed with Old Holborn were dropped off in all sorts of ingenious caches near the prison. Occasionally those who scurried out to pick them up were caught and lost ninety days.

There were 'runners' every week, usually occasioned by 'Dear Johns'. They were always recaptured and returned to closed prison. The fear of 'shanghai' is the greatest corrective influence on a prisoner's conduct. No one wants to see that infernal place again.

No one, that is, save one man who could not reconcile himself to imprisonment. Martin Trimble wandered the camp, pale as a Hammer film zombie, dreaming of his wife and his children. He saw them bleeding by sides of roads, saw them raped and garrotted by night, saw them die a thousand times in every day. He saw his wife on top of Chinamen and splayed under black men, sucking off white men and being gang-banged by red Indians, morning, noon and night. When she wasn't dying, she was screwing, and it was cracking him up.

133

He knew that to run for home would cost him three more months away from his precious family, but he didn't have the strength to stay.

He explained all this to me one afternoon as we sat at the top of the playing field. We were looking out through the low wire fence across the fields which now were sprouting young wheat.

'Why not ask to be transferred to a closed nick?' I asked. 'At least you'd be safe from yourself.'

'I want to,' Martin sighed. 'I can't cope here any more. I'd be better off in closed nick, but there are shorter visits there, only half an hour . . . ' His voice cracked on a little whimper.

'I know,' I said, 'but it'll be over soon, and you won't have to fight yourself all the time.'

'Will you write the application for transfer for me?'

'Yes,' I said, and pulled a sheet of paper from my pocket.

'I can no longer tolerate the temptations to which I am subjected by open conditions,' I wrote. 'My constant fears and worries as to my family's welfare goad me to the point where I feel that I must do something or go mad. I therefore request that I should be transferred to closed prison as soon as possible.'

'Is that enough?' Martin asked, staring admiringly at the note.

'It should be, for God's sake.'

It wasn't. Martin's application was refused. One week later, he jumped over the fence, ran three miles and hitched back home. His wife and his children were out at the shops when he arrived. He sat down in the living-room to await their return.

The police arrived five minutes later. He lost three months for ten minutes and a ginger biscuit.

Part Two
CUI BONO?

14

After twelve weeks at Ravenhill, I had adapted to the new regimen and to the new regime. In my own way, I suppose, I had mastered it. I thanked God daily for the disciplines of my education and for Fiona, without either of which I might too easily have slipped back into depression. It would have been damned difficult to clamber back.

The trouble was that I had well-nigh forgotten my reason for being there.

Trevor had lived as I now lived. Trevor had died, beaten up and then cursorily executed as he coughed up a busted gut. I had to try to find out why, but I simply did not know where to begin.

It was May, and the spring pruning of the roses in the parade ground had been careless. I suggested that I might be allowed to cut them back. My suggestion was accepted.

I spent three days getting myself scratched to shreds by rose-thorns as I hunted for anything peculiar which might explain Trevor's allusion. I scraped the soil back around their roots, looked for some pattern in their planting, read the labels attached to their stalks and found nothing.

Deep gloom oppressed me. Maybe Trevor had been mad. Maybe he had meant nothing more than that the roses would stand as his only monument. I'd destroyed myself, my old way of life, my career, for nothing. The roses had no tale to tell.

God knows, there were enough suspicious circumstances. I saw screws and cons engaged in secretive transactions, I saw screws' cars backing up to the kitchen store-room and driving away again with boots just barely tied down with string. I had already seen enough crimes to keep a professional journalist in work for life, but none of them reeked of murder. I needed a motive, I needed a murderer, and I had no clue as to what or who that might be.

When I learned that Mickey Rourke had found Trevor's body, I approached him cautiously. He was receptive enough. Mickey had never been popular, and now, after his contact with sudden violent death, he was shunned with a mixture of awe and contempt. He longed to be bullied again, but his lifelong fear had at last been fulfilled. No one wanted Mickey now.

He slouched around the camp with his hands in his pockets and dreamed about Mars Bars. When Mickey came to the canteen on pay-day to spend his hard-earned £1.14 credit, he knew that he should buy tobacco, letters, soap and toothpaste, but there were Mars Bars on display, and Mickey liked Mars Bars. He bought seven: 'One for every day of de week, you see', and could just afford half an ounce thereafter. He then guzzled all seven Mars Bars that afternoon and unsuccessfully begged tobacco and fag papers off everyone for the rest of the week.

The fates would never treat Mickey kindly, but somehow they had found him a wife. A winsome, whining, black-haired creature who called me 'Mister Sebastian sorr' on Mickey's instructions. She had dealt him in turn a load of snotty children with red hair and freckles. Everyone, so Mickey told me, joked that he could not be their father, but Mickey wouldn't believe that, not of his Maureen. I wasn't so sure. From what I saw of her on visiting days, she seemed the sort who'd just lie back, grateful for the attention and anxious to please. It wouldn't even touch her. A gang-bang would just be a chore to her, like a surprise children's party. She would just carry it off with a good grace, wondering vaguely when she could have her tea.

Mickey showed me his little passport photograph of Maureen about six times a day. Eventually, I drew her portrait for him. He said I'd got it wrong. I asked where had I got it wrong. He said he didn't know. Four attempts later, he grudgingly took all my sketches, and thereafter carried them about with him too.

'Now you can do the kids for me,' he announced.

It cost him four ounces. He lost a lot of weight and I lost my patience. Mickey was never satisfied. When everyone in the billet had examined the drawings and found them good, Mickey would shrug and say, 'Yeah, it's good, but there's something wrong.'

Damn it, Mickey didn't want portraits. He expected me to recreate his children for him. He wanted the drawings to squeak and giggle and pull his hair and tell him to fuck off as they did on visits. Everyone except Maureen told Mickey to fuck off. His three-year-old said little else.

During a tea-break, I asked, 'Would you like to learn to read and write, Mickey?'

'No. Fuck off. Course not.'

'Why not?' I asked. 'You could read your own letters and write to your Maureen.'

'Fuck off, Foy,' Mickey snarled in a manner that he had learned from another. He turned to walk away.

'All right, Mickey,' I said, 'I don't give a damn. I just thought you'd like it, that's all.'

Mickey scurried away, and didn't speak to me for the rest of the day. We were weeding the same bed, but he ignored me completely. Whenever I came near him, in the garden shed or in the dining-hall, he turned and whispered something to the nearest man, who invariably paid no attention.

The next evening, I sat in the billet reading *Catch 22* and giggling like a madman. It had never seemed so funny as in Her Majesty's prison. Every time I laughed, big Bill laughed too and threw something at me.

Mickey came in nervously and tried to saunter up the dormitory, greeting imaginary friends on the empty beds. When I looked up, he jerked his head quickly toward the door. I nodded.

'Ah, well,' he sighed to no one, and sauntered back to the door.

'Fuck off, Paddy!'

'Fuck off, Rourke!'

'Funniest Irish joke on earth!'

Mickey said, 'Watch it, mate!' in his high, quavering voice. He clenched his fist, and everyone laughed. Mickey smiled, happy, though he had no idea why they laughed.

A minute or two later, I put down the book and followed Mickey. I found him standing by the water-boiler, trying to look as though he were waiting for tea. It wasn't very convincing. He had no mug.

'Hi, Mickey,' I said casually.

'Hello,' said Mickey, and scampered along beside me, putting in two steps for my every one. 'Seb, look, I was thinking ...'

'Yes?'

'Could you just show me how to write a few words? I'll tell you what.'

'I thought you didn't want to learn.'

'Ah, fuck!' He stroked his vole-like soft hair. 'It's not that. You know, I'd like to learn just a few words. Give Maureen a bit of a surprise, learn the kids a few things, you know?'

'Sure, I know.'

'But no fucking fancy stuff, you know, and don't tell nobody?'

'I won't tell anyone. Why should I?'

He shrugged. 'People's odd,' he said, 'but I reckon you're OK. You won't tell no one, will you?'

'No, Mickey, I won't tell anyone. And just to show you how easy it is, I'll give you something to learn tonight. What do you want to write?'

'Happy Birthday I love you,' he said rapidly, then, 'fuck me yeah, well.'

'Hey, Mickey,' I said during the second lesson, 'what was it like when you found the stiff?'

He shrugged casually, 'Oh well, you know, the usual.'

'I don't know, I've never seen anyone dead.'

'You haven't? Oh well, it's like this.' He leaned forward to expound, just like my old tutor at Cambridge. 'He's got this strange smile, you see, just as if he's seen heaven. His face is twisted like. And blue. Yeah, blue. Mind you, Trevor wasn't that young anymore.'

'Did you know him?' I asked.

'Yeah. Yeah, I knew him. I liked him. He was OK. Like you in some ways. Educated, you know, good at the verbals. Less posh than you.'

'They tell me he was hounded to death by the screws.'

'Hounded?' he frowned, but worked it out. 'Oh, hounded! Yeah. They kept nicking him and putting him in the block and giving him days and everything.'

'Where did he live?'

'D block.'

'You don't know which room?'

'D.15,' he said without thinking, then he frowned, 'Why do you want to know?'

'Oh, I've got this thing about people haunting places.'

Mickey said something like 'pshaw' and shivered at the same time.

'Why don't you go back to Ireland, Mickey?'

'No bread there.'

'D'ye make any over here?'

'No.'

'So again, why?'

'Oh, we've tried. I can never get the fare. I tried last year, but I met a friend on the way to Fishguard and we got pissed instead.'

A friend, someone who'd take his last penny, and as long as he left laughing, he was Mickey's friend. Anyone would leave laughing.

'Anyhow, how did this guy Trev die?'

He shrugged, 'Don't know. Screws, I suppose. He was liked by the lads.'

'Yes.'

'Yeah. I suppose it was screws, at that time of night.'

'Which screws?'

'Oh, Forsdyke or someone. I don't know.'

'Why did they hate him?'

'I dunno. No one knew. It was funny. He was funny. He was broken down at the end. He was on the gardens too, you know.'

'Which section did he work on?'

'Mostly the top of the football pitches and round the back of the huts. He did the roses in the beds, though. He liked roses. The gaffer said he was good with roses.'

'Thanks, Mickey. Here ...'

He looked at the Mars Bar in my outstretched hand. 'Hang on, what do you want?' he asked.

I smiled. 'Mickey, I want absolutely nothing. It's just that I've got a bit more burn then you and have nothing to spend it on. Take it.'

Mickey took it as though it were fragile. 'Fuck, thanks, Seb,' he said, and shot from the room.

The occupant of D.15 worked on the prison farm and so was away from the prison all day. It should have been easy to explore the room, but anyone seen on the landings during the day would be nicked and punished as a thief. That meant thirty days.

One wet morning in the middle of May, I stole away from my place of work and down to the parade ground. The rain had driven every one indoors. The square seemed empty.

I ran through the main doors of D block and up the stairs. The corridors were long and narrow. There were rooms on both sides. I didn't know where the landing cleaner was, and I didn't want to meet him. A con suspecting theft might dole out a punishment worse than thirty days.

The corridor was empty. I've never seen a corridor quite so empty. It was empty of furniture, people and dust. Walls and tiles gleamed white and grey. My vile rubber soles squeaked on the tiles. The door at D.15 opened smoothly and silently. I closed it behind me.

The room, too, was spotless. On the left there was a sort of locker-cum-desk arrangement with a blue formica top. The pin-board above it was covered with birthday cards and pictures of half-naked girls on motorbikes. The bed stood on the right.

I scanned the walls. There was nothing there. I lifted the pictures and the cards. The board, too, was bare of clues.

I crouched. Something was written on the wainscoating under the bed. I crawled under to study it better. It was a list of autographs. There were three names.

Jim Brooke, 7.11.71 – 4.1.73. Fuck the lot of them
Patrick Morrison, Dec 19th, 1974. Tranmere Rovers rule OK
Trevor Abbott, May 75-Sept 76. Runner. Damn the doctor

I frowned. Perhaps he had gone nuts. There was nothing to be learned there. I rolled out from under the bed.

I rolled back in again, fast.

Footsteps approached, clicking, assertive footsteps. Steel tips meant screws. I tried to think why he should choose to come into this particular empty D block room. I couldn't think of a single reason.

But he did.

I held my breath. The feet clicked twice so that they were just opposite my head. I admired the shoes. They were meticulously buffed. That was a spit and polish job.

'Get up, Foy,' said a high-pitched voice.

I lay still.

'Get up, Foy!'

Brer fox, he had nothing on me.

Forsdyke's head appeared where his shins had been. 'I said get up!'

I got up.

'What are you doing here, Foy?'

'I lent Sykes my pen,' I lied. 'I came here to get it back. I needed it.'

'Liar,' he said.

I don't know why, but the word 'liar' offends me more than any other. I must have coloured. I certainly clenched my fists. Forsdyke stepped back.

'All right, ask Sykes,' I said.

'Oh, I will,' sneered Forsdyke, 'I will. It doesn't alter the fact that you're out of bounds, that you've left your place of work and that you're going to be charged with intent to steal.'

'Fine,' I said, 'It's a fair cop, guv, or words to that effect.'

'Come with me.'

'How did you know I was in here?' I asked.

'None of your business. I saw you coming in.' He smirked.

'I didn't see you on the square.'

'I was in the PO's block.'

'Yet you knew which room I was in?'

'Don't fucking argue, Foy!'

'Right you are,' I said. 'Lead on, executioner.' His hand tightened on my arm. He made a sort of hissing sound, and led me in silence to the block.

The block is meant to be unpleasant. There's no furniture, just plain grey pocked walls and a plank bench. It's like a police cell, but at least there's reading matter. There is more graffiti than wall.

Glad of the solitude, I sat down and enjoyed the literature. All the classics were there – 'Balls to Picasso', 'I choked Linda Lovelace', 'On a bridge stood the Bishop of Buckingham' et alii.

I added 'The young man of Belgrave' and 'When in Disgrace with Fortune and Men's eyes', the prisoner's sonnet.

Somewhere between 'The Shape of Things to Come' and 'Do your Bird', I recognised Trevor's scrawl again. He had drawn a circle, put a line through the middle, and had inscribed 'Cave' above it. Someone had substituted the word 'Cunt'.

Cave . . . beware. Beware what? A circle with a line through the middle . . . I puzzled over it and came to no conclusion. Maybe he had just been amusing himself working out the diameter of a concave shape at a given depth.

That's how thick you can become in nick.

But I attained a small triumph as I thought about the words he had left in D.15 – 'Damn the doctor'. I had only seen the Ravenhill doctor once, when a cut had gone septic. He had seemed harmless enough.

I went over the words again and again – 'Damn the doctor' – and then I had it. Doctor, leech, Leach. Damn, dam, dam the dyke, Forsdyke. Beware of Forsdyke and Leach? Well, maybe.

At one o'clock, I was led forth to face my doom. John Sykes had been brought back from the farm to bear witness. He was a broad man with crisp dark hair and a jaw like a shovel.

He glared at me across the room.

The governor did his moustache bristling bit. Glaser stood at his side, Forsdyke at mine.

'Stand up straight, Foy!' Glaser barked unnecessarily.

The governor frowned at him irritably and turned to me. 'Foy,' he said, 'what were you doing away from your place of work?'

'It was very foolish, sir. I am sorry. Tea-break approached, and I wanted to do the crossword. I had lent—'

'Wait a minute,' Glaser interrupted.

'My pen, my only pen, to sykes, and so—'

'And so you thought that you could break prison rules and enter his room.'

'Yes, sir, it was foolish.'

'You realise,' said the governor, 'that being in another inmate's room during the day is a serious offence.'

'I do, sir.'

Forsdyke piped up, 'I think we should ask Sykes.'

The governor growled, and turned to the big man. 'Sykes,' he said, 'Foy says he lent you a pen. Is that true?'

Glaser looked complacent. Forsdyke shifted beside me. They knew that I was lying.

Sykes looked at me, then at Forsdyke. 'Yeah,' he said, 'he lent it me.'

God bless John Sykes. Glaser clenched his fist and puffed like something punctured. 'When did you borrow it?' he demanded.

'Yesterday tea-time.'

'When did you say he could have it back?'

'Before bed-time last night,' answered Sykes.

Forsdyke was almost jumping with frustration. 'I don't believe him!' he squawked.

Sykes raised an eyebrow. 'You calling me a liar?'

'I believe Foy was stealing from your room.'

'You do? And why should he choose my room, considering it's about the most difficult to get to without meeting a screw? He was after his pen. That's all.'

'Very well, Sykes,' said the governor, 'you may go.'

Sykes cast a glance dipped in curare at me as he closed the door.

The governor had no choice. Despite Glaser's protestations, he had to believe me. He docked seven days from my remission. Seven more days from freedom, and Fiona.

I was not going to wait for Sykes to come to me. I returned to D.15 as soon as tea was over.

'All right,' he growled as I entered, 'what's it all about?'

'I was not thieving,' I said.

'That's what I reckoned,' he answered, unsmiling, 'otherwise I wouldn't have done what I did. You're richer than most of us and you're Maurie's mate. So what's the game? It'd better be good, or the whole nick's going to know about it, and your life won't be worth living.'

I made a decision. It was gambling time. 'Will you come with me?' I asked.

'Where to?'

'To Maurice's room.'

'What for?'

'I want to tell him about this too. You'll forgive me, but I

145

don't know you, and I can't afford to have you talking about this around the nick. I've got to tell you, and anyhow, I've got to get some help. I trust Maurice. Maybe I'm wrong, but he's the only person with the power to shut you up in case you should feel talkative.'

'OK. You know that Maurie'll do you, too, if you're not straight.'

'Yes.'

I had deliberately put off the moment when I recruited aid. To start off with, not knowing my enemy, I could trust no one. Second, I knew that, if there was anything to know, it was safer not to know it.

Only Maurice had the contacts, both inside and outside, to help me with my investigations. Only Maurice could deal with Sykes if he should have anything to do with Trevor's death. If Maurice were involved, I'd had it.

I had to take the risk. Not only had Maurice been imprisoned long after Trevor's murder, but he would surely be of more use to any conspirator on the out than in nick. Above all, I had to trust someone. Complete solitude in this alien environment was driving me mad.

Maurice had a bridge foursome going. They were playing for high stakes. I counted twelve half-ounce packets on the bed behind them. Maurice looked up from his cards.

I nodded towards the door. He laid down his cards. 'Games over. Out!' he announced. 'I've got business.'

The other three left without a word. The last to leave slammed the door and it bounced open again. 'Barry,' said Maurice softly. Barry stuck his head through the door. 'Please shut it quietly this time, Barry,' Maurice smiled.

Barry shut the door as though his baby were in the jamb.

'Now then, Sebastian,' Maurice frowned, 'what were you doing in John's room?'

'That's what I've come here to tell you, and I want your word that you'll repeat it to no one.'

'You have mine, provided that the story's good,' Maurice said.

'And mine,' grunted John.

'Right. It's good, all right. It's also crazy. Listen.'

I told them the story from the beginning. From time to time

during the narrative, Maurice nodded.

At the end, there was silence, then John said, 'Fuck me! Is it true?'

'Yes, it's true,' Maurice grinned. 'I checked Seb out. He's OK. He did know this Abbott guy.'

'Christ!' John whistled. 'First time I ever heard of anyone actually wanting to get in.'

'What have you discovered so far, Seb?' Maurice asked.

'Bugger all,' I admitted. 'I have a clue as to where I'll find the truth, but I'd rather not tell you about that at the moment.'

'Fine,' said Maurice. 'Now, I think I can probably help you. Whatever is going on, I'll bet it's connected with the nocturnal activities about this camp. I thought it was burglary.'

'Nocturnal activities?'

'Yes. I've kept my nose out until now, but this is the position. There are a few cons who've been getting out at night. I've heard them in the corridor, we all have. Now, it's normal enough for people to get out. They go to pick up parcels or to get their legs over or something, but they don't go out every night. These guys do. Second funny thing: although they go out every night, they don't get nicked, which means that there are screws involved.

'The point is, we know about this, but we shut up, right? If we ask them anything, they just say they went to get a parcel or something and that's that – and you're not going to get any con going out of bounds to check on them, are you? He'd lose ninety days and get shanghaied, so everyone shows good sense and keeps his nose clean. Let them get on with it.'

'Yeah,' said John, 'I hear them, too. I've seen a few of them. They've been at it ever since I've been here.'

'My theory is, they've got a creep syndicate,' said Maurice. 'It may sound far-fetched, but think about it. A con goes out of the nick, does a creep, comes back with the goodies and hands them over to the screws. If he should be identified, he's got the original cast-iron alibi, 'cos he was tallied in here that night. Only one screw does the D block tallies on any one night. If he's involved, he just records that the empty beds were full all night. If any of them did get nicked, they'd just be runners trying to get some cash, and they'd be useless from there on.'

'Makes sense,' I admitted, 'but why aren't you in on it,

Maurice, if you don't mind me asking?'

'Creeps aren't my line, boy. I've got my hands full enough as it is without creeping. I sometimes come in at the other end, but that's all.'

'But why should they get nicked?' asked John. 'You see, I am a burglar, and I know. Doing a creep, you only ever get nicked by one person. It's night-time, right? And the owner of the house comes down and says "Gotcha!" and you either say, "OK, you got me," or you run for it and hope they don't get you on an identity parade. They always do. You don't fight back, ever. Professionals never carry shooters or anything like that. We don't want a life rap for the sake of a few snuff boxes. That's why these guys who want to arm the Old Bill are so far off the mark. If you might meet a trigger-happy rozzer, you're going to carry, aren't you?'

John warmed to his theme. 'But if you're in nick and you go out for a job, it's easy. Someone nicks you and you run, and there's never going to be an identity parade. "That's 'im!" says the old dear, pointing at your photograph. "Terribly sorry, mum," says the Old Bill, "that's not 'im, 'e's in nick."

'Of course, if it happened too often, then the police would get suspicious, so these burglars would go out armed. Someone sees them, that someone gets croaked. Easy. And by the time the stiff is found, the creep is back in nick like a good little boy, waking up and saying he don't sleep too well these days.'

'Bloody hell,' I said, 'that'd be worth killing Trev for, if he knew.'

'That's right,' said Maurice. 'We're talking about a foolproof system of organised crime, and they'll kill you too if I'm right in my guess. After all, as your Trevor found out, there's no escape and no law to protect you in here. I'd leave well alone, Seb.'

'Don't be a silly arse, Maurice,' I said, 'would you?'

'Nope.'

'Who are these guys?'

'Who are they, John?' Maurice asked. 'Let's think. There's Fred Oakes. There's Dom, Dom on the twos, nice guy.'

'There's them dagoes,' said John, 'They're next door to me. That's obviously why they got the orderly jobs.'

'What's that?' I asked.

'Well, they're only in for shoplifting, aren't they? Each of

148

them got a stretch, so they should be in the dormitories, same as what you are. But they got nice cushy jobs in the Officers' Mess, see? So they have to work late at night some days and therefore get rooms in D block as if they was long-termers.'

'Interesting,' I said. 'What are their names?'

'Oh, some bloody wog names. One's called Osman, I think, like the light bulbs. I don't know the other – Ali or something.'

'How old are they?'

'Hard to tell. No more than twenty-three, I'd say. Yes, maybe . . . yeah, twenty-three, twenty-four.'

'Who else?'

'Oh, Jesus,' said Maurice, 'I don't know. I'll find out. There's a fair number but, you know, we only know about the ones we've actually seen. What the eye doesn't see, the heart doesn't grieve over, right?'

'Right. If you're going to investigate, Maurice, you'll have to do it yourself. You can't ask around. You realise that?'

'You think we're daft, Seb? We're not getting our throats cut for anyone. You can go all kamikaze if you feel like it. We'll bring flowers to the funeral.'

'If they use their usual method, there won't be any need. There'll be daffodil bulbs stuck in my eye-sockets. Just one more question. What have these guys, the few you know of, got in common?'

Maurice raised his eyebrows and shrugged. John shook his head. 'S.F.A.,' he said.

'Nothing at all?'

'Not that I can think of. You, Maurice?'

'Nope,' Maurice shook his head. 'Not a bloody thing. Dom's in for extortion. A million or two, and they never got it back. He's over fifty, but he's tough. Ex-commando. He's got as many gongs as I've had hot dinners.'

'Fred Oakes is in for burglary,' said John. 'Nothing special about him. Plenty of previous.'

'Yeah, I've fenced for him,' mused Maurice. 'He's a loudmouth and a bore, and he's not a pro., like John, for example.'

John Sykes bowed and looked rather coy.

'And the Arabs?'

'I don't know anything. Small-time shoplifters. They speak English bloody well and seem to be quite bright.'

'But don't worry, Seb,' said John, 'there are plenty more. We'll find a pattern soon.'

We didn't. John and Maurice sat on the bog, peering over the doors, for two successive nights. Between them, they came up with thirteen more names. All the men left their rooms between 11.30 and midnight. We could not observe the ground floor, so I was still in the dark as to who was, or was not, a member of the conspiracy. Furthermore, they seemed to operate on alternate nights. Only two men, Dom and another older man, Kevin Gough, came out on both nights.

There was no connecting factor. Some of the men were old lags, some stars. Some had five years to serve, some eighteen months. There were men of sixty and men of twenty. There were Irishmen, Englishmen, Arabs and Scots.

There was only one thing for it. I would have to risk the whole ridiculous enterprise 'on one throw of pitch and toss'. I would have to follow and observe. If I were caught, I'd spend the rest of the sentence gratuitously and unpleasantly in a closed prison.

The thought did not please me. I put off action day. I continued to teach Mickey, to write petitions, to draw portraits and to annoy screws. I continued to read, to write letters and to receive visits from Fiona. I continued to garden.

'Bloody funny place for a rose,' said the voice. I spilled my tea and turned.

My gaffer was holding forth at an afternoon tea-break. It was early July. 'No reason why it should grow there,' he was saying. 'Some git must have planted it deliberately. Bloody fools. Nice job, though. It's taken well. Right slap on the ditch.'

So maybe I wasn't mad after all. Maybe Trevor had intended that I should follow him.

Heedless of possible traps, I ran round to the back of the nissen huts. A ditch ran the whole length of the playing fields. I walked down its edge.

And there, just halfway down, almost obscured by brambles and twitch, was the dark pink satin head of a recreant rose.

I imagined Trevor's grim face nervously glancing over his shoulder as he shoved a pre-prepared shoot into the bank.

Someone would have been watching him. Supposing that that someone stood at the bottom end of the ditch, his movements would have seemed innocent only in August or September when the weeds were at their highest.

I had no such protection. I dug that rose up in stages, returning to it throughout that day and the next. I loosened the earth for a clear foot on either side of the stalk. Each time that a screw turned up, I grabbed a handful of twitch and looked as though I should be there.

Leach came by at one point, looking officious. When I saw him approach, I dived for a clump of nettles two yards away and occupied myself with stinging myself.

'You'll sting yourself,' said Leach.

'I am stinging myself,' I replied.

'You should use gloves with those nettles.'

'Yes. I forgot.'

'So much for fucking brains! You're stinging yourself!'

'I know, Mr Leach. I can feel it.'

'You're fucking soft in the head.'

'Ah, but you should see my hands.'

'Shut up, Foy!'

'Lovely company we get around here.'

'You don't deserve better, Foy, you're a traitor to your class, your country and your mother. God, what I could have done with your advantages!'

'What's my mother got to do with it, Mr Leach?'

'If you don't know ...' He shrugged. 'I despise you.'

'And after I've given you four of the best months of my life!'

'Fuck off, Foy,' he sniffed, and strode away.

I don't want to give the wrong impression. Screws' conversation is not monotonous. It is full of variations and modulations to the dominant. It's just that it always ends on the same chord, and it's not the tonic.

At half-past three, I returned to my rose. I scrabbled at the loose earth until there was a pit a foot deep all around it. There was nothing there. I sat back on my haunches and gazed at the ravaged patch of earth. I had felt sure that Trevor had transplanted the damned thing for a reason. It was at once the most obvious and the least obtrusive indication that he could give us to the whereabouts of any information. In fact, it was

151

brilliant. Invisible for all but two months of the year, it was at once a freak, word of which must inevitably come to my ears, and a matter of insignificance both to screws and to cons.

'Damnation!' I cried at last. 'Damn bloody paranoid Trevor and damn his bloody messages! May he rot!'

In a fit of vindictive fury, I tugged at the rose, jagged my hand, and as petals fluttered to the ground, I found what I'd been looking for.

It was a single sheet of paper, rolled in a ball and wrapped in the cellophane from a one-ounce pack of tobacco. The neck of the screwed-up plastic had been tied around the root.

I shoved the little bag into the pocket of my overalls and rapidly made good the damage that I'd done. The rose, I replanted. Those old roses are tough. *Si monumentum requiris,* I imagine that you'd find it there still.

I ran to the loo and forced the package up my rectum. I was not going to die simply because some screw took it into his head to give me one of their random body searches.

I eat liver and bacon that night in a mood of elation. Not until I was again in the privacy of Maurice's room did I, with much tugging and heaving, retrieve my precious quarry.

'To whom it may concern,' I read. 'I can't mention your name in case the wrong chap finds this. Anyhow, I hope you're OK, if you're who I think you are. I don't know what's going on. I hope to run when I've found out details. I'll go straight to my editor's house, provided that no one gets me first.

'This is all I know. Under the electrical workshop, there's an arsenal sufficient to blow the whole of Lincolnshire sky-high. Guns, grenades, high explosives, the lot. There are quite a few cons involved, quite a few screws, but I don't yet know who. I'll find out, though, and indicate it as best I can about the nick.

'God bless you, lad. I know you won't really come here, but still. Take care of Cindy. This really looks like the biggest and the last. I can't turn to anyone in a nick like I could elsewhere, that's the hell of it.

'Don't, for Christ's sake, go on the forty-threes. They'll have you where they want you.'

I handed the note to Maurice. He whistled. 'So much for fucking burglary,' he said.

'Terrorism?'

'Could be. The same advantages would exist. Jeesus, Seb, what're you getting us into?'

'I don't know,' I admitted, 'but I suggest you keep well out.'

'I don't need lessons in cowardice, Seb, I was born an expert.'

'Get me some bent letters out?'

'Can't,' he said.

'What d'you mean, you can't?'

'You're being watched, Seb. That means I am, too. I can pass on requests orally, but sure as hell I can't be seen handing anything to anyone. What would be the consequences for both of us if that note were nicked? How do you know the bloody postman isn't involved? Not only can't Seb, won't. This thing's getting big league.'

'OK,' I sighed. 'Can you insure that I've got a reliable con with me all day from now on? I don't care who, so long as he's one of yours. I want to insure that no one gets me alone.'

'Easy,' he said. 'I'm owed about thirty ounces. That's enough to buy twenty hit-men for twenty jobs. You're guarded.' He paused, then said in an avuncular tone, 'Look, kid, you've got enough now to feed to *Private Eye* or someone. What's the point of going further? I like you. I don't want to see *you* pushing up daisies before your time.'

'What can I give to *Private Eye*?' I asked. 'The word of a discredited lawyer, a discredited journalist and, if you're prepared to be quoted, a pretty notorious gangster. Even if someone published it, this lot would know before ever it reached the presses and would just move everything out pronto.'

Maurice sighed. 'All right, Seb, I'll give you what help I can.'

He meant what he said. He was, after all, an honest man.

15

That night I followed them.

From the window of my billet I saw them emerge. They clung to the walls like last summer's flies, but they made no great effort to keep out of sight. They came one by one; they vanished one by one. At half past twelve, the last one emerged. I hoped he was the last. He'd better be. I scurried after him.

It was pitch dark and very still, but I saw his figure tinged with liquid blue in the lamplight. He turned the corner in the direction of the electricians' workshop.

I reached the corner in time to see him climb the stone steps. He knocked on the door. It opened at once. I saw his face in the light from within. It was the man they called Dom.

The basement lights were out. I had no choice but to creep up those stairs after him.

A wild cat screamed, and I almost disappeared into myself so rapidly did everything contract. I'm no commando. I'm the sort of guy that goes on Aldermaston marches and keeps spaniels. It's all right humanity, I'm your friend. I took a deep breath and pressed on.

I raised my head just above the window ledge.

I lowered it again. It was two minutes before I realised that the men in the room couldn't see me as well as I could see them. It was another two minutes before I convinced myself.

I looked in again.

There were seven cons and two screws in there. They were stripped to their shirt sleeves and they were hard at work.

Two Irish cons whom I but vaguely knew were busy with wires and solder. Leach, the screw, and Dom were demonstrating something to the others who lounged about but listened intently. A large chart like an architect's blue-print hung on the far wall, and Dom kept walking over to it and tapping it. He was a small, wiry man with neat grey hair. Gentle eyes sparkled in a well-worn setting. He seemed to be the boss. The second screw, Farrell, sat in the corner looking bored.

Suddenly something clicked in my mind. These men shared something in common after all. They were all keep-fit fanatics. They were always at weight training sessions or running round and round the fields, wrapped in plastic. It figured. It also scared me just a little bit more.

Then I saw the glint of black steel and Dom came up with the next of the night's surprises. He assembled the gun as though he'd spoken guns before ever he had learned English.

He smiled, and soothed the thing. It was a sort of rifle-cum-machine gun with a plastic stock. It looked nasty. They didn't seem to think so. They all rushed over and cooed and clucked at it like a load of broody mothers. One of the little Arabs took it, swung his left leg round and crouched with the gun at his hip. It pointed straight at me.

I ducked down and thought of nice warm beds and Veuve Clicquot and waking up with Fiona's head on my chest. I had to think of something.

I thought I'd seen enough, and crept back down the steps.

Someone else thought I'd see a bit more. He just stood there, arms folded, at the bottom of the steps, and I damn nearly ran into him. It was Forsdyke. Only then did I realise that he'd been charged to watch me from the moment I arrived at Ravenhill. Sebastian Foy, barrister, thumb in bum, mind in neutral.

I wondered whether this was an official or an unofficial bust. Would he carry me to his friends, or to the block? If I went to the block, then I'd go to closed nick. If I went to see his friends, I didn't reckon I'd go anywhere else.

'Foy again,' Forsdyke whined.

'Forsdyke again,' I said.

'You've had it this time.'

'Don't think so, Mr Forsdyke. How are you going to explain an arsenal to a visiting court?'

'They're on our side too.'

155

I tried a bluff. 'All of them?' I asked. Four local worthies constituted the visiting court. One at least was an old dear with a holy hat. I couldn't associate her with what I'd seen.

Forsdyke said, 'There's not going to be a visiting court. Come with me.'

'No,' I said.

He put a hand on my arm. I remembered what Billy Turner had taught me at the Cliff. 'Look, Mr Forsdyke,' I said.

I stretched my right arm out in a helpless, harmless gesture, then I put the nut in.

I think I did it quite well, for a beginner. I kept my eyes on his mouth so that my forehead struck the bridge of his nose. There was a scrunching sound, and Forsdyke keeled. His hand left my arm. I swung round and did what used to be called a donkey kick – they call it a dragon kick these days.

Billy was right, knees don't bend backwards, but they do make a hell of a noise.

Forsdyke dropped groaning and choking. I ran for my life.

I was back in the billet in one minute, undressed and in bed in two. I reckoned it would take Forsdyke quite a time to alert his friends. They could scarcely come to get me in the dormitory because I knew one thing now; they didn't want me on governor's, they didn't want me before a visiting court. They didn't want me returned to a closed nick either. Whilst I was at Ravenhill, I was safe from Shanghai. The wanted me to stay there forever.

Maurice was as good as his word, I was guarded all day. Every time that anyone came near me, someone else was there, chatting to me about the test match, or the weather. Forsdyke had been assaulted by an unknown convict, we were told.

Of course, they could not have me in a hospital, so they put Mickey there just to show me. They uncorked him behind the Nissen huts, just where I'd found Trevor's rose.

Maurice and I walked round the playing fields after tea the next day. The cons were playing a cricket match, and the sound of bat on ball punctuated our conversation. Bowlers grunted, fielders puffed and swore.

It was one of the few beautiful evenings we were to have that year. A few swallows skated around, dipping, cresting, winging over the cricket square. The smell of grass was strong, and the barley fields of Belvoir Vale waved like green fields of breeze blown fire. Everything was shadow dappled. It was one of those evenings when you pity Californians.

'Maurice,' I said, 'can you find out for me what this it?'

I handed him a sketch of that gun.

Maurice took one look at it, said 'Christ!' and sat down on the grass. 'Get out of this, Seb, whatever it is,' he said. 'Have they got these things?'

'Yup.' I said, sitting cross-legged beside him. 'Do you know what they are?'

'Yes.' He sighed wearily. 'Believe it or not, I was once SAS. This is crazy. This is fucking crazy.'

'What are they?'

'AR 15s, Sebastian, M.16s. High velocity, .22, weighs nothing and has a light-weight bullet which explodes on target impact. It's a nasty piece with a nasty bullet which goes mad when it hits you and tears most of your inside out. We had them. The Yanks had them in Vietnam.'

'Where would this crowd get them?'

'Christ knows, Seb. They're not even legal in warfare. The bloody thing will kill you if they hit your little toe. It almost atomises the blood. They're American. That's all I know.'

'Thanks, Maurice.'

'You're going to have to run and take your chances, Seb, I'm sure you can wield a big enough stick to get people to listen.'

'I doubt it,' I said. 'I don't even know what it's all about, do you? And by the time they've got warrants and everything sorted out, the place will be as clean as a whistle.'

'Yup, 'fraid so.' Maurice nodded. He handed me back the sketch. 'Better eat this or something,' he said, 'we're being watched.'

I looked over in the direction he indicated. Farrell stood in the corner of the field, his huge form silhouetted against the sinking sun. The drawing tasted lousy.

They got me alone on the Sunday. It was easy enough. They simply called me into the governor's office. Maurice's men hung around the PO's block, but they could not follow me in.

I did not know what the governor and Glaser already knew,

so I could pull no stunts. They went through the old routine.

'Foy,' said the governor, 'it has been decided that you constitute a security risk. As you are aware, letters are usually censored on a random fifteen percent basis. In future, you will be on the special censor's list, which means that all your letters, in and out of prison, will be censored.'

'I see, sir,' I said.

'Don't answer the governor back!' barked Glaser.

'No, sir.'

'Foy, I've warned you ...'

'Right, sir.'

'Right, watch it. Out!'

I walked out to find a reception party awaiting me. Farrell and Leach took my arms and bore me kicking along the passage. A door opened. I was dumped down.

I was in a little office. Facing me sat a man whom I had never seen before. He was tall, blond and bronzed. He wore Wranglers, Harvey Hudson and the most beautiful shoes I'd seen in ages. His hair was perfect – the Trumpers' haircut which isn't a haircut – just clipping the collar, but neat as God made it.

'Come in, Mr Foy,' he said unnecessarily.

'I have little choice,' I said.

'Yes, sorry. Farrell, Leach, can you leave us alone please?'

'Right, sir, 'said Farrell. They left like dutiful Nubians.

'Now, Mr Foy, would you like a drink?'

I was dreaming. Second only to Fiona, my dreams had concerned drink. They were almost erotic dreams: vats of claret and swimming pools of Dom Ruinart. Or I'd be working in the garden, being a good reliable prisoner when suddenly I'd think of a pint of Abbot, slipping smooth and soapy down my throat, chased by a vigorous straight malt. And now I'd gone mad, and here was this guy leaning back as though he were at Lord's and saying 'Would you like a drink?'

'I'd like thirty-two, please.' I said.

He grinned. 'Help yourself.' He waved towards the cupboard in the corner. 'I'm afraid I've only whisky.'

Well, that wasn't quite true. He'd only Laphroaig. I poured myself half a pint, sipped, shuddered and sighed.

'Now offer me a Sullivan Powell,' I said, 'and I'm all yours.'

He smiled his sunny smile again, and offered me a Sullivan

Powell.

'Do sit down, Mr Foy,' he said. I sat.

'My name,' he said, 'is Heron, Carol Heron.'

'How do you do?'

'I run this show that you've stumbled over,' he said. I rather resented the word 'stumbled'. 'I must say, I admire your persistence,' he went on. 'You dealt with that idiot Forsdyke splendidly. He'll be useless from now on.'

'Good.'

'Yes, yes, I admire you, but fairly obviously I can't let you ruin the whole thing.'

'Obviously.'

'And I think you will see why when I explain to you what it's all about.'

'I know what it's about,' I said. 'It's about murder and torture.'

'Torture?' He blinked and looked genuinely hurt. 'Oh, you mean Mickey Rourke! That was not my doing, Mr Foy. That was the cheap, petty vindictiveness of two officers who did not like what you did to Forsdyke. They have been disciplined.'

'And Trevor?' I said.

'Abbott?' He frowned. 'He did much of what you are doing now. He threatened our whole existence, and thereby endangered many thousands of innocent lives. Incidentally, we knew all along why you came here, but we also knew that Abbott had left some information about, and we wanted to find out where. You were the best means.'

'Thanks.'

'We also knew of your politics and your abilities and therefore trusted that we might be able to work something out.'

'Go on, Mr Heron.'

He got up and walked over to the window, his hands linked behind his back. 'You are a pacifist, are you not, Mr Foy?' he asked.

'I am not.'

'But you went on Aldermaston marches in the early sixties and have made large contributions to the Committee of a Hundred?'

'Yes, Mr Heron. I am anxious to preserve our culture and those people whom I love, but I am more anxious to preserve

159

life itself. I see no purpose in destroying all life in the specious name of defence. Once eradicate such weapons, and I'm all for our men dashing off and bashing one another on the head as much as they like.'

'Ultimate deterrent?'

'Ultimate deterrent be damned!' I said. 'Sure, there's a chance that those weapons won't be used in the event of invasion. I doubt it, but there's a chance. Chance is restricted to gambling, and I do not believe that we are entitled to gamble with the lives of our children, with all life indeed. The crime is not in running a child over, but in driving drunk in the first place. It's taking chances that we have no right to take.'

'I'm glad you feel that way,' he said. 'Those weapons have so far reduced man's sense of purpose and pride as to make all action immoral. You have observed, of course, the resultant disregard for the welfare of others which now characterises the young?'

'I have.' I said. 'With no we-consciousness, and the natural desire to assert an identity, they are forced into an anti-social role.'

'So you sympathise with them?'

'Sympathise? Yes. Contrary to the assumptions of the sanctimonious liberals, that does not mean that I do not believe that society has a duty to defend itself as best it can for so long as it exists in its present form.'

'So you believe that, in a world devoid of pride, in a godless, hopeless world, full of violent crime, murder, rape, disregard for property, and all the other manifestations of anti-social individualism, society must yet suppress such evils?'

'Only thus does a society define itself,' I said, 'though I wonder whether I would seek to defend this society or its ideologies against the exponents of a new structure.'

'That doesn't matter,' he said with a wave. He ran his finger along the window-sill, inspected the dust, and sniffed meticulously. 'What you think of Ulriche Meinhoff?' he asked.

'Personally, I admire her. I admire anyone of her intelligence with the courage to assert a moral conviction in the face of her own, and her society's morality.'

'So do I. I should have phrased my question otherwise. What would you do if you were threatened by a Red Brigade terrorist?'

'That depends on my position. If I were observed, I hope that I would have the nerve not to resist . . . No, of course, I would resist.'

'You would try to kill him?'

'If it were the only means whereby I could stop him, yes.'

'And if he threatened your house, your family, or even a school or a town which you did not know?'

'If I could prevent him, of course, I would.'

'Good, good,' he said, like a doctor inspecting my tongue. 'Well, Mr Foy, there are thousands of innocent people being raped, maimed and murdered by such people throughout the world. By logical extension of your ethic as you have just expressed it, you would attempt to prevent this by force, if possible and necessary.'

'Go on.'

'If, that is to say, I could point out to you a man and say, "This man intends to kill defenceless men, women and children tomorrow, and only you can stop him'', then you would forestall him if you could not dissuade him?'

'Yes, provided that I were not contributing to the escalation of nuclear weaponry.'

'Provided, in short, that you had anonymity?'

'Yes.'

He smiled broadly, and sat behind the desk again. 'That,' he said, 'is exactly the problem faced by the judiciary and the official military. They cannot, or rather, they dare not go against that wishy-washy liberalism which is the mainstay of their power. The net result is that, while the public receives no protection, the so-called terrorist is protected by the full might of the law. There are countries which will give him sanctuary and, when he is caught, he is given a nice, extra-luxurious prison cell for a few years. We protect the public. The terrorist now knows as never before that he faces summary justice in proportion to his atrocities.'

I took this in slowly. It was incredible. He must be mad. So why wasn't he gibbering?'

'And you operate from Ravenhill?' I said at last.

'We operate from a large number of different bases, many of them prisons. As you will no doubt have recognised, an open

161

prison offers well-nigh total protection from snoopers, cast-iron alibis, all the facilities which we need for training and plenty of storage space. It's also damned economical because our staff is fed and housed by the Home Office, which strikes me as only appropriate. We can staff a place like Ravenhill, as you know full well, by having our men do just as you have done. They merely pick the crime, commit it in a given area, and the system inexorably spews them up in the desired prison.

'Our permanent staff is even easier to establish. The prison service is desperate for men, which isn't surprising since they are indisputably the worst employers in the country. Screening is minimal, and anyhow, most of our men are good ex-service material.'

'It's clever,' I admitted, still incredulous, 'but what are we talking about? Another Walter Walker private army, ready to fight MIGs with executive jets if an emergency arises?'

That really cracked him up. He grinned that dazzling slow grin again. 'God forbid!' he said. 'Ours is a professional fighting force permanently in the field. Let me tell you the story.'

'May I have another drink?' I asked. I knew what he was going to ask me. I also knew what my answer must be. It wasn't going to be as easy as I had thought.

Heron waved at the bottle and crossed his long legs. I filled the glass. He hummed.

'Right,' I said, 'fire away.'

'My father,' he started in his best listen-with-mother tone, 'owns mines in South Africa. I was born and brought up in Johannesburg.'

He saw my raised eyebrows and smiled. 'Charterhouse,' he said. Which explained why I had never met him and, to my mind, explained quite a few other things. 'Now, when terrorists began to threaten our mines and to put pressure on the buyer governments, gold almost dropped out at the bottom. No one can afford that sort of insecurity. As well you know, a secure government depends upon a secure economy and vice versa. It only takes a few crazed dissidents threatening the stability of the great industries or of governments for the whole economic system to teeter.

'All known security systems were useless. They're OK for armed robbers and so on, but they're about as much good

162

against highly-trained operatives with a cause as a load of boy-scouts with water-pistols. I decided to form my own team. I trained them, I equipped them, I turned them into a highly efficient counter-offensive force. We have had no problems since first they were developed.'

'Very impressive,' I said. I was getting tight, and enjoying it.

'Other industries came to me, wanting to learn, and I realised that there was a market for an international anti-terrorist squad. The largest companies in Britain wanted our services, so did those in South Africa, in Ireland, in Italy, France and Germany, everywhere. I approached them all on the QT. Over eighty percent of them wanted the sort of service that I offered.

'I formed a holding company. It runs a clinic near Geneva. Each consolidate paid me a subscription. My brief was to defend their companies from terrorism and subversion. We were successful. But since these bastards established bloody great training camps and the sophistication of the whole thing grew, we received increasing demands that we should protect the currency per se. That means striking before the enemy does. Two years ago, we undertook to do just that. We know where the enemy is holed up, we unearth him, we liquidate him. We bring back some evidence to show that we're earning our keep, and everyone's happy.

'We do, in short, exactly what the police would do, what the average citizen would do, if only he were allowed to. We're weeding the buggers out. Think about it,' he commanded. I was thinking. 'In effect, we are employed by the governments of our client nations. They depend on the security of their political parties and industries for the welfare of the money market and hence for the continued existence of democracy. Many of our biggest clients are nationalised industries. We've got trade union pension funds invested with us. Many of your friends, I may say, and even your relations, are among our supporters, consultants or operatives.'

I offered token resistance, taking shelter in clichés. 'It gives you an unparalleled and very dangerous power to play God,' I said.

'Jesus Christ!' he cried, standing again. 'You're a lawyer, aren't you? You're a member of a profession which of its very nature 'plays God', as you put it. It condemns, punishes, sanctions and rewards. Someone has to. Someone's bloody got to play God, otherwise there is no law and no society. You know that as well as I do. Someone has to arbitrate on social contracts. Someone has to have the courage to ordain what is permissible, what is not, what is punishable by what and so on. It's bloody uncomfortable, it's *bloody* cold, but it's got to be done. Remember your Hobbes?'

'Hobbes saw his arbitrator as subject to natural or divine law,' I said. 'Are you?'

'I am subject to no absolute idea of good, no. I am bound only by my convictions, my sense of honour, and I have the guts to believe that I'm right.'

'Yes, I admire that,' I admitted, 'but in the same way do I admire Meinhoff and Co. How do you distinguish between them and you?'

He came round the desk now. I'd touched a nerve. He frowned and jabbed his finger at me. 'Look,' he said, 'you are an Englishman, and have in the past displayed considerable pride in being so. And why? Because it's a pretty place? Because it occupies a certain longtitude or latitude that you just happen to like? No! Because the English way of life represents to you certain freedoms which you deem to be worthwhile. Would you not fight to preserve them? Would you not die to preserve them?'

'I would.'

'And yet you have not the courage to kill to preserve them?'

'Oh yes, I have,' I said. I refilled my glass.

'Well, show it then!' Heron slumped in his chair.

'With pleasure,' I said. 'I have no compunction about killing to defend something or someone that I love when it is threatened.'

'Well, for heaven's sake, man, who is fighting for freedom and peace if we are not?'

I saw his point, of course. I remembered a fifteen-year-old girl who'd never smile into a mirror again. I remembered Jamie, my cousin and my friend, who had been 'executed' in a quiet field in Londonderry. I remembered, too, an impractical, crazy beggar called Mick Murphy, who believed in Kropotkin and mutual aid and thought we should all be like little flowers.

Heron threw in one of his aces. 'Your woman's father is with

164

us,' he said, 'he's one of our senior executives.'

'Major Gunn? That doesn't surprise me.'

'Charles Virtue is with us.'

Charlie . . . Lord Charles Virtue. Charming upper-class twit, he had shared rooms with me at Cambridge. Did he know about Trevor Abbott? Did he even know what death looked like, smelt like, except in foxes and pheasants?

'Almost every mason you know . . .'

'All right! All right!' I shouted. 'I know it's reasonable. I suppose we've all been expecting such an organisation for years, but none of us had the nous to do anything about it. None of us had the expertise or the initiative. We just complained.'

Heron grinned and sighed. 'Thank God,' he said. 'I was afraid we were going to have to dump you. I didn't want to.'

'That's no reason for not doing so, as you must know better than most.'

He nodded. 'True, and I must confess that I was in favour of keeping things tidy by removing you as Abbott was removed. Mine, however, is an organisation staffed entirely by volunteers, and I can ill afford the sort of disaffection which professional cold-bloodedness might engender. You have some very powerful friends, Mr Foy, friends with a firm belief in your abilities and in your loyalty. After this conversation, I believe that their faith is justified. We could do with your help.'

'I'd never have come here if I'd known what it was all about,' I sighed.

'Of course not. Still, you're here, and we might as well profit from it. You have consistently shown in the past that you believe in our cause. Had it not been for your unbalanced mode of life in London, indeed, you'd have been approached by us some time ago. You'll have to prove yourself, you know, but at least if you'll take the oath . . .'

'The oath to whom?'

'To the Crown, of course.'

I finished the bottle, shook his hand, and staggered out, feeling dirty and very drunk.

John Sykes was waiting for me on the parade ground. 'Sebastian, you OK?' he asked.

'No.' I replied. 'I'm pissed. Lend me your bed for an hour or two.'

'OK,' he said in his characteristic, lugubrious fashion. 'How come you're pissed?'

'I've been drinking.'

'Are you really OK?'

'Otherwise, fine,' I said.

'How come they didn't do you?'

'We're all good friends now. We're all together. It's all right!'

He asked no more questions. We walked back to D block together. It was a long way and I kept looking around for a taxi.

'Mickey's back,' John said quietly.

'Back where?'

'He's back from hospital. In his old room. I saw him this morning. He was crying.'

'I'll go and see him.'

'He'll be on a liquid diet for a year. I think he's still in great pain. He refuses to go on the forty-threes.'

'No. He couldn't stand closed nick. I'll go and see him.'

'He probably won't see you. He was still crying.'

We reached the door of D block. I must have been mumbling contentedly for John was looking faintly disgusted. I didn't understand. Life was good again. I wasn't scared anymore. I was happy. No one was trying to kill me anymore.

'Can't remember the number of Mickey's room' I said.

'D.21.'

'Of course! Thank you, thank you, thank you!' I dribbled, and swayed up the stairs.

John followed, dour.

'I'll go and see Mickey,' I said. 'You'll wait, will you?'

'All right,' he said. 'I'll hang on.'

I bumped into Mickey's door. 'Mickey!' I bellowed. 'Mickey, it's me!'

He did not answer. I turned the handle and pushed at the door. It did not move. I pushed harder. Something gave. The door banged open, and I fell in over a chair.

Mickey was hanging by a torn sheet from the top of the window frame. He was blue, all right, but he didn't look as though he'd seen heaven.

166

16

The next weeks passed slowly, as if in a dream. I was numb with shock. I felt beaten. I'd escaped the constant terror of the past weeks, and that afforded me relief. But at the same time, I felt wrong. I just wanted to get out, to go to sleep in some warm and welcoming arms, to rest my aching head on a soft breast, 'to cease upon the midnight with no pain'.

Instead, most midnights brought training sessions in the workshop. I learned lots of useful things, like how to make a bomb out of a box of matches, or a shirt and a cigarette, how to assemble, load and fire the M.16, how to dodge airport metal detectors and how to throw grenades. I learned how to kill a man in twenty different ways and when he was dead at last, how to bring him back to life again. I learned about pretty drugs like Susceanol, about the exploitation of phobias and about Middle Eastern politics. I learned all sorts of things I'd have given anything not to know. I'm no obscurantist, but I was happier just knowing about Baudelaire, Sung, hunting and haute couture.

Twice a week, 'our' screws had the night shift to themselves. That meant that the prison was ours. On those nights, we'd learn woodcraft, practise knife-fighting and climb sheer walls covered with tarpaulins. If we had a spare moment, we'd run a mile or two.

Dom was our instructor. I came to like him. Farrell, who also turned out to be ex-SAS, was his deputy.

I kept telling myself that this was impossible but, ridiculous as it may seem, it was all too easy. There were only three screws on any one night-shift, and the 9 pm-5 am shift was the least popular. Our men simply volunteered, were accepted, and were thus left in sole control of the prison.

The other screws and the governor lived miles away, the cons were safely confined to their dormitories and their rooms, and no one – screw, civilian or policeman – was permitted to re-enter the prison having once left. The whole system was perfect, and should any convict, illegally out of bounds, see anything moving, he would run for his life, and would scarcely report what he had seen to the governor.

The governor was not of our number, nor, I knew, were most of the senior officers; but I had no idea who was. There must have been at least two other officers in the organisation and, I was told, there were seven other convicts.

Each party, of course, was deliberately kept in ignorance so that none of us, becoming scared or having problems of conscience, could reveal anything to anyone, without risking discovery and, I assumed, execution.

Our oaths demanded total devotion to the cause, so every evening after tea, I showed lumps of metal what I was made of. They didn't seem very impressed. I did bench presses, bar presses, curls, snatches and squats. I had deadweights pulling out my arms and legs, and people dropped ten-ton medicine balls on my stomach. Some people are like that.

I became soft, weak, slow and incapable, then, mysteriously, I became hard, strong, quick and deadly.

I also became tired. Loveday the screw, asked me almost every day, 'I say, are you all right, old chap?'

'Fine thanks, sir.'

'You look rather the worse for wear, you know. You must try to sleep.'

'Oh, I'm OK, sir, honestly. It's just the strain I suppose.'

'Yes. Well, take care. It'll all be over soon.'

I was still followed, and was forced into the unenviable position of the traitor.

Maurice was totally bemused. 'What's it about, then, Seb?' he asked me kindly.

'I'm going along with them, Maurice,' I said, and left him to work out what I meant.

He did. He said nothing, but ignored me totally from then on.

The trouble was that I really did not know whether I was going along with them or not.

If Heron had told me that he was head of a neo-Nazi group, I would have played along with him for as long as I reasonably could. It was that, or die, and martyrdom without an audience is a singularly futile fate. I'd have worn my armband, strutted and sieg heiled, found out as much as I could, and revealed all, should I ever be allowed to leave.

But this was different. I was surrounded, not by recognisable fanatics, but by ordinary people completely dedicated to a good cause in which they believed profoundly. I began to understand the peculiar form of madness demanded of resistance fighters. The propaganda says that the new status quo is good. In a very short time, your language itself tells you that the new status quo is good. It cannot be bad, just as black cannot be white.

Yet you retain some ill-defined certainty that the status quo is wrong, all wrong. Until you win, therefore, you are just a wrecker, a murderer, a common criminal. You can justify your actions only by your own convictions, which are frequently less than rational.

I admire no men in history so much as I admire Brutus and Cromwell who, for just such a conviction, condemned themselves to eternal self-hatred and uncertainty. Brutus killed his friend whom the people saw as a god. Cromwell killed a divinely appointed king. In doing so they affronted themselves and became no man. They were but temporal interfaces. Their mothers, who had taught them the ABC, their gods, and their own languages, condemned them, but they dared to reach beyond their terms and those of their times. They recognised some common, essential human quality which they saw to be affronted and they effaced themselves. They saw *sub specie aeternitatis,* as only he can who has shared in the unity of all things and ceased to be subject and his universe object. They had seen themselves in trees and stars, had seen themselves as minute fleckings in a universal eye and so they dared. They dared to play God.

Just so did I find myself torn between inner conviction and 'self-evident' truth. The more I stalled, the surer I became that these men were indeed serving a necessary and righteous function.

At times I thought, as I had always thought, that no man

169

should be a law unto himself, that a nation cannot have two kings or two armies, that the end does not justify the means.

But it is characteristic that all such ideas can only be expressed in such platitudes, for all nature is pragmatist, all ethics are survival ethics. It is merely the function of every dominant ideology to pretend that time has been arrested, that some divine arbitrator has ordained an absolute right, an absolute wrong. 'It has always been thus' we say, meaning that it has been thus for a generation and that we are afraid of transition and supercession.

I realised too, that to all intents and purposes we were an official police force, with contacts in Special Branch, in the SAS, in the seal squad, in the army and in the police. We had the tacit sanction of the highest in the land. It was all, quite literally, too close to home. We were fighting to preserve those freedoms which I believe, and still believe, are being eroded by corporatism and by the deliberate corruption of the language. We were fighting, as our fathers had fought, not for capital (though Heron saw it thus), but for our unwritten constitution, which has thus far transcended feudalism, livery and maintenance and capital.

In past generations we would have had a war, but war meant death to the world, so we were going to war quietly, efficiently.

But what of the courage of those whom we destroyed? They too believed that they were right. They too dared to be ostracised, vilified and laid in a criminal's grave for a personal conviction. We all had the same problems. Liberty can only exist by the suppression of liberty. The only trouble was, we disagreed.

It appeared that my dedication satisfied them and, early in August, I was rewarded. I was summoned on a night when usually I would be left abed. There were plenty of nudges and winks amongst the men, but I did not guess what I was in for.

I duly arrived at five to midnight. The cons who had gathered there looked scrubbed and glossy. They had greased back their hair, sloshed themselves with after-shave, and had donned their best sets of prison greys. They fidgeted and shuffled from foot to foot.

'What's it all about?' I asked Ali, one of the mysterious little

Arabs.

'You are going to get your leg over,' he announced seriously.

I think that I said, 'Oh!'

This, I discovered, was a regular weekly treat. When we were all assembled. Farrell conducted us to the Officers' Mess. It was a large square room with a bar in the corner. A vinyl-covered bench affair ran all around. The lights were low.

Three girls awaited us. They wore mini-skirts, shirts, and nothing else.

Six large bottles of nasty Spanish plonk stood on a low table in the middle of the room. They were emptied in minutes as the cons, with the diffidence which characterises the villian in his approach to women, sat around for a while, chatting to the girls about the Jubilee celebrations and the weather.

Then the girls started to go about their business.

'Maidens, like moths, are ever caught by glare/And Mammon wins where angels might despair.'

Maybe that was why I received special attention. Maybe it was just that I was from the same world as they.

For these were not whores. They were young, limber, beautiful women, and they spoke what my mother would call 'The King's English' – as acquired at Tudor Hall or Heathfield. They were Heron's friends or the daughters of his friends. They might even have been his sisters.

In my Paris days, I was conducted to several 'partouzes' in a little house near Fontainebleau. After the first kick at shared abasement, they depressed me. No one caressed anyone. We squeezed and probed as though we were pressing buttons on a console. We did not fuck with our bodies but with genitalia alone. Like the love earned by the orator, it was a matter of tricks. A kiss suddenly seemed the most erotic thing on earth, a real kiss in which two people tried to break down definitions, to sink into one another.

It was not like that here. I lay back, half smothered by sweet-smelling breasts and hair falling on my face, and the two girls who concentrated on me responded with a fervour which astonished me. They kissed, sucked, fucked and whispered like young girls in love. The responded, however, not to me, but to some idea. Quite literally, they closed their eyes and thought of England. Of power. Of death.

They gave themselves with the sort of wild enthusiasm with which a soldier might scream obscenities, cursing himself into courage, for only a scream will silence the whisper of mother's milk morals.

I found myself caught up in their excitement and took one of them, a lovely fair-haired girl called Caroline, with a fervour like a fury. She loved it. I was fit, I was frustrated, and almost at once the smell of rut, the touch of naked flesh, the kisses of another of the girls, aroused me again. I did not want to follow the others, to make my own contribution to the fifty-seven varieties which now churned about inside her. My morbidly sensitive imagination was picturing the gastronomic goldfish in her bath, so I had her suck me off. She did it expertly.

As she bent over me, Osman came up behind her and thrust into her. She raised her head, hissed and laughed. He pounded into her while she completed the task that she had already begun on me. Her hips circled, her nose ran. She drank every drop, and looked up, drooling and murmuring.

After, the girls lay stroking me, whispering in my ear, telling me how marvellous I was. Their hips heaved. All those ischial folds throbbed like sailors' throats.

I looked down at their faces, the faces of young girls, reflecting absurd ecstasy and devotion.

I think that it was then that I decided I'd rather die a hero.

'I hope you don't mind my pinching one of your precious visits, darling.' My mother leaned forward and rested her elbows on the formica table-top.

'Of course not, Mum. I'm glad to see you.'

'Oh, rubbish,' she grinned. 'I'm quite sure you'd rather have one of your young ladies here, but I had to see you just once during all this silly business.'

She bent to rummage in her bag. 'I've brought a few things for you,' she said, and a dry bang of grey hair flopped over her brow. 'I don't know whether they'll allow you to have them but I thought they might help. Cigarettes, chocolates and things. Oh, where are they?'

She pulled a handful of pens, handkerchieves, keys and compacts from her bag and slammed them on the table. For a moment, a frown of annoyance replaced her composed smile.

Her mouth curled downward. The pouches beneath her eyes drooped. In that moment, she was a very old woman and a very sick old woman.

She looked up and caught my gaze. She knew that I had seen. A corner of her mouth twitched angrily, then she smiled. 'You're looking very fit, Sebastian, love. Tougher, somehow. No bad thing. Are you allowed chocolate? And what about money and books now? I remember Bertie used to say he had terrible trouble getting books in those days, but I suppose things must have changed.'

I shook my head. 'They haven't changed.'

'Oh dear, Sebastian,' she sighed and looked up at me coyly, 'I do wish I could do something?'

For fifteen years I had scarcely dared to look her in the eye for fear she might steal something of my tenuous independence, but now, as she stole a girlish glance at me, I met her gaze and smiled. She crossed her legs and looked down at the chocolate in her hands.

'How are you, Mum?' I asked.

'Oh, thriving, thriving, darling. Don't you worry about me. You're the one with problems. I gather the Gunn girl has been visiting you.'

'Yes. How did you learn that?'

'Sylvie, of course.'

'Oh, damn!' I closed my eyes.

'She's slightly distressed, I reckon, though of course she'd never let on. I mean, she knew that you and the Gunn girl were seeing one another before she turned up.'

I felt a blush suffusing my cheeks and a fierce throbbing under my eyes as I remembered Sylvie's regular, uncomplaining letters. My mother broke off eight squares of chocolate and passed them to me surreptitiously. Her long fingers plucked and tore at the silver paper.

'The Gunn girl, Sebastian,' she said. 'I'm worried. I've been hearing things: you know the way one does, and one doesn't give them a second thought as a rule, but there's one thing I've got to say because obviously, you know, I'm concerned and all that.' She paused for breath, looking down at her working fingers and snatched her hands away. Again she looked me in the eyes. Again I met her gaze. With shame I realised that she was scared of me.

'All I'm going to say, and I know you'll be very cross with me, is that she's spoiled. It's not her fault, but she's spoiled and just isn't equipped to face things when they get tough. What I'm trying to say is ...' She looked about her. Her head was high. Her eyes scanned the tables all about us. One of the last of the grandes dames.

'Look,' she resumed, 'that fellow over there – the one that looks like australopithicus with the scrawny little woman who keeps pecking like a chicken. Got him? Right. How often has he been inside?'

'Frank?' I said. 'Oh, on and off since time immemorial. He's a recidivist. Nice chap.'

'And spoiled,' she said firmly. 'Spoiled by orphanage and by borstal, by army and by prison. He cannot live without an institution. I bet he longs for freedom. I bet he dreams of it while he's in here. But so soon as he's out, he needs the freedom from responsibility which an institution affords, so he commits another crime. Right?'

'Right,' I nodded gloomily.

'Well, she's like that. You are freedom to her, and I'm sure she'd love to be able to stay out in the cold, but she just isn't strong enough. She's an emotional recidivist. There.' She sighed, relieved to have got it out. She leaned back in her chair.

'You're wrong, Mum,' I said without conviction. 'She's been very brave. She's kept every visit, you know, and she writes frequently.'

'Did she ever do so while you were free?'

'Of course not. I saw a lot of her then.'

'Of course not. She loves the idea of her commitment to someone who cannot touch her, someone romantically locked away. It's a woman's ideal, Sebastian; a dead or imprisoned lover. She knows she's wanted, and it can't affect her or burden her with responsibility. Lovely. It's like television violence. You can fight as your hero fights, but you never get hurt.'

I was growing annoyed. Reproofs swarmed in my mind. Any one of them would have hurt her enough to ensure her silence. Just this once, I kept them in check.

'Please, Mum, let's talk about something else. You, Redway.'

She looked at me with sardonic affection under heavy-hooded

174

eyes. Then the old smile returned, an eyebrow arose. 'Never liked advice did you, Sebastian, love? Never mind.' She sighed and grasped my hand. 'You haven't long now.'

'Nope.' I squeezed her dry open-pored hand. 'Not long now.'

My first real mission took place on the last Friday in August. I had just one month more to do. Fiona and I were already planning the holiday that we would take on my discharge. We were to spend a couple of days in London and would then fly to Tuscany, where my mother had a little villa.

All was not well with Fiona. She was tense and nervous on visits. Where once we had laughed and kissed and told one another that we were in love so much that we forgot everything else that we had to say, now she prattled out the news as though she were at a debby cocktail party.

Her letters, too, disturbed me. Occasionally she wrote enjoining me to remember that, whatever she might do, she would always love me. I did not find that very consoling. I did not, I could not reasonably expect fidelity whilst I was locked away, but she gave it nonetheless, and was insulted by the imputation that she might do otherwise.

Then after one of those nights when we came so close, I would tell myself that I was merely being paranoid and that the old rejection syndrome was playing up again. All the old lags to whom I spoke told me that such tensions were 'only to be expected'. We had survived seven months. We would surely survive the rest.

The mission was simple. I was to travel to Sussex on the 'flier', supervising a small consignment of arms which had recently arrived from Liverpool.

The 'flier' is the bus which travels from Durham to the Scrubs each week, stopping at other prisons on its way. When you read of a top-security prisoner being transferred from one prison to another, you know that he has travelled on the flier.

Leach and I were to board the bus at half-past nine in the evening, travel down to Austin Open Prison, near Chichester, where another member of the organisation would meet us. He would take charge of the crate in the boot and we would find our own way back to Ravenhill before five o'clock the next morning. Farrell would meet us at the fence to escort us back to

175

our beds.

I was Leach's excuse for being on the flier, should any reason be demanded. As far as the screws from other prisons were concerned, I was just another con being transferred. The governor, and any that might have questioned my presence, were, of course, safely at home watching Kojak by the time that we boarded.

We were simply to ensure that the wrong person did not handle our luggage.

It all went according to plan. We reached Austin at midnight-thirty and were dropped off without a second glance from the driver or the other screws who dozed, handcuffed to their charges.

We were greeted by two screws who glanced nervously over their shoulders, explained that there were a few non-members on duty that night, showed us to a Citroën Safari and bundled us in.

Leach unlocked the 'cuffs and handed me a box from the back of the car. I cut the strings. I would have cried, if I had remembered how.

My clothes.

Deborah and Clare had never seemed so Deborah and Clare. I loved them for it.

'What's this all about?' I asked.

'You're a civilian now,' he said. 'It'd look bloody funny if we were stopped for any reason and they found a con in the front seat, wouldn't it?'

I enjoyed the feel of the clothes, creased as they were, enjoyed the trite prattle on the car wireless, enjoyed the sight of cars and people and houses.

We pulled onto the motorway at Watford. 'Fancy a cup of coffee at the services?' Leach asked me.

'May I? I'd love it!'

It felt strange and almost frightening to be a man again. I flirted with one of the girls behind the counter just to reassure myself. She called me 'sir', she called Leach 'cock'.

I ate a plastic egg and some packed powder chips. I drank some coffee which tasted as though someone had taken a mouli to a mummy. It was great.

Leach stood. 'I'm off to the bog,' he said, 'then I think I'll go and fill up at the garage. Take your time. I'll be back soon.'

It was hard. There were public telephones immediately opposite me in the lobby. I had only to get up and make a reverse-charge call for Catkin to have a load of improbable and useless information and for both of us to be as good as dead. I had only to bolt through the door to find myself snatched up by two strong pairs of arms, dumped into a car, and driven straight across the Styx. I sat still.

It seems that I had won their trust. I was offered the usual reward the next week, but I cried off, pleading fatigue. I was genuinely frightened of following Mistah Kurtz. Two days later, Heron briefed us as to our immediate purpose.

He looked sensational in a Huntsman blazer with old gold buttons, the predictable Brown's flannels and unclotted ox-blood brogues. You'd never have guessed that he was a Carthusian. Only his socks gave him away. They were green, and they annoyed me.

Chairs had been set out for us in the workshop. Heron strode back and forth at the far end of the room, gazing out over his audience's heads with that studied myopic look favoured by RSC aspirants.

'Good evening, gentlemen,' he said, all charm. We said rhubarb.

'In the past months we have successfully accomplished a number of missions in this country and in Ulster. Each of them was the result of a tip-off from our friends in Special Branch and UDR. Each involved one, maybe two known enemies who had been run to their lairs. Their liquidation was necessary, and has doubtless saved a large number of innocent lives.

'In the next month, however, all such disparate missions will be suspended by the Ravenhill and Austin divisions. We have a more important programme to fulfil, a programme which will result, indirectly, in the eradication of several thousand murderous fanatics.

'You are all loyal volunteers, not conscripted soldiers, so, as is my usual practice, I will explain to you the nature and the purpose of the mission, omitting only the precise practical details.'

He stopped pacing and stared at us.

177

'Before I do so, however, I want to remind you of the thoroughly unpleasant nature of our duties. We have to kill people in order to save others. This is never agreeable, and I do not want the sort of men in my organisation who would find it so. The sadist is useful as a kamikaze thug, but he's of no use to us as an operative. Your courage and your commitment in overcoming a natural reluctance to kill have been wholly admirable, and I thank you.

'This mission is going to be more unpleasant than any other, because we will not be dealing with violent activists as such. We are going to have to sacrifice innocent lives in order to save many, many more. Now, most of you have already shown that you are prepared to sacrifice your own lives for the greater good, but I will quite understand if you should be unprepared to sacrifice those of others. If you have any qualms, please say so now, leave this briefing and return to your room or your billet. You need feel no shame in so doing. You will be doing us all a grave disservice by undertaking to do something for which you have not the stomach. I need not point out to you that, should you change your mind halfway, you will put us in an unenviable position, but one with which, as well you know, we are equipped to deal. You constitute only one third of our Ravenhill personnel, and you have no idea as to who is, who is not with us either in here or on the outside. Anyone who stays for this briefing and then decides that he cannot go through with the mission will endanger the whole organisation. Leave now if you want to.'

He turned his back on us then, and busied himself with the lighting of a Davidoff cheroot from a box left out for us on the table. He gave us two minutes. We all sat still and stared straight ahead.

At last he turned back, sat casually on the corner of the table and rewarded us with a big smile.

'Right,' he said, 'I'm very grateful to all of you, and I assure you that your trust has not been misplaced. This will be our most productive single enterprise to date. In terms of saved lives, we are going to accomplish something roughly similar to ending a major war.

'As well you know, there is only one specialist anti-terrorist force on this earth with greater reach and power than our

178

own. That force is the Israeli military. The operations at Entebbe and Mogadishu were as intelligent and disciplined as any that we have accomplished. They were magnificent.

'Now, Dayan's boys play it close to the edge, but their policy of automatic retaliatory strikes is working and, provided that their retaliation is not disproportionate to the provocation, it meets with no moral disapproval, embargoes and so on, from the great powers. Washington goes all righteous and sells them more arms, Moscow whimpers and growls alternately, but no one moves. No one can afford to.'

Heron drew deeply on his cheroot. 'The greatest single threat to the safety of the individual in the Western world today is that of the so-called Palestine Liberation Organisation. Our purpose is to discredit and annihilate this pernicious group, which is enjoying a deal too much sympathy from the liberal lumpenproletariat in the universities and, still more contemptible, in Hollywood.

'There are camps where these people are trained in atrocity, camps not unlike this, in essence, but only half as thorough. They are located on the southern border of the Lebanon, most of them in the high country about Hasbaya and Jezzin. Again, we find psychopathic murderers enjoying official protection. These camps must be destroyed. They must be destroyed now.

'As well you know, we can, and do, strike in the Lebanon, but to knock out these camps would demand bombers which, obviously, we cannot use, or a huge force of commandos which must suffer massive casualties at each of the targets. It would mean the uncovering and, in effect, the annihilation of our whole personnel.

'Our friends in Israeli intelligence have now pin-pointed these camps and their supply routes. They only await sufficient reason to strike. That is our mission.' Smoke slid from his mouth as he spoke. 'We give them justification, and we totally discredit the PLO in Europe. In the guise of the Palestinians, *we* are to hit a number of prominent Semites in Europe thus furnishing Dayan's boys with just cause for retaliatory action. We are going to launch those bombers, gentlemen, bombers which will wipe out thousands of these animals and thus save hundreds of thousands, possibly millions of people and millions of pounds.

'That is why I say that this is going to be unpleasant. We are going to have to hit ordinary Jews in order to achieve this end, but it seems to me that, given the two alternatives, there is only one which can be considered morally responsible. We can do the job, or we can allow the PLO to continue unimpeded. Here are a few examples of their work to date.'

From behind him he drew a large sheaf of glossy black and white photographs. We passed them around. Each picture had a half-inch strip of typescript affixed at the bottom in case we were in any doubt as to the nature of the subjects.

'Shelley Russell, secretary. Age seventeen. Lost both legs in Heathrow bombing, 1976.'

'Marie and Thibault Regis, aged thirty-two and eighteen months respectively. Killed instantly, Rue de Rivoli dept. store, March '76.'

There were lots of them. They constituted a powerful argument.

There was silence. Heron grinned. 'Yes?' He pointed towards a raised hand.

'Well, um, what if we get nicked, sir?' asked a keen young con who had joined us just the week before. 'I don't look very Palestinian.'

'You won't get nicked,' said Heron casually. 'Most of our targets are unprotected save by the most primitive methods. If anyone sees you, you know what to do. After all, you're totally safe. You were in Ravenhill at the time. Only positive identification will do, and you will prevent that.'

I was getting very annoyed with those socks. 'How do we indicate that we are PLO?' I asked.

'We will be PLO,' Heron answered. 'Ali and Osman here will be released from this prison in one week's time. They are here under assumed names, so nothing can tie them up with Ravenhill. They will get nicked at one of the targets. They will know all the details of the other hits. Ali and Osman are Palestinians.'

'Very neat,' I said.

'We have two more in France, one in Germany. There is no problem.'

There never was. So we were going to kill innocent Jews in order that their countrymen might prevent other people from killing other innocent Jews; and guilty ones. It was all very logical, very praiseworthy. There was no problem.

'Are we hitting known Zionists alone?' I asked.

Heron smiled, annoyed. 'Most of them are active Zionists, yes, but I have already explained to you that one of our purposes is to discredit. We want to create the greatest possible outcry.'

'When do we move?' asked Dom.

'In order to create maximum shock effect, we want all the operations to be completed within the space of two days. At our friends' request, we will attempt to move within the next three weeks, that is, before the trainees' winter dispersal takes place. Obviously it cannot be until our Arabs are released, on Thursday 8th. Our captains on the continent and I must select the optimum moment, that is, the moment when as many of our targets as possible are at their homes or are together in one place. At Ravenhill, of course, there are only two nights of the week on which you can perform an operation of this kind. Austin and civilian operatives will take care of the second wave. We therefore have a choice of five possible nights. The first of these is Friday 19th. I will give the signal on the day before.'

'How many hits will there be?'

'In this country? Sixteen. We want to get at least ten.'

'We deal with how many?'

'Seven, if we have a complete pack.'

'What form will the signal take?'

'The death will be announced on the six o'clock news of a prominent Semite in the West Country. His initials are T.M. I will take care of that pigeon myself.'

I gulped. It wasn't original, but there it is, I gulped. There wasn't much else to do as I pictured Tommy Mansell with a hole in the back of his mottled neck.

If Heron wanted 'maximum shock effect', he was starting in the right place. Mansell, in his late eighties now, was one of the best loved of all our elder statesmen. He was an amiable socialist who had caused a load of trouble in the Commons over the years with his abrasive Cockney-Jewish ardour. He hadn't eased up since he had become Lord Mansell, either. Everyone in the country had disagreed with Tommy Mansell about something.

He was a devout Jew, and old school Socialist and, to the best of my knowledge, he had none but an academic interest in the Zionist cause.

On this occasion, Heron was careless. I suppose that he had no choice but to leave the house-plans for us to study. No detail was omitted. Pressure pads, alarms, trip-wires, ultra-violet scanners, locks, cellars, servants' quarters and water systems were meticulously charted. As Messrs Philby, Maclean and Burgess had shown, there is nothing more adapted to the purpose of espionage than the British class system. Who needs 007s when a house guest, even a stranger, passes anywhere unquestioned.

The houses looked impregnable, but Dom and Farrell grinned. 'That one's a bloody walkover,' they said, pointing at a plan of Fort Knox.

'Yeah, easy!'

'God, look at this one! They'll never fucking learn, will they?'

'Not Yale? Christ!'

I picked up the plans as they dropped. I recognised two houses from the plans. One was a Henry Holland Palladian mansion in Northants. Any amateur student of architecture would have recognised it. It was the property of a television and film magnate.

The second was a rectory near North Cerney. I knew the owner quite well. He collected eighteenth-century watercolours and department stores.

I ran up to Maurice's room after tea. He looked up at me slowly, sardonically.

'All right, Maurice,' I said, 'enough of your damned moralising. Can I have a guard again?'

He smiled, leaned back, and said, 'My dear Sebastian.'

'Yes, well . . . I haven't much choice.'

'No. Let's celebrate.' He reached under his bed and pulled out a bottle of Bollinger B.V.

'Bloody hell!' I whistled.

Maurice raised his eyebrows. 'I try to keep a few small luxuries about,' he said. 'We must try to keep up standards.'

'But if they found it . . .'

'If they found it, they'd nick it, but they wouldn't nick me. I don't think they want me shanghaied to the big 'ouse. It's easier

182

for them to have me here amongst the amateurs.'

'They're not all bloody amateurs,' I said. I held out a plastic mug. Maurice filled it to the brim.

'No, I'm afraid not,' he sighed, 'nicks aren't what they used to be. What are you going to do?'

'Run.'

'When?'

'Don't know. Tomorrow, I should think.'

'How are you going to do it?'

'I don't know. The official pursuit won't be very hot. The unofficial one will be pretty desperate.'

'Well, a car won't do, then.'

'No.'

'And leaving on foot won't do, either.'

'Fuck it, no. Short of sprouting wings, I don't know how in hell I escape this lot. They're highly-trained commandos, Maurice, and they're convinced that they're right. There's no mercy when you know you're right.'

Maurice sipped his drink slowly. 'Wings?' he mused. 'No, I don't think that would be very good. It'll have to be a horse.'

'A horse?'

'Of course. It's ironic, isn't it? The more they develop new-fangled means of transport, the more the outlaw depends on the horse. Many of my friends have found this when they're on the run. It's almost impossible for Old Bill to keep up with you. Cars don't help 'em, and you can always go where their bikes can't. Another thing, if their bikes do catch up with you, what can they do? You're a bloody tricky target for any easily hidden shooter, and most townies are scared stiff of gee-gees. Where d'ye want to go?'

'London, eventually.'

'You'll have to find your own way into the actual city, of course.'

'Yes. I've just got to lose this lot.'

'Right. There'll be a friend of mine in a car at the top there, on the main Grantham road, between midnight and one tomorrow night. He'll take you to the nag, and you should be away cross-country before either the screws or the bad boys know you're gone. Have another drink.'

'It sounds possible. Thanks, Maurice.'

183

'OK, kid. Now, you'll need some bread.'

'God, I suppose I will.'

'I'll lend you fifty. That should see you to London.'

I laughed. 'Maurice,' I said, 'money and alcohol are illegal in here, in case no one told you. They're forbidden on pain of grave penalties, and here are you, swimming in both. I don't know why they bother to send you here.'

'Neither do I,' he said modestly. He resumed his businesslike tone. 'The bread will be with someone in your billet who will give it to you at lights out tomorrow evening. You can't afford a strip-search at this stage in the game.'

'No.'

'The interest rate is 15%,' he grinned.

'OK, Maurice. I'll inform the executors of my will.'

'Per month,' he added. 'Have some more bubbly.'

That night was 'open' night. I felt sure that my colleagues knew of my intended perfidy, but I joined them as usual. At half past twelve we were back in the field, practising our killing routines. It was pitch dark. The winds were up and the trees sucked and sighed around the ground.

We stood in a ring in the middle of the football pitch. We were watching a danse macabre. Dom circled slowly with a knife in his hand, not the traditional flick-blade, but the thin navaja that he had favoured since the war. Osman, who had grown a dead mouse under his nose, circled too. Their left hands reached out, smoothing down the darkness. Osman's feet shuffled in nervous little dance steps; Fred Astaire and Cyd Charisse.

Fred lunged at Cyd. Cyd bent from the hip and slashed cross-arm. Fred executed a perfect pirouette. Cyd stepped backward, being led. Fred crouched lower. He hissed, and whispered, 'Come on, you bastard, you're not a bleeding amateur. Come on, kill me!'

Cyd was aroused, she rushed in and made a feint. Fred was faster. He parried. Cyd thought she was clever, deceived the parry and struck upward at Fred's guts. The classic mistake; she'd forgotten to use her body as well as her weapon. Fred jumped, grabbed Cyd's arm and threw her. She flew about eight foot, and landed with a grunt. Pure escapism.

Dom wiped his mouth on his sleeve and looked down on his

victim. 'You'll have to do better,' he spat. 'That was kids' stuff.'

Suddenly, everyone stiffened. Months of woodcraft training had taught us who was and who was not amongst our friends. This was no friend. He had about as much idea of woodcraft as a crazed bull-elephant.

He was just twenty yards away. It was too late for us to scatter. Dom just said, 'Hush!' and we waited.

We had seen runners and men collecting parcels on other 'open' nights, and had hidden until they passed. This one careered straight into our midst. He had blacked-up his face with shoe polish, but had left his mouth and eyes untouched. He looked like a fleapit nigger minstrel. I did not recognise him.

'Hey, you lads,' he panted, 'I've seen you out here before. I – I've got to get to see my missus, see, and I reckoned you must know the best way, I mean ...'

He had been looking about him in increasing alarm. Now he saw Leach and Farrell. He saw two knives, and he stopped talking.

'What the fuck? I mean ...' His world had turned upside-down. He wasn't going to have time to get used to it. 'Jeez ...' He turned back towards the buildings.

The circle closed about him.

'Look, I don't know what the fuck's going on. I don't care!' He tried the casual approach. 'Do what you want for all I care. I just thought you might know the way, that's all.' He paused again. 'Please,' he said.

The wind slashed through the circle. The nigger minstrel spun. 'What's up, lads?'

Dom sighed. 'You,' he said, pointing at me, 'tidy up.'

Lead charged into my intestine. My heart made room for it. Here, then, was the choice: martyrdom without an audience or sound pragmatist survival law. The old sympathy v. survival war which had dominated my existence ever since I learned to love now crystalised in one battle. Pragmatism told me that I could save several lives by taking one already lost. By doing so, of course, I would be preventing others from saving even more lives by taking a few that weren't much worth preserving. Distinguish between pragmatism and high utilitarianism. Can't. Distinguish, then, between utilitarianism, the extension of self interest, and serving one's sensibilities. J. S. Mill wins hands down. We admire a man who lays down his life for the greater good, how much more, then, must we admire he who lays down his principles, which are his self? Myself, I discovered, was no pragmatist. It couldn't connect logic with whimpers, screams and pouting wounds puking gouts of blood.

But I stepped into the circle.

'Look, I didn't ...' was all that my victim had time to say. I could not let him say any more.

I feinted at his diaphragm, at his neck. The man turned. I grabbed him. My right forearm clamped around the front of his neck and I grasped my own left elbow.

Now all I had to do was to jerk sideways and upwards.

I was ready to do it.

Suddenly, my feet left the ground. I was spared further moral dilemma by the fact that I was flying forward. I landed nose down on the turf.

'Careless,' said Dom. 'Too damned confident by half. This man's army.'

He pointed to the new kid. 'You,' he commanded.

The fair-haired boy moved into the middle. The dance had become a grotesque eightsome. Keen as ever, the executioner wasted no time. The minstrel's head was spinning like a spaniel's tail. The young boy grabbed it, placed his right forearm around the neck, his right leg around his victims, his left knee in the small of the back. He pulled.

There was a click, like the sound of a typewriter key falling. The body twitched twice in his arms. It was a full minute before he let the man slump to the ground.

'Poor begger,' he said. 'He just wanted to see his missus. Damn!'

Which made him a braver man than I.

Dom struck his forehead with the heel of his hand. 'Bugger!' he sighed. 'All of you, tidy that lot up.'

We buried him in the flowerbed by the dining-hall. 'Two into one won't go.' I said. It wasn't funny, it wasn't clever. *Accidie* was closing about my brain, and creeping into the crevices like smoke.

Dom did not hear. He just said wearily that it was a bloody shame. I felt sorry for him. He'd been fighting all his life, and

186

was now training a new generation to fight. There could be no sadder fate for a good soldier, who set out initially with a vision of peace as his prize, his justification.

17

The next day, I gardened: I talked to stocks and pansies. I spared earthworms.

That night I ran.

I left Obolenski standing and ran for the corner-flag. It was raining hard. It lashed at my cheeks and stung my eyelids.

The rain reflected the light of the lamps about the fields. I ran towards the garden shed. Once there, I had only to jump the fence, plunge into the woods, find my way through one hundred yards of unkempt woodland and onto the road. Any parked car would be checked and its registration number recorded, so my car would be rolling up and down the road with its hands in its pockets, looking as though it had never heard of a prison. Provided, of course, that my car were there.

I was not scared of discovery by ordinary screws. No officer in an open prison would risk his neck to stop an absconder. Discovery would simply mean that I would have less time to get away.

I *was* scared of meeting 'our men'. I did not know whether I was watched at night, nor who amongst the screws apart from the ones in our group, might be of Heron's crew. I only knew that I wanted no company for a while.

This was how Trevor had spent the last minutes of his life, running as I now ran, urged by an absurd conviction. Trevor had known, as I knew, that if he were caught, he would lose more than ninety days. He'd get a plenary indulgence.

Trevor was caught.

So was I.

Two screws stood by the garden shed. I heard them before

they heard me, but it was a matter of seconds only, and I was a hundred yards from any cover.

'Hey, Bill,' one of them shouted, 'there's one out there!' He ran along the perimeter fence to my right, hoping to head me off. He passed under a lamp. It was Superscrew, out to prove his mettle. He passed into the darkness. The other screw switched on his torch. I was just twenty yards from him, and, though I dropped, he saw me and recognised me.

He switched off the torch. 'Carter!' he shouted, 'he's doubled back towards the gym! Get down the bottom!'

It was Loveday.

Superscrew ran down the field and out of sight, and Loveday stepped forward. 'All right, get up, Foy.' I got up, and walked into the lamplight.

'What the hell are you up to, Foy?' sighed Loveday. The rain dribbled constantly from the slashed peak of his cap.

'I'm sorry, Officer Loveday,' I said, 'I'm running. I've got to. I can't tell you why. I'm not going to stop now.'

'Look, old fellow,' said Loveday, 'I can't just let you go.'

'I know, sir, but equally you can't really stop me. I'll lay odds that I'm faster than you.'

'That's not what I mean,' he said slowly. 'Damn it, I can't let you ruin the whole thing. You must understand. Too much is at stake. I'm sorry, Foy.'

'You!' The nightmare grew, and like all nightmares, the horror was the greater for its commonplace materials. Officer Loveday with his fishing and his golf and his scraggy turkey of a wife, was standing before me with a Browning 9mm. in his hand. He was a timid soldier, but he had his job to do, for England, home and beauty.

Suddenly an unconscious association cohered in my consciousness. Trevor had warned me! 'Cave diameter!' It was a rotten pun, but so obvious that I'd have kicked myself if I hadn't been rather preoccupied with that gun.

Dom's voice: 'Rule number one: run for the man with the gun, run from the man with the blade. It's bloody hard to hit a man coming at you. It's bloody easy when he's running away.'

Easier said than done, with a black muzzle pointing at your groin. Loveday looked a lot more frightened than I felt. He had nowhere to head for.

'I don't know what's got into you, Foy,' he jittered.

'I don't like murder,' I said.

'Oh, come on, we're not talking about murder. Politicians are in this, for God's sake. I met John Porter at one of our meetings the other day. The MP. He was a nice chap. I had a drink with him, actually. He's not talking about murder, now is he? My old CO recruited me. He's scarcely a murderer. Everyone's in it, Foy, soldiers, chief constables, politicians, everyone. They can't all be wrong.'

'I think they are,' I said. 'So what are you going to do about it?'

'Well, I'm going to have to stop you, aren't I?'

'Are you?' I said, and prepared to charge.

I didn't see him coming, nor did Loveday. For all his bulk, he knew his woodcraft and he knew how to incapacitate. Loveday's head jerked back. His face twisted. Two hands pressed firmly upward just behind his ears. Loveday made a noise like a tonic water bottle opening and crumpled on the grass. Rain thudded on his cap.

Maurice said, 'Fuck off, Seb. We'll truss him up in the shed. They won't find him till morning.'

John Sykes emerged from the shadows. He carried long strands of baling twine.

'Thanks, Maurice,' I said.

'Just protecting my investment,' he said. 'Get lost.'

I crashed into the woods. They had never been tended. Brambles tore my trousers, branches slashed my face. It was like charging through barbed wire. I hardly noticed. I was thinking of Loveday and I was feeling sick.

Damn it, the man was right because he believed himself to be right, and he was like me in that he dared not kill for his cause. Was my cause, then, no more than a rationalisation of moral cowardice?

I broke out on the roadside, stumbled over a ditch and into the road. The car cruising to my right stopped and zapped back in reverse to where I stood. It was a low yellow De Thomaso. I would have been impressed if I had thought about it, but I wasn't in an Earl's Court cooee mood.

I walked around the car and squeezed into the passenger seat with much squelching.

190

'Who sent you?' asked the young man beside me.

'Maurice.'

The back of the seat hit me hard. The trees started to rush past at one hundred and twenty miles an hour, telling us to shut up as they passed. He drove well. His movements were smooth and relaxed. He was tall, thin and bespectacled, and looked more like a student of applied physics than a villain.

'Hear you've got problems,' he said.

'Yup, big problems.'

'We'll have the mare tacked up and ready for you at five. You won't be able to see a thing before then. I think you'll like her. She's a blood horse, but she'll hunt all day, so she should do you. By the way, my name's Tony. Her's is Silence in Court or, at least, it was in her hunter 'chasing days. She's known as Mossy.'

'OK, thanks.'

'Where you going?'

'I don't know,' I said. 'London, eventually.'

'Go north or east to lose them, then get a train where you can.'

'What about the animal?'

'Just ring me when you get to town and tell me where you've left her. Maurie's paying.'

'What's your business?'

'Me? I'm a farmer.'

'So how come you're mixed up with us bad boys?'

He laughed. 'I'm in the tack business. It's a good screw these days.'

'You nick it?'

'Yup. Germans buy it. I do a bit of rustling, too.'

'Operate in Gloucestershire?'

'Certainly.'

'Ever do a place called Redway?'

'Yup. Nice one. Up on the wold. Read about it?'

'No, I live there. It's my mother's house. She didn't like you, you know. I'll have to tell her that she misjudged you.'

He laughed and hit the steering wheel. 'Bloody hell!' he said, 'that's really funny! I screwed your house! God, that's a joke! Lots of good stuff there.'

'I know, I grinned. 'You got my hunting saddle.'

'Maxwells, with a sheepskin?'

I nodded. 'That's the one.'

He smiled. 'I remember that. You shouldn't really use nickel bits, you know; they break. Still, I'm damn glad you did.'

'Scrap market good?'

'Sky high.'

The car swung into a well-fenced drive, kicking up a great spurt of gravel. Half a second and half a mile later, we were before a large stone house held together by Virginia creeper.

A warm orange light and two black labradors came out to greet us. Tony's wife followed. A mignonne little blonde, she shook my hand and said was I really all right, maybe I'd like something to drink and oh it was nice to see me. Her name was Evelyn and I fell in love with her.

I drank whisky as I lay in a hot bath, and came downstairs again in a new pair of jeans, a check shirt, a suede jerkin and a pair of jodphur boots which they had laid out for me.

My hostess met me at the foot of the stairs. 'Right,' she said, 'hold still.' She dropped to her knees and started to stick pins into her mouth and then into the jeans. 'Can you take them off for a minute?'

In five minutes, she was back with a pair of neatly-stitched shortened Lee Coopers which could have been made for me.

We sat around the kitchen table for an hour or so, picking at grouse carcasses, drinking good ale and discussing the treatment of tainted hog meat, the subject of Tony's Ph.d. at Reading.

Evelyn fussed about me. Had I got everything that I needed? They assembled a few Ordnance Survey maps, a compass, a sandwich box, a hip flask, a foldable plastic mac, a hunting whip just in case there were gates to open or nasty people to frighten away, and oh this was so exciting.

A child squawked upstairs. Evelyn brought it down and cuddled it until it went back to sleep again. The child's name was Sonja and she was beautiful. We listened to Miles Davis. I didn't want to leave.

'What time's the first tally of the morning?' asked Tony.

'Five.'

'That's fine. If you can leave at about a quarter past five, you should be well away before they come round here.'

'They'll come here?'

'I should think so. I've got form. They wouldn't bother if you were just any absconder, but I gather from Maurice that you are wanted by someone other than the nick.'

'Yes.'

'Well, I'll make 'em go and get a bloody warrant before they come in here.'

'No, you won't,' I said. 'Let them in as soon as they arrive. Be nice to them. They won't be worried about warrants.'

Tony frowned. 'I've got a shotgun which says that no bastard will enter my house without a warrant.'

'Tony,' I said seriously, 'if they think I'm here, a Holland twelve-bore won't do you much good. Let them in and just be innocent and ignorant. There's nothing for them to find, is there?'

'No. Your clothes have been mashed up for the pigs.'

'OK, let them in and you'll be all right.'

'Are we talking about the police now?' Evelyn asked.

'It may be the police,' I said, 'I don't know. As Tony says, I shouldn't think the police will bother. I'm not exactly a dangerous villain.'

'But who then?'

'Some thoroughly nasty people. I won't tell you any more for your own good, but if they think you're holding out on them, they're not going to arrest you. Just believe me.'

'OK,' they both said at once.

'If Maurice says it's all right, it's all right,' Tony added.

'Dear Maurice . . .' mused Evelyn.

I was watching Sonja. She snuggled up in her mother's arms, her thumb in her mouth and her eyes tightly closed. My eyelids suddenly seemed very heavy. I started to nod, surrendered without a struggle and rested my head on my arms. Miles Davis understood and helped me on my way. Soon, I had joined little Sonja in a beautiful world in which no one ever shot anyone.

Evelyn woke me with a cup of black coffee. The first sip shivered through me like an electric charge.

'Sorry to have to wake you, Sebastian,' she said in a low voice, 'it's a quarter to.'

Tony padded in. He had put on his pyjamas and dressing-gown, but he didn't look as though he'd been sleeping. 'Good sleep?' he asked. 'Good. They'll have missed you by now.'

'Yes. Is it light?'

'No, not yet. It's just creeping up over the horizon. You'll see clearly enough in a few minutes.'

I walked over to the window. The sky was the colour of watered blue-black ink. It looked very cold out there. A road stretched across the middle of the valley below. A few lorries trundled along it, but I saw no car headlights.

'Quickly now, Sebastian,' said Evelyn. I turned. There was a half-pint mug of orange juice, and a plate piled high with eggs, bacon, Melton sausages, kidneys and tomatoes. I wasn't hungry, but I wolfed the lot. Tony stayed at the window while I ate.

When I had finished, Evelyn handed me a folded sheet of paper and a straw. I unfolded the paper. There was a gramme of coke inside. I made a couple of lines on the oilcloth tablecloth and snorted them. Ice trickled down the back of my throat and suddenly I felt much better. 'God,' I said, 'life is good again. I'm actually looking forward to this trip!'

'Keep the rest of it,' she smiled, 'you'll need it.'

I gawped and stammered my thanks, but how do you thank someone who treats you like a member of the family and then gives you a cool forty pounds worth of instant energy just because you're the friend of a friend and you're in trouble?

'Come on,' said Tony.

'OK.' I turned to Evelyn. 'Bless you.'

'Go on, Sebastian. I hope we'll see you soon.' She leaned forward, kissed my cheek, and pushed me gently towards the door.

I followed Tony into the yard. The wet cobbles glowed like beetles, and the earth seemed refreshed. Every smell was accentuated; that of horse as Tony led the mare out into the yard, that of soaped leather as I gathered the reins and mounted and the horse snorted and clattered on the cobbles, and then all the rich fragrance of harvest as I rode through the gate into the field. Every footfall on the wet turf set up a crackling like a swarm of ants on cellophane. A fresh breeze surprised me, fanning the hair back from off my brow. I leaned down and took Tony's hand. 'Thank you,' I said.

'Oh, I reckon I owe you something,' Tony grinned. 'Good luck, Sebastian.'

He turned. There was a crunching on the drive. Headlight beams swung around a bend below. 'Off you go!' he said. 'I think you'll like the saddle.'

I rode at a walk down the hill and into the woods. A cock crew. The car growled on the drive above. Someone hammered on the door. I nudged Mossy into a trot and, ducking under low branches, left the yeomen of England to plead ignorance and innocence. They would not fail.

Maybe it was something to do with Tony and Evelyn, maybe it was just the effect of the coke, but suddenly any doubts that I had had about my purpose seemed miraculously resolved. After a while, the coke wore off. My certainty did not.

I had decided to ride to Newmarket. My friends there were sporting rogues and would treat my assistance in the same careless spirit as that in which they approach their seductions – if, that is, they were not also Heron's friends.

I avoided major roads and travelled cross-country as much as I could. I trotted for half an hour, walked for half an hour, and every four hours I rested for half an hour. Mossy did everything that I demanded of her. At first, she showed a too companionable spirit towards every bird that burst free of the hedgerow, but she soon settled down.

Although I seemed to spend the whole day in opening and shutting gates, it was easy going. Maurice had been right. There could be no safer or less obstructive means of transport. I skirted Folkingham and Bourne, but felt confident enough to pass through Market Deeping. Two police cars passed me, but no one showed any interest in a man hacking through the countryside. Convicts and horses are not associated in the popular imagination.

The weather was perfect for my purpose, overcast and cool. I rode through Holland and down to the Fens. Night fell as Ely cathedral arose from the plains before me, a massive lone demonstration of the temporal power of the church. No wonder that the mediaeval peasants in their fenside crofts believed so implicitly in all that they were taught, no wonder that eschatology was so central to their lives. Here was a creation already halfway to heaven.

I tethered Mossy with the aid of the hunting whip and hid the tack in a ditch. I could only hope that no sharp-eyed, light-fingered passer-by happened to have an eye for a horse. I found a room at the next village inn. I ate cod's roe at a chippy and then rang Catkin's number from a telephone box. She was out. I rang back every half hour. Not until midnight, six pints and two lines of coke later, did she pick up the phone.

'Who the hell is that?' she said groggily.

I chose the name of one of her persistent disappointed suitors. 'Quentin,' I said.

'What the bloody hell do you think you're doing ringing at this time of night?'

'Hello, Catkin, it's Quentin.'

'Oh my God!' she said. 'Where are you?'

'I'm on my way down to London, darling, and I wondered if you'd come to the cinema with me in the next couple of days. Maybe spend the night.'

'OK,' she said quietly, 'I'd love to come.'

'Great,' I said. 'Can you have a reassuring word with my mother? She'd love to hear from you.'

Catkin hesitated. 'Yes – of course.'

'And you remember that nice girl we went to "Equus" with?'

'Of course.'

'Can you tell her that I'll see her very soon. Be down in her area.'

'Right you are. The monster's shooting in Scotland. He'll be back in a couple of days.'

'Tell him when you see him. He might be able to help. Miss you, Catkin.'

'Oh, I miss you, Squentin. Take care of yourself.'

'I will. See you soon, love. 'Bye.' I rang off, staggered to bed, and slept.

I bought five papers the next day. My escape recieved a half-inch column in the *Express* and the *Mirror*, nothing in *The Times* or the *Sun* and a half-column in the *Telegraph*. It described me as 'Notorious renegade lawyer'.

As soon as I came to Newmarket at half-past two that afternoon. I threw the sandwich box and the saddle-pack into a convenient ditch, shortened my leathers until I was in that 'monkey on a thistle' position favoured by all would-be Lesters today, slouched in the saddle and started to 'row a boat'.

I don't think that I looked very convincing, but Newmarket sleeps of an afternoon. I arrived at Tim Farquhar's yard undetected. The yard was empty. A few horses turned and snorted in their red and white painted boxes. I found an empty box, unsaddled Mossy, washed her down and filled both haynet and manger. She had served me courageously and well.

I walked over to the office, a wooden annexe of the main house. Tim lay snoring peacefully on the sofa amidst piles of paper. An open bottle of Mumm stood on the table.

'Wake up, you lazy bugger!' I threw my whip and gloves on the desk, sat in the swivel chair and poured myself a glass of flat champagne.

He executed a perfect Disney double-take. He opened his eyes, said, 'Hello, Sebastian, what you doing here?', closed his eyes, opened them, jumped up and bellowed, 'Bugger! What *are* you doing here? You're in clink, aren't you?'

'If you'd spent a little longer listening to old Criddle at school, you'd've learned to read something other than formbooks, Tim. Don't you read the papers?'

'Only the pages which concern me, to whit, financial, sport and three. What is it? Appeal?'

'Nope. I've absconded, escaped, run.'

'Bugger me!' he sat down again. 'When?'

'Day before yesterday. I rode straight down here from Grantham.'

'What can we do for you?'

'Get me to London.'

'Catch a bloody train.'

'No. It's not the police I'm afraid of. It's organised crime, big organised crime, and they don't wear uniforms. They'll be watching every station for me.'

'I've got a horse booked for Bath tomorrow, but I didn't intend to declare him. Tendon's playing up.'

'Declare him. Pay the fine for last minute withdrawal.'

'All right.'

The nice thing about those for whom a game is a living is that life is a game. These were the people who disappeared like Lucky Lucan.

Lucky Lucan.

18

The next morning, Tuesday, I climbed into the horse-box. My companion was a four-year-old bay colt. I was the fitter, but it was a close-run thing as to which of us sweated most. Both of us wasted it. He wasn't going to have to run, and nor, for the time being, was I.

I dismounted at Chiswick, bought a *Times* and walked to Gunnersbury Park, hiding behind Bernard Levin all the way. In the tube, too, terrified of being seen by friend or by foe, I crouched behind the paper. If this organisation was as widespread as I believed, there were no friends and, strangely, I did not know whether I would have admired a committed member who had disregarded me on the grounds of past friendship.

There was only one place in London where I could be confident of escaping observation and that was right in its heart. I came up at the Talk of The Town exit of Leicester Square station and dived at once into tiny, dirty streets.

I knew that Catkin's house would be watched. If Heron was half the organiser that I thought him to be, I reckoned that he would be keeping tabs on all those whom he knew to be my friends. Today was Tuesday. Heron had said that Friday was the first possible day for the murder of sixteen Jews. I had two days in which to stop him. He had two days in which to find me. Thus far I had kept ahead of him, but to be unknown and unobtrusive in London is not easy.

I walked to a place where people made it their business. I strolled down Old Compton Street keeping my eyes on the film stills outside blue movie clubs, on the salamis in the delicatessens until the whole world seemed flaccid and fleshy.

I turned up Dean Street, relishing the smells and colours clashing. The shameless vigour of the place always causes a shot of adrenalin to jolt through me. Car horns and saxophones blare. Massage parlours, topless bars, strip-club spivs and film clubs promise a hundred forms of easy love. Leave your emotions in the bank, all we ask is your money.

In a little dark alley just by Berwick Street market, I ducked into the doorway of a two-storey, crumbling house. There were two bell-pushes on my left. The lower bore the name, 'JOANNE', the upper, 'FRENCH MODEL, YVONNE'. I pressed the top one and ran upstairs.

'Yvonne' was really called Sue, and despite her extravagant claims in newsagents' windows, she was no more French than Max Miller. She was a highly intelligent girl who had freely chosen to be a prostitute, and believed that she, and others in her profession, were entitled to the protection of the law and union representation. I had first met her at a rally for that cause.

It is a strange paradox and characteristic of English hypocrisy, that prostitution is legal but that its practitioners are so far beneath the lofty gaze of the law as to be unworthy of the protection which any other citizen enjoys. They are exploited by pimps, charged exorbitant rents, derided by public and police, and their rape is considered fair game. It is a huge industry, but is represented by no union, and so has no strength with which to assert the rights of its members. Sue, a graduate of Durham University, resolved to fight. She's still got a long way to go.

Her ancient, puckered 'maid' opened the door. 'Good morning monsieur,' she said. 'Please come in. Yvonne is busy at the moment, but if you will please to wait in here?'

She showed me into a scrubbed pine kitchen. A portable television sputtered on the fridge. Paddington Bear was pottering about his garden.

'You have been here before, monsieur?' asked the little old woman.

'Yes,' I said. I had paid Sue for her services on a couple of dreary evenings when anything else would have seemed parody and debasement. For the information of those who pay fourteen or fifteen pounds for the privilege of being jerked off by a pseudo masseuse, there are professional whores who will give a gentle, unabashed blow-job for a fiver.

After five minutes, I heard footsteps going down the stairs. Sue came in almost at once. She wore a white mini-dress which was more like a one-piece bathing suit. She was an attractive blonde with legs which made strangulation seem rather appealing. I smiled at her and put a finger to my lips. She nodded but her lips curled downward in a barely suppressed grin at my appearance. My jeans were filthy.

'Hello, would you like to come in?' she said in her best professional tone.

I followed her into the bedroom under the approving eye of the old madame. It was a large, opulent room decorated in a restful shade of orange. A huge mirror ran the length of the wall by the bed. The lights were low.

So soon as she had shut the door behind us, Sue came to me and hugged me.

'Sebastian, love, what do you look like?' She giggled. 'And where on earth have you been? It's been fucking ages!'

'I know,' I said, 'I was sort of held up.'

'What have you been up to?' She spun out of my arms and scampered over to the cupboard in the corner, 'Here, have a drink and tell me your news. You're not here on business, are you?'

'No, my love,' I admitted, '"fraid not.'

'Don't worry about it,' she said with a wave, 'Business has been quite good of late. There's nothing like a period of recession for us lot. Strain is our business. Here.' She handed me a half pint of Bloody Mary, sat down on the bed and crossed those legs. Her stockings hissed. I hissed back at them. 'Now,' she said, 'tell me what you've been up to.'

I told her, omitting the details about Heron and attributing my problems to that syndicate of burglars that Maurice had suggested. She giggled at the idea of me as a convict, nodded sagely as I told her of Mickey and of Trevor's murder, frowned as I explained what I wanted of her.

'Stay here?' she squeaked. 'Can't you come home with me instead?'

'No, my love. I have to be in Great Windmill Street tonight and possibly tomorrow. I've arranged to meet an old friend – oh, I forgot, you know Catkin – well, I've got to see her and give her a written account of the whole business before I set off to try to stop these bastards. Travelling to and fro from Parson's Green would be asking for trouble.'

'But, Sebastian, there's only this room, the kitchen and the Nona's room upstairs. I can't stop working for two days.'

'Of course not. Can I buy your services for two days, then?'

'Oh, Sebastian, what a lovely idea,' she sighed, 'but it's just not on. When I go on holiday, I have to find another girl to take my place here. There are regular clients. There'd be a bloody riot if I had them all piling up on the stairs.'

'Sue,' I said slowly, 'I'm sorry to do this to you, but I need your help. This is very, very serious.'

'You shit! You total, grade one shit. OK, 'need' is different. You wouldn't say it unless you meant it.'

'Thanks.'

'Now, let's see,' she said, businesslike, 'how are we going to arrange it?'

'How many regular clients have you got?'

'Um, five on a daily basis, one who comes on Wednesday evenings, and whoever my bastard of a boss sends round for a freebie.'

'OK. Supposing I went upstairs when they were here and at peak hours in the evening, and we ignore the daytime passing trade. I'll give you a couple of hundred for the two days, and we can spend the rest of the time together.'

'No trips to Bond Street this time?'

I got up and kissed her. 'Not this time, darling.'

I don't want to represent Sue as one of those sloppy slags so beloved of the nineteenth century. If she had had a heart of gold, she'd have sold it at scrapweight value. She was just a woman. Two years before, she had confided in me her secret ambition. Believing that something about her other than her pubis might be glamorous, she wanted to dress up. She asked me to escort her along Bond Street and Sloane Street. I spent the whole day in chattering speciously to shop assistants while Sue tried on every beautiful evening dress that she could find.

She emerged from the fitting-room at Bill Gibb looking like a fairy-tale in one of Bill's white crêpe things with ostrich feathers floating all around it. She had grown by a foot in that room.

Sue shut up shop. The old Marseillaise grumbled until I gave her a tenner.

Thereafter, she seemed to enjoy her role. Throughout the lunchtime rush, she was perfecting her lines.

'Mam'selle Yvonne is terribly ill, monsieur. She is like Marguerite, you know, of Dumas fils. She coughs like a cow. She cannot be seen, not even by her best clients, monsieur. I am sorry, but she says she will be better the day after tomorrow and hopes to see you.'

The languishing 'Mam'selle Yvonne' and I, meanwhile, sat in the bedroom, discussing the state of the world and what we were going to do about it, and watching Gable camping it up in a bad early movie.

At five in the evening, she turfed me out and returned to work. I went upstairs to the maid's garret. Sue had equipped me with a block of loose-leaf paper and a couple of Bics. I rested the paper on the low bedside table and, almost bent double, I wrote down everything that I knew about Carol Heron and his organisation. I named those of his past and projected victims of whom I knew, and roughly reproduced as many of the house plans as I could remember.

As I worked, I heard Sue with her clients in the room below. The prostitute's life seemed depressingly silent.

'Hello, would you like to come in?'

Mumble.

'Have you got a tenner, then?'

Mumble.

'Can you manage something for the maid, please?'

Mumble.

'Thanks, love.'

A pause.

'Come on, love, aren't you going to take off your clothes, then?'

Mumble, creak, muffled thud. A serpent's hiss as she untied her sash.

'There now, that's better, isn't it? We'll get rid of all those horrid tensions. Now, relax, that's right, just relax. No. Just leave it to me. No. Relax ...'

There followed a few grunts and sighs. One man shouted, 'Fuck!' as he shed his load. Once, when the silence seemed interminable, I heard Sue ask, 'Do you want to put it in me, then?'

Then she would say, 'There,' and usually kissed her client. 'Come on, then, I'll give you a wash.'

Five minutes later, the routine started all over again.

Despite the distracting sound effects, I managed to complete my story. I copied it out twice, and had only just finished when Sue came in, looking as bright and breezy as ever.

'How's it going, maestro?' she asked.

'Finished. Here, love, would you keep this copy for me? Don't read it.'

'OK.'

'And now, let's get some dinner.'

'Sebastian,' she said firmly, 'you've forgotten your bloody manners in nick.'

'How's that?' I asked, surprised.

'How do you know I'm not going out to the theatre with my lover tonight?'

'Bugger!' I said. 'You're absolutely right. I'm sorry. Are you?'

'Am I what?'

'Going out with your lover?'

'No,' she grinned, 'I haven't got one.'

I raised my eyebrows, 'What happened?'

'He complained about the job.'

'Would you want the sort of man who didn't?'

'Not terribly, but he didn't have the guts to beat me out of it and take the responsibility. He just moaned and whined at me. Anyhow, I'm really rather into celibacy at the moment. Makes you feel good. And I'm not joking.'

'Didn't suppose for a moment that you were. So shall we get ourselves some dinner?'

'I thought you couldn't go out.'

'Nor can I, but that doesn't prevent us from getting something in.'

'Not a bloody take-away?'

'Why not? Let's try Wilton's, shall we?'

'What the hell are you talking about?'

'Any restaurant can be a take-away, and I haven't had an oyster in months. Ring up, make your order for half an hour's time, pop down, collect it and a couple of good bottles, and bring the whole shooting match back here. Just because it's not called a take-away, it doesn't mean you can't shove your dinner into a carrier-bag rather than into your stomach. We'll have a posh *souper intime* back here.'

We dined on oysters and fresh sea-trout in Sue's place of work. Like the professional that she was, she made me feel like the master of the house and her man. It was a damned good feeling.

She said, firmly, as we cleared up. 'If you think I'm staying in a Soho pro's room alone while you're out, you've got another think coming. I'm coming with you.'

'OK,' I said. 'I'm afraid it's not going to be very amusing. We may have to sit there half the night.'

'God, I'll look bloody marvellous tomorrow if we do,' she groaned, 'but I'll sacrifice my beauty sleep to the nobler cause.'

'Your gallantry overwhelms me, darling.'

'Go to hell, Sebastian. Hey, I've just remembered! I can lie in all day tomorrow! Gurreat!' She kissed me, and started to sing 'Sleepy-time girl' out of tune.

We left the flat at ten o'clock and walked down to the all-night cinema in Great Windmill Street. Both Catkin and I knew about this place because one of Sir James's clients, a well-known variety entertainer, had been charged with committing a gross indecency there. For just three pounds or so, it offers to the vagrant the cheapest, least restful billet in London.

Sinuous strip-club music followed us down the street. Lean young men slouched in doorways, looking for clients or for victims. A dark girl in a full-length floral print rushed by on the other side. She carried a black bag.

'Hi, Sue!' she called.

'Hi, Jeannie! Happy days!'

A hot dog stall stood in the light coming from an amusement arcade which buzzed and clanked and whirred. A wave of oily air struck us from a basement kitchen. It smelt of brussels sprouts.

The placard outside the cinema promised, 'All Night SEX FILMS. Tea supplied FREE'. Eat your heart out, Aladdin. We charged through the doors and into the lobby. If Catkin should arrive now, and if Catkin should be followed, I would be just another Soho statistic. I crouched behind Sue as she bought the tickets. The old woman in the kiosk didn't even look up from her magazine. With me still trying to be invisible, we ran up the thickly carpeted stairs, through the swing doors, and into the darkness.

We sat there for five hours watching late-sixties, shoestring, soft-core porn. It was hard on the eyes and on the sensibilities. I'm all for good pornography. But the sight of would-be movie stars but barely hiding their goose-pimples and their sense of shame as they simulate ecstasy is about as erotic as tapioca pudding.

Few of the audience watched the screen. They just stretched themselves out across the seats and tried to sleep. Clogged breathing, rasping snores and coughs which sounded as though each one brought up a bucketful of phlegm did nothing to enhance the effect of the films.

One young man came in at about one o'clock and lay on the seats beside us. He then removed his shoes and socks and started to caress his feet. With a beatific smile creasing his pustules, he groaned and giggled as he stroked and scratched his toes. This macabre business continued for half an hour until Sue hissed, 'Right, that's enough!' She leaned over, grabbed the youth's hand and slapped it like a cook with a thieving child. 'Stop that at once,' she commanded, 'you're a very dirty little boy!'

He stopped.

At three-thirty I concluded that Catkin was not coming that night. Sue and I returned wearily to the flat, and I cuddled her until she slept.

We got up at midday with much languorous stretching. Sue insisted on 'just one more cuddle' five times.

Old Nona was grumbling again, so I gave her another twenty and she shut up. After a vodka breakfast, Sue went out to ring chambers from a public telephone box. I told her to ask Catkin, on Quentin's behalf, if she had the secateurs. Catkin thought for a moment and sent back the message, 'Yes, I've got the secateurs. Shall I bring them with me tonight?'

'No, leave them at home,' Sue ordered, 'we'll pick them up some time later.'

Secuta sum . . . I am followed. I had not underestimated Catkin's memory.

Sue and I dined at A L'Ecu de France in her bedroom that

night. We returned to the cinema. At midnight, Catkin came down the aisle. She peered about her as she tried to accustom her eyes to the darkness. I hissed at her. She sidled along to the seat beside me.

'Hello, Foy, you silly bastard,' she whispered. 'How are you?'

I hugged her, reassured her about my state of health and checked on hers. She then greeted Sue with almost as many 'gosh it's been so longs', and 'how are yous'. I felt about as inconspicuous as a pillar of fire.

At last we got down to business. 'Why in hell have you run away?' Catkin demanded.

'This'll tell you everything.' I said. I handed her two envelopes. 'Take one of them straight to your bank. You'd better take the other off to the loo now and have a good read, then deliver it to Jack Drake first thing in the morning. I'm afraid that means that you can't go home tonight. It's vital that the papers get this story fast. It's our only hope.'

'OK, Foy. This is bloody ridiculous, you know. There are two heavies constantly outside my front door. They follow me quite openly. It's like a spy-thriller.'

'It's a lot bigger than any spy-ring,' I said. 'Don't worry about your escort. They won't hurt you so long as they have no reason to suppose that you know anything.'

'Thanks.'

'Where did you shake them off?'

'Quentin's.'

'What?'

'Well, I thought I'd better make your telephone calls seem realistic, so I arranged to have dinner with Quentin tonight. I got him fearfully pissed and then agreed to go home with him to bed. They followed us to his flat in Prince of Wales Drive. I plied him with a few more drinks until he stopped puffing all over me. We went to bed and I told him that I wasn't on the pill, so sorry. By then he was past arguing. He's snoring like a fat, drunk baby right now. I got out by the fire-escape, so the nasties should think I'm still inside.'

'And tomorrow morning when he wakes up, there you'll be cooking breakfast.'

'That's it.'

'Brave girl.'

Catkin went off to the loo and left us to a further study of mammaries. She returned in a quarter of an hour, sat down and whispered, 'Bloody Nora!'

'Good stuff, isn't it?'

'But Sebastian, are you sure about this? I mean . . .'

'I'm sure, love. I wouldn't be here otherwise.'

'Of course, it was only to be expected from some quarter. It was inevitable.'

'Yes. I even sympathise with them, but it must be stopped. Murder, I mean. You do agree with that, don't you?'

'Yes,' she said dreamily, 'I suppose so. It's incredible.' She shook her head. 'Yes, Sebastian, of course. You know my opinions on the law. What do you want me to do?'

'Lend me the Kawasaki for a few days. I've got to get down to Tommy Mansell's house.'

'Yes, of course. Where shall I leave it?'

'It'll have to be plausibly near chambers tomorrow morning.'

'Outside the tube station?'

'That'll be fine. Put a spare key and a hundred pounds in cash under the saddle.'

'Right. I'll have to wait until the banks are open. How long have we got?'

'God knows. Ali and Osman are discharged at eight tomorrow morning. If Heron is already in the area, it could be any time from there on.'

'This morning, it's Thursday now,' she corrected me. 'Bugger!'

'Yup. I'll have to try to ring Mansell, but I can't until I'm on the road. They'll trace the call. I shouldn't think I'll get through anyhow. That's why you can't ring him either.'

'I'll tell the monster about it. He knows Mansell.'

'Yes, all right, but don't tell him that you know anything about the organisation. Just say that I said to ring Jack Drake for the details. Pretend that I didn't trust you with them.'

'All right. You will take care, won't you, Sebastian?'

'As much as I can. You know, I've almost given up thoughts of survival. It's so big that there's really no way out. These people are *the* people, the government to all intents and purposes.'

'Don't be gloomy, Sebastian, darling. You've survived this far. You'll make it somehow.'

Sue and I left the cinema first. For some reason, I felt choked up as we left Catkin there. I was once more alone, and that brief taste of companionship had not helped me.

19

I took a taxi to Temple tube station at ten the next morning. I had left Sue happily returning to normal duties. She was all too glad to see me go. She was a friend, but above all she was a professional; a survivor.

The sight of London seething made me feel freakish and sub-human. This had been my pitch, these, my landmarks. And now I had no place in it all. I was blackballed, strictly P.N.G., and it rather offended me to see that the club got on perfectly well without me.

I had a feeling I wasn't going to see these places again for a long, long time – if, indeed, I was ever to return. That, and the unfamiliarity of the familiar, gave hard, Acapulco gold edges to my perception. I was a different man from he who'd loved and laughed here. I felt dissociated from it all, like an old boy watching a new generation of schoolboys.

The taxi slowed as we neared the station. My arsehole twitched. I saw the flash of Temple Gardens and leaned forward.

There was Catkin's motorcycle, all nice and green and shiny. There, beside it, looking more than ever like a thick Olly Hardy, was Farrell.

'Keep moving!' I yelled to the cabbie, 'for Christ's sake, keep moving!'

The driver put his foot down. I ducked. The taxi swung to the left.

'Problems?' he asked over his shoulder.

'Yes.'

'What can we do about it?'

'I don't know. It's just someone I don't terribly want to see.'

'Owe 'im money?'

'Not exactly. Something like that.'

'I'll move 'im for you.'

'How?'

'The usual. Call a policeman and accuse 'im of being a nuisance or something.'

'No,' I said, too fast, 'no police.'

'Oh,' he grinned, all knowing. 'Like that, is it?'

'Can you park somewhere along here, please?'

'Sure.' The cab rocked, turned, and stopped. For some reason, I was still crouched down below the level of the windows, studying the Woodbine butts. I raised my head. We were just downriver of HMS *Discovery*.

I set a soggy brain to work. I depended on that bike, but unless I had a large crowd of witnesses, I had no chance of escaping Farrell. Even should I be able to assemble such a crowd, I would inevitably acquire a policeman or two in its wake, and then Farrell need only change hats and become again a prison officer on leave. 'There was I, just strolling along, when who should I see? Well, constable, it fair amazed me ...' I doubted that it would matter much to Heron whether I was arrested by the police or by his own men. Either way, his influence would be brought to bear, and I would be 'tidied up'.

But if Farrell were watching the bike, someone else must surely be keeping an eye on Catkin as she worked.

'I think I've got it,' I told the driver.

'Bad luck, guv. Straight to the clinic, is it, then?'

'Go round by Fleet Street, please. I want to see if this guy's friends are watching for me at chambers.'

'Right you are,' he hummed, a study of equanimity, and let out the hand-brake.

Fleet Street looked sickeningly the same as when I'd left it eight months before. The same gowned and wigged figures swept in and out of chambers, looking self-important. Rob still sold his newspapers and knew everything about everyone. I got all self-pitying then, and started wondering how all these people reacted when the name of Sebastian Foy was mentioned. Escaped convicts were so far removed from their conception of the normal world as to be implausible and unseemly fiction.

Prison, like death, the fool on the heels of materialism, is something that happens to other people.

The lights turned red when we were just fifteen yards from the Inner Temple archway. I had plenty of time to scan the area from behind my newspaper. There was no one there.

'Can you drive to a safe parking place just up the road, then walk down to the courtyard and see if there's anyone hanging around, you know, waiting for me?'

He shrugged, grumbled, said, 'What the frigging hell,' and stopped the cab in Chancery Lane. Dismounting, he slouched down the road and disappeared round the corner. I sat still and sweated.

I watched two men unloading a lorry of brown cardboard packing-cases. They didn't seem to know that there was a major war going on around them. I began to think again that I might be mad, for the rest of the world seemed either impervious or on Heron's side. Maybe Catkin and Sue were just nurses and I their patient to be humoured. Maybe, alternatively, I was the only sane man left on earth.

The taxi-driver returned after five minutes. 'No one there,' he said, 'and don't worry, I know what I'm looking for.'

'No one?'

'Nope. Just lawyers and so on romping about. No one waiting or watching.'

That did not make sense. Someone must either be watching the entrance to Lord Chesterfield Buildings or that to the Temple itself.

'Come on, guv,' said the driver, stroking a huge lump on the back of his neck, 'it can't be that serious. He's probably scarpered by now. There's no one down there, honest.'

'No, wait.' I didn't like any of the thoughts which now occurred to me. The nicest of them was that Catkin was watched from Dr Johnson's Buildings by one of Heron's men at the Bar. The next was far-fetched. The last, the nastiest, the most probable, was that Catkin was no longer on my side. In all fairness, I had never had any reason to suppose that she was. This was an ideological, not a personal dispute.

If Catkin were watched by a barrister, then I had no hope of reaching that bike. I must play the other hunches.

'Look', I said, 'would you drop me here? I'll leave my helmet

211

and gauntlets with you. Go down to the newspaper seller on the corner and tell him, ''Mister Farrell says come at once, urgent.'' OK? Then watch his reaction. If he runs off, get back here quick. If he shows no sign of understanding what you're on about, go on back to the Inner Temple and deliver the same message to the clerk in Lord Chesterfield Buildings, a red-haired girl, and then get straight back here. There's a tenner in it for you. Just say, ''Mr Farrell says come at once.'' Got it?'

'Bloody hell,' he sighed. 'I don't know. Playing fucking cops and robbers I can do without. Right, I'll do this, but this is the lot, savvy?'

'Savvy.'

I jumped from the cab and scurried into the nearest doorway. 'Mr Farrell, right?' I reminded the poor, beleaguered driver as he started up the engine once again.

He waved disdainfully, 'I got that guv. Don't worry, I could sell a vaginal deodorant to a bloody skunk.'

I tried to look casual as I lounged in the doorway and studied the brass plate of The International Temperance League. I read it fast, then slow, then backward, then in Braille. Faye Dunaway could have raised her skirt and begged me. I'd have stayed in that doorway. Nothing would have lured me out into that street.

The taxi returned so fast that I automatically crouched. I associated roaring engines and complaining brakes with television policemen.

''Ere, come on, guv!' cried the driver. 'Get your arse in here, and quick!'

I ran to the car and clambered through the already open door. 'Was it the clerk?'

'Never got that far,' he grinned. 'Your friend with the smutty rags jumped like a blue-arsed fly and scarpered off towards the tube.'

'Thank Christ,' I sighed. 'When he gets there, they should realise that it's all a set-up and run straight back here, and reckon that I've got into the Temple in the mean time.'

'Yeah, I got that far,' he said condescendingly, 'so you want to get back to the station sharpish.'

'Correct – just as soon as we've seen them on their way.'

We slid into Fleet Street again. I saw them almost at once.

Farrell ran as fast as he could. Allowing for his seventeen stone handicap, it was a pretty impressive performance. Rob followed in the path that he'd cleared, shaking his head and excusing himself to the big man's back. They were intent on one end and looked neither to right nor to left. I watched at leisure as they swung in through the archway.

'Easy peasy lemon-squeezy,' chuckled my driver. 'Haven't done that one in ages.'

He sang happily to himself as he steered us down to the rose-strewn Temple gardens.

I jumped out of the cab, handed him a ten pound note that Sue had lent me, said, 'Hold on,' and ran to the waiting bike. The keys and money were still there, deo gratias, neatly wrapped in a plastic bag and tucked under the saddle. I plucked out another tenner and gave it to the cabby. He grinned, saluted, and drove off without a word.

It took me five seconds to don the large white helmet and the gauntlets, five more to take the gauntlets off again when I discovered that I couldn't unlock the ignition with them on, and another minute to get the engine going. Two jumpy minutes later, I was speeding along the Embankment. For the first time in weeks, I was in control.

Mansell lived just outside Frome. I reckoned that the journey would take me two and a half hours maximum.

Heron would soon be told that the bike was gone. He would also know where I was headed. I could only depend on the speed and manouevrability of the machine. I had no time to go by any but the direct route.

Heron had said nothing about the time at which Mansell was to be executed. He had merely specified that it would be in time for the six o'clock news. I was on the loose, and they'd be anxious to get going before I could forestall them. For all I knew, Tommy Mansell might already be dead.

I zapped down that motorway, anticipating at every turn a sudden spurt of M16 bullets ripping through the suede jacket spewing my guts out onto the asphalt.

It was a beautiful day, and the more beautiful for that fear.

I am a patriot. Not the sort who'll defend his country at the expense of his world, nor yet one of those narrow-minded berks who prefers Blackpool plaice and chips to Baumaniere, but a sentimental idiot who just happens to gulp a little when John of Gaunt croaks his last, or when all those drunken revellers bellow 'Land of Hope and Glory' on the last night of the Proms.

It's not pure jingoism. It's logical; it's based on the simple and self-evident principle that God was English and his son an emigré. If I were asked to select a suitable site for an earthly paradise on a glum Brummy morning, I might choose the Alpilles of Provence, or Fiji. Place me for five minutes on an Avignon terrasse, knocking back the Ricard for survival's sake, or subject me once more to the impenetrable plush of a Yasawa night, and I could nominate none but my own land.

You just can't tire of the place. So far from sating your taste for one sort of landscape, one sort of weather, England is always provocative, always changing. She is the great prick-teaser, all female, and allowing no complacency. Custom cannot stale her infinite variety. Better such a volatile, wilful creature than any constant and dutiful mistress.

She's also got taste. There are no seasons, but only predominant shades. Grey, blue, russet, rose, and a million shades of green, she rarely indulges in excess, and is never the same from one day to another, from one acre to another. So she makes of us stoical, humorous madmen who say 'Yes' to anything that the fates throw at us. We're all perverse lovers of contrasts and incongruities. Heat on cold days, cold breezes on hot, light crashing through a trance of trees, shadows shifting across sunny lawns, these, the tit-tautening frissons of sudden contrast, are the source of English pleasures and poetry.

I roared down the M4, past Windsor castle, ochre with streaks of flake white, through the father-at-the-fireside, honey-hubby rhododendron belt, and down into the vale of Kennet. There were shadow-stippled tracks that curled through woods like streams, there were Herefords grazing in low-sleeping, low-sweeping fields, there were dips in the road which made me believe that 'freedom' has a meaning. The sky screamed, sheer as steel. I told myself that it was for all this that I was rushing down to Somerset, for, with the anthropo-morphism typical of patriotism. I associated the land with its laws and its lovers.

Then I remembered a guy called Heron who felt towards England as I did. I remembered a sad soldier called Dom who

214

loved his country with the same passion. I remembered the terrorists who, because they were prepared to die for something other than themselves, must also love the very fabric of their worlds. I valued Habeas Corpus and freedom from coercion, Heron, the prosperity upon which such luxuries depend, Dom, a status quo that he had not learned to regard as less permanent than the valleys and hills. The only enemies were the loveless money-grabbers.

I decided not to stop to telephone anywhere near Windsor or Slough for fear of recognition, so I took the Newbury turn-off and headed for a pub that I had long known and liked. It was a simple spit-and-sawdust place with a well-kept tap-room. I hoped that there I would be able to telephone Mansell and grab a pint and a cheese-roll at the same time.

I couldn't believe that I was at the same place. The old pub had been tarted up like a Californian corpse. The little bar had been extended until it constituted an agrophobic's nightmare. There were enough pseudo-ethnic implements of brass and copper to start a scrap-yard. Even at midday, the effect was of subdued lighting. The customers, far from being the local yokels that I had expected, wore aluminium suits and patterned shirts and ties. They were the sort of congenital middle-management men whose greatest fears were death, dirt, individualism and any form of guts, vigour, bawdy or passion.

I had hoped to be unobtrusive, but every polished little head turned as I entered. There was no point in retreating now, so I ducked under the saucepans and walked straight up to the bar.

A squat little woman with scrotal sacs under her eyes and a goitre which competed with her tits for possession of the waist area, said, 'I don't allow motor-cycle helmets in my bar.'

'Right you are,' I said amiably, 'I'll take it outside. What I really wanted to know was whether you have a public telephone?'

'No. This is a pub.'

'Do you know where I will find a pub with a telephone?'

'No. Please take that helmet out of the bar. This is a respectable pub, and my clients are used to certain standards.'

I snarled, but otherwise controlled myself. I turned to leave. It wasn't her fault that she was fat, ugly, unpleasant, stupid and amateurish, I told myself charitably. But then, it wasn't a runt's fault, either, but it died all the same.

As I reached the door, a fidgety little grey-haired man got up from his chair. 'Excuse me,' he said softly, 'but if you go on up the road, you'll find a pub up there with a telephone. A nice pub. It's got a telephone.'

He spoke with the breathy keenness of one selling pictures of 'woman with donkey, monsieur, *exposition trés difficile.*' Maybe I was getting paranoid, but thanked him and rode off as fast as I could, in the opposite direction.

I rang Mansell's house fifteen minutes later, from a petrol station. A man answered.

'May I speak to Lord Mansell, please?'

'I'm sorry, sir, but Lord Mansell is very busy. He is not to be disturbed. Can I take a message? This is his secretary speaking.'

'May I speak to Lady Mansell, then? It's very urgent.'

'Lady Mansell is unavailable, sir. Who is speaking, please?'

'Listen. I've got to warn Lord Mansell of a serious threat to his life. He is in considerable danger from a para-military force whose members intend to kill him today.'

There was a deal of whispering at that, then the calm voice returned.

'Can you give us any further details or prove your bona fides, please?'

'Lord Mansell is to be executed today by a para-military force under the leadership of one Carol Heron. It is to be the first of a series of murders calculated to provoke Israeli retaliation against PLO training camps in the Lebanon.'

'I see, sir. Who is that speaking, please?'

'He must get police protection immediately. Do you understand?'

'As a prominent Jew, Lord Mansell is fully aware of his position in relation to all sorts of activists, sir, and has a perfectly adequate security system. Who is that speaking?'

'The hell it's bloody adequate!' I shouted. 'He has two guards at the main gate lodge and one on permanent patrol at night with an ex-police dog past his prime. He has an ultra-violet scanner along the road stretch of wall. The monitor is in the porch-room above the front door and is checked by the same man as is

216

responsible for the rest of the interior. There are conventional Stoneham pressure pads by the windows on the ground floor, but none on the first or second ...'

The secretary and his companion were making noises like angry wasps now. 'All right, all right, sir! Who is that speaking?'

'May I now speak to Lord Mansell?'

'Lord Mansell is not available, sir. I'll pass on your message. If you'd hold on a few minutes ...'

I wouldn't. I looked at a nearby clock and realised for how long I had been speaking. I put down the receiver. I could only trust that the message would reach Mansell and that he would know what to do.

I enjoyed every minute of the journey from then on. I was filled with that rare elation which comes with the acceptance of the inevitable. I was on the downward slope and had let go. Nothing really mattered any more. I had a job to do. I would do it as well as I could. Thereafter, I couldn't give a damn what happened. The past no longer mattered. The future no longer existed. I was totally alone. To go back was to die; to hide, unthinkable. Everything from now on was straight-forward comic strip adventure.

I crested the hill above Mansell's house at a quarter to one. No one, to the best of my knowledge, had shot at me. That was nice. The next problem was getting in.

Such a security system may have been a joke to Farrell and Dom. To me, it was a major tragedy. Aristotle would have approved it. It was nasty enough.

It was a large, Strawberry Hill Gothic house with a stucco façade and castellations and niches for statues and a huge, tent-roofed conservatory at the east end. The walls all around were equally fancifully fortified. From the main lodge to the front door, there were five hundred yards of straight, unprotected drive. I saw men moving at the lodge. A St. George's cross on the flagpole scarcely stirred. The windows seemed opaque.

Two triangles of thick woodland descended behind the house on the other side of the valley. Between and behind these, there were open fields. I might as well don an Ascot hat and move in on an elephant as try to steal in from that direction.

So I was going to have to play the hero. I had no idea whether the guards at the main gates would be armed. It wasn't a subject I liked to think about. Assuming that my warning had reached Mansell, I had no doubt but that he would now have an armed guard. So why didn't I just turn up at the lodge and declare myself? Because the guard would be the police, and because, if I were arrested, Mansell might be saved, but I would be discredited and Heron would continue his activities unimpeeded. Becaue I possessed about as much credibility as Lyndon Johnson at a CND meeting. Because the guards might be Heron's.

It was a good old trial by ordeal. If they shot me, I would know that my warning had been heeded or that Heron was already there. If they didn't, then there'd be an enemy to greet me at the front door.

As I rode down the hill towards the house, I considered suitable last words. What should one say as one's guts spilled out? 'Thank God, I have done my duty' was pretentious junk. Duty had nothing to do with it, and gratitude was just silly at such a moment. *'Mehr licht'* and *'Tête d'armee'* seemed a little inappropriate. Eventually, I decided that 'Fuck!' was probably the most succinct and immediate expression of my position. It wouldn't merit O.D.Q., but I might at least have time to say it.

I was in a little country lane with steep banks on either side. The gates were now two hundred yards ahead of me on the right.

Halfway along, I turned left into a blackened stubble field. I switched off the motor, and pushed the Kawasaki along the inside of the hedge. As I neared the gates, I ducked down.

There were two eagles on top of the gateposts. They were looking inward, just for starters.

Then there were two men. They wore a sort of uniform: faded jeans, checked shirts and Levi jackets. Both men were young, tall and fit. One was black, the other white. They carried guns. I recognised them. They were standard issue Martini action .303s. I remembered the pink steel dogscock bullets and the whole of my stomach slotted into my thighs.

The gate was pretty. It was of wrought iron, and some farrier had worked it skilfully into a clean, formulaic version of those primaeval whorls and presumptuous, thrusting lines which adorn the Dordogne caves. The farrier had obviously spent months over it, a great craftsman with pride in his work.

I was left with some interesting possibilities. I could clamber over on the chestnut branch which spanned the lane. I could climb the bank and the wall. Either way, I would probably be noticed immediately, and would have to make my way on foot through the grounds. High velocity rifles like people on foot. They're not averse to people on Kawasaki 1000s, but give them a man on foot and they lick you all over with gratitude.

Another interesting alternative was that of doing an Evel Knievel over the lane and the wall. It was interesting, like death is interesting to metaphysicians. You don't want to take research too far.

I had only one chance. It was founded upon the simple empirical observation that the guardhouse was inside the gate. If they were to arrest me, they would therefore take me where I wanted to go. If, that is, they were police – if they failed to recognise me; if they weren't trigger-happy; if Heron had not warned them; if someone up there was rooting for me. Pots and pans.

I went back to the bike and started the engine. It pulled me back down to the road and up to the gate. I kept the helmet on.

The black man, who stood on the left hand side of the gate, turned to me with the apparent casualness of one who knows better than to waste a movement. His gun turned towards me, too. I didn't like either, so I looked at the ground.

'Yes?' he chewed his gum noisily, cha-cha-cha.

'Lord Mansell is expecting me,' I said.

'Oh, yeah, cha-cha, and who might you be?' He peered through the gates at me.

'A homicidal maniac intent on garotting him,' I said. 'That's why I've come to ask your permission first.'

'Take off that helmet.'

'Not bloody likely. When you've got .303s pointing at me?'

'What's your business with Mansell?'

'Interview. I'm a journalist.'

'Name of?'

'Chapman Pincher.'

'Sure,' chimed in his white friend. 'Go away, friend. Mansell has cancelled all engagements today. He'll be in touch.' I looked up at him. He had eyes of Gestapo blue, and the skin over his cheekbones was pulled back tight as though in a permanent tic. He, too, thrust his hips forward as he talked.

'No friend of thine, thou haught, insulting man,' I yelled. 'I want to see Mansell now!'

'Bad luck.'

'Stop shoving that shrunken organ towards me, jerk,' I sneered. 'Nice for you that you've got a metal substitute. Sublimate the lust for boy scouts that way.'

'Fuck off.'

'Go ring your boss, nancy.'

'Fuck off, I told you.'

'Or do you get it together with the shine here? Careful you don't pick up any stains.'

The black man stiffened. 'You trying to get yourself mashed, man?'

'Don't make me laugh, boy. Do what massa tells you. Go ring your boss.'

'Jesus, I want to put one on this moron,' he told his colleague.

'Don't bother. Cheap is cheap.'

It wasn't working. I played my last card. 'All right, I'll go and find Her—— I mean, I'll go and find *my* boss!' I shouted. I revved up the engine and swung a leg over the saddle.

It was bad acting, but they couldn't afford to be drama critics today. Both guns jerked. 'Get off!' said the negro.

'No!' I bellowed. 'Why should I?'

For answer, he just tapped the gun barrel with his left forefinger. Bloody rhetoricians. I got off.

'Turn off the engine!'

'No!'

The gun moved, but rifles like that make a lot of mess. Maybe they didn't want it all over the road. Maybe they were curious as to who I was.

The white man walked into the porch of the lodge and buzzed something. The latch clicked. The gate opened inward. The black man stood back, his gun unslung, and signalled to me to enter. I pushed the bike through.

'Right. Take off that helmet!'

'No. Ring Lord Mansell and tell him I'm here.'

The black guard was cha-cha-ing very fast. He looked to his

colleague with raised eyebrows. I knew the next move. They would both come at me at once, push me off the bike and pull off the helmet. Game, set and match.

I clicked the bike into gear, and pulled back the throttle. It took off and dragged me with it. The front wheel hit the negro at the point of his pride at thirty miles an hour. He shrieked, went down, and the bike went over on top of him. It fell on its side, wheels spinning.

His colleague stole my last word. There was a rattle as he unslung his gun. I put my head down and ran at him.

He was stronger, fitter, faster, better trained and armed. I won. He relied too much on the rifle. I grabbed it by the barrel and pulled it down. He pulled the trigger. The bullet must have passed straight between my legs. It blasted a hole in the drive and went on to play in the woods. The guard came down with the gun in order to get leverage. My helmet arose of its own accord and struck him hard on the jaw.

It didn't knock him out. He still held on to the gun, but he sat down heavily on the gravel. One shake of his head and he'd be over that. I ran over to the bike, whose rear wheel was still kicking up a Catherine wheel of gravel and dirt. I wrenched at the handlebars. The negro was lying still.

The engine roared. I crouched down, all my weight on one leg, and did a wheelie. I walked a wheelie at forty miles an hour, then I bore the machine down. It skidded as I swung my right leg over the saddle. I got my foot down just in time. Two little spurts of gravel in front of me told me that my friend had recovered and had pulled a revolver from somewhere.

I lay flat. The bike was even more scared than I. It pulled hard. Weaving on loose gravel at high speed is for circus performers. I relied on speed, and rode straight for the house.

I was just a hundred yards from the front door and travelling at ninety miles an hour when my right leg fell off, and my forehead thumped on the sky. I saw the bullet smash into the gravel before I realised that it had hit me. I was out of control.

The bike slewed onto the grass at twenty degrees to the horizontal. Automatically, I put down my leg. It gave. The Kawasaki went down. I tumbled forward, telling myself that each involuntary jolt would be the last. The bike followed. It stopped just a yard behind me.

There was a lot of blood streaming down my jeans, but it was someone else's leg. I felt sorry for it. The conservatory above me was full of purple flowers. St. George's flag stirred. Cry God for Harry. The grass smelt of wet dog. The sky spun above me. I wished that it would stop. It made me feel sick. I tried to try to get up, but couldn't be bothered. I was panting, I was hurt. I just hadn't the energy. I rested my cheek on the cool grass and prepared to sleep.

Then a bullet thudded into the earth just a foot from my nose, and I found myself on my feet again. It wasn't I who found the will. It was the man with the bleeding leg. I was sobbing and tugging at the bike. I was astride it, again being pulled as if on strings towards the house. I ought to slow down, but the engine kept turning at full revs.

I turned the bike over at the very foot of the steps. My head hit the bottom step. I didn't care. My right leg was under the machine but I felt only a slight twinge of pain. I looked down at the wound. Congealing blood had picked up a thick coating of gravel.

Somehow, I levered the bike up and pulled myself out from under it. Using a step as a handhold, I stood. It was all right. I was going to limp for a while but, so long as I did not put too much weight on my right leg, I could walk. Much the same applied to my brain. I might yet suffer from delayed concussion, but for the time being, if I avoided unwanted and over-energetic exercise, it would work.

I climbed the steps one at a time, stood up straight and removed the helmet. I had made it.

The white front door swung inward open.

There, resplendent in striped trousers, blue cravat and butterfly collar, his huge beard splashing out in all directions, stood Sir James Crashaw, Q.C.

20

'J.C!' I gawped, 'what the bloody hell . . .? I mean, thank God you got here!'

'Yes,' he growled, 'all is well. Got your bed-time story from young Catherine. Good stuff. Bit discursive at points.'

'Forget the Prac. Crit.,' I said. 'How's Mansell? Is everything OK?'

'Fine, fine,' he said, putting an arm around my shoulders. 'He's resting at the moment. So's Florence. Come on in. I'll ring through to those guards. I'm sorry about all this. I didn't realise what was going on. I suppose you couldn't identify yourself and so on?'

'How could I? I didn't know that you were here. If they'd been Heron's men, they'd have shot me dead as soon as I mentioned my name.'

I gabbled out a hundred questions as he led me into the hall. It was a room as high as the house, papered in orange. The staircase curled above a large marble fireplace. Brass dogs caught the light from the lantern windows. I noticed a few seascapes and high-backed Carolingian chairs. Everything seemed strangely silent.

Sir James barked a few gruff words down the telephone. 'Now, for God's sake, Sebastian, shut up and relax,' he commanded as he shut the library door behind us, 'everything's all right. Have a drink.'

'Lovely,' I said.

I stretched out my hands towards the fire, and suddenly I understood. 'By God, I've done it!' I murmured. 'I've bloody well done it, J.C! I've stopped the bastards! We . . . we won!'

So great was the release of pent tension that I was overcome by a fit of the giggles and collapsed onto a huge sofa. Mansell was safe, the story was safe, Heron and Co. were scotched if not destroyed, and all thanks to a mad impulse that had led me to follow a friend into prison. *I* had defeated a huge organisation. The individual had won.

I recovered at last and sat up to see my boss standing before me with a concerned expression on his face and two liqueur glasses in his hands.

'Here,' he said, 'for God's sake, take this, and calm down.'

'What is it?'

'A treat. You tell me.'

'Oh come on, J.C., I'm not much in the mood for gastronomic snobbery. Tell me all that you know. Tell me what's happened.'

'Later, later,' he smiled. 'You just taste this and tell me what it is. It's fascinating.'

'OK, boss,' I sighed, 'but haven't I done well? I mean . . .'

'Oh, shut up, Sebastian! Just for a moment, let's try to be civilised and talk about what's in these glasses. You bloody well need a drink anyway.'

I felt aggrieved but, still chuckling contentedly, I obediently sniffed the contents of the glass and concluded that Sir James had gone mad. 'At this time of day?' I asked. 'Before lunch?'

He grunted, and his beard changed angle. 'So what is it?'

I tasted it. The flavour exploded on my tongue like a grape crushed against the roof of the mouth, and slowly spread.

'I don't know,' I said, 'but I'd guess that it was a very fine old Armagnac. Very old.'

'Not bad,' he grinned, 'but you're wrong. It's whisky.'

'You're having me on!'

'No. Napoleon whisky, my boy. Probably the only original Empire period stuff left in the world. Apparently, Tommy got it with the house. You'll never taste this stuff again, nor will anyone else.'

I sat back with an inane grin on my face. I intended to show due respect to this drop of history, whose warmth was now tickling the backs of my knees. To my horror, however, Sir James had already drained his glass and was now at the cabinet, sloshing undistinguished blended whisky into a tumbler.

224

'God, sir, you're cavalier with the stuff, aren't you? I thought it was my nerves that needed calming.'

He returned to the bumrack and sat down. 'Not just yours, my boy,' he said, 'the whole business has been pretty harrowing for all of us. I was . . . I was terribly sorry about your mother, by the way.'

'My mother?'

'It was rotten luck.'

I now knew, but asked all the same, 'What was rotten luck, for Christ's sake?'

'Didn't Catherine tell you? Oh, God,' he moaned, 'I am sorry, old boy. I thought you knew.'

'She's dead?'

'Yes. The day after you bolted. Cancer. Apparently she had known for some time, but no one else seems to have known until the last few days. I'm amazed that no one told you.'

'I haven't seen anyone who would know,' I said dully, 'only Catkin, and she . . .' She had not told me for fear that I might abandon my immediate mission.

I felt no grief, just a mixture of rancour and a cold sense of emptiness which frightened me. I would have been somehow consoled had I been able to cry, but my eyes remained resolutely dry. One of the last ties with my old life had gone. I now owed my honour to no one. I had complete power.

'Tell me all that you know about Heron,' I said. 'Did you know him at all?'

'Yes,' he said, 'I knew him, and his father. Surprised that you—'

There were three sounds from the back of the house. In the past, I might have dismissed them as malfunction of the heating system. Now, every nerve in my body awaited them, as a tooth awaits the touch of the drill; three silenced gunshots – pht! pht! pht!

'Jesus!' and I pulled myself up clumsily from the sofa. I turned, and limped towards the door as fast as I could.

'Sebastian!' bellowed a voice behind me. I stopped, and turned.

Sir James was looking sadly at me. He had a gun in his hand. 'Hold still, damn you, Sebastian,' he sighed, 'there's nothing you can do now.'

225

'I can get Heron!'

'Heron is probably the only reason that you, or any of us, are still alive in a sane society.'

'You *what*?'

'You heard me, my boy. You've made a right cock up of this whole business. You've forced us into a position where there's only one thing that we can do.'

Now I really wanted to cry, as much for him as for despair.

'How in hell are you involved in this?' I asked, bewildered.

'If you must know, I was approached by a member of one of the highest families in the land. I'm sorry, Sebastian, but you've got it all wrong. We've got to take the place of the law where the law fails because of public opinion, and like the law which sent you to prison, we've got to enforce principles which are hard, immutable, and frequently unsympathetic. Do you think I like it? Do you think I liked prosecuting murderers in the days when the gallows awaited if I succeeded? Such things are necessary, that's all. Necessary for all of us, necessary for the welfare of society.'

'Don't talk rubbish, J.C.,' I said. 'How can murder be necessary for a society?'

'What do we do to a man who kills? We send him to prison for life or we kill him. Either way, we deprive him of those liberties whereby we define life. Of course, murder is necessary for a society.'

'The law holds itself above the wild justice of the vendetta, J.C.'

'No, it doesn't. What other purposes does imprisonment serve in cases of psychopaths? You're not going to tell me that it rehabilitates?'

He'd got me there. 'So, you're Heron's man?'

'Be damned to that, Sebastian! I'm what I've always been, the people's man!'

'You think that the people favour execution and vigilante squads?' I asked as I wandered towards the desk.

'You think that the people favour taxes, wages policies or even laws of decency? Try taking whisky away from Eskimos. You've said that often enough.'

'So who is the arbitrator, you or me?'

'The man with the courage to arbitrate.'

226

'The man with the gun.'

'The man who dares to use it.'

'You, J.C? For England, Home and Beauty?'

'No need, if you stand still, Sebastian. Tommy's dead. I don't like that. I was very fond of Tommy, but he's done as much good for his country by his death as ever he did in his life. Tommy's dead, and you killed him.'

So that was it. They would leave me here, bleeding and unconscious with a gun in my hand. They would make no mistakes in getting me convicted.

I looked down at Sir James's gun and counted my blessings. It could have been Kalashnikoff. It could have been a sawn-off elephant gun. Instead, it was a pretty little Ortgies 7.65 which couldn't have blown my head off. It would just make a neat, halfpenny size hole in it. I had seven inches of medieval steel in the form of a ballock knife which lay on the desk. J.C. had six far smaller pieces of twentieth-century lead, and they were still stone to my scissors. That's progress.

I weighed the alternatives as Sir James tried to justify himself; life imprisonment with guilt enclosing me as much as stone walls, or a quick bullet. I've never understood the concept of sacrifice. Given the limitations of any man's position, he can only do what he wants to do. I made no sacrifice in choosing a short life.

'You are really prepared to kill me, then?' I said. I took up the knife in my left hand and turned towards him.

'Damn it, Sebastian, as I see it, you're a *traitor* to the cause and to your country. I'm not such a fool as to suppose that treason can be defined other than subjectively once two people actually dare to fight. All assertions are *a priori* guesswork. I like you, Sebastian, you know that. I think you're a great fellow, but you're misguided. You're full of damned-fool, idealistic guff. You're a threat to us, the established and acknowledged protectors of order in this country. Of course I'd kill you, just as I killed in the war.'

I limped slowly towards him until I stood beside the sofa. He was just six feet away. 'You're sure that you're prepared to kill me, J.C.?'

'Yes, damn you, Sebastian!' he shouted. 'Yes!' He shifted on the bumrack.

227

I put all my weight on my left leg, bent my knee, and jumped. His head jolted up. The gun jolted up. The blade burst the skin just under his beard.

He never even pulled the trigger. He made a gurgling sound, like the last twist of bathwater going down the plug, and started to topple back toward the fire. My left hand curled round the back of his neck and pulled him forward onto the blade. My face was buried in his beard. Blood ran down my right hand and under the cuff, up to the elbow.

I struggled for a footing, and eventually managed to pull myself into a standing position, free of the embrace. I looked down at his flapping right arm. The left held me around the waist like that of a dancing partner. I looked down on his eyes. They rolled back and stared straight at me. I pushed the knife more firmly home and turned away.

His legs kicked in a pathetic little movement like that of a child on a swing, then he died.

Retching up gobs of air, I eased his body down onto the rug before the fire. His weight bore me down with him. I knelt. My right arm was stuck under his shoulder-blades. I tugged, gave up, and let my head slump forward onto his chest. A little squeak bubbled up from my throat. Something thudded at my cerebral cortex and I found tears trickling down my cheeks onto the waistcoat. The tobacco smell of his clothes and hair awoke some memory whose initial source I had long forgotten, a memory of warmth and strength and the confidence engendered by love. My head rocked of its own accord as though trying to wear a hollow in his too, too, solid flesh, a hollow into which I could fit, in which I would belong, in which I could sleep a deep, deep, childlike sleep.

'I'm sorry!' The echo of my own howl awoke me, and a sort of wild levity suddenly possessed me. I tugged my arm free, grabbed J.C.'s gun and ran out into the hall. Absurdly, I was not only smiling but had an erection.

'Heron!' I screamed, 'come out, you pansy bastard! Come on, come on! I want to tear your guts out!'

There was no sound. My mind was suddenly filled with erotic fantasies. I wanted identical twins with long blonde hair and tits heavy to the hand. I wanted to sink my nose and lips and tongue into a crisp pubic bush as deep and dark as night.

'Heron, you fucker, come out and have your balls blasted. Come out, damn you!'

I was sane now, but sanity meant fear. I could ill afford it. I tried to keep my muscles taut, tried to think about Sir James and Mickey Rourke and the anonymous nigger minstrel in the Ravenhill flowerbed. It didn't work.

I opened the first door on the left. It was a dining-room. There was cheddar cheese and granary bread and cloudy rough cider and the heads of three people on the mahogany table. It was all very clean. Heron had done his job, as always, tidily.

Mansell's body was slumped at the end of the table nearest to the door. Lady Mansell was at the other end. Their daughter appeared to have been the only one who had thought to struggle. Her hair was flung forward over the table. Her hand grasped a broken glass. A trail of spittle still lay on the table by her head. It sparkled in the beautiful cold light from the window behind her.

I shut the door quietly and walked to the front door.

21

'Jack?'

'Sebastian, for Christ's sake, where are you?'

'Not far from Mansell's house. I was too late. He's dead.'

'You're sure?'

'Of course, I'm bloody sure, Jack. You got the bumf?'

'Yeah. It's fantastic. It's with the editorial board now.'

'Not the original?'

'Don't be a berk, Sebastian. I had it photo-copied as soon as I got it.'

'You've got to stop the release of the news about Mansell.'

'That crossed my mind, Sebastian, but how in hell? I've got the rozzers coming over in half an hour. I'll see what they've got to say. Only the Home Office is going to keep that under wraps.'

'Yes,' I sighed, 'not much hope there, I suppose. You must try to persuade them, and get the other targets protected.'

'I've started on that already. You did a good job with those plans. We've identified five of them and have located two so far.'

'Good. When will you get clearance from the top?'

'The meeting should be over in the next hour, then it's got to go to the legal boys. I'll know for certain by four, four-thirty. Ring me back then. What are your plans?'

'God, I don't know. I'll have to go back to complete the sentence, but I'd like to see Heron done first.'

'He'll be done, all right. I've got one hell of a story ready. Heron is going to be top of the world's floating shit-list.'

'Do we warn the Palestinians?'

230

'Don't know that I can bring myself to do that, Sebastian. I reckon that they deserve what's coming to them. You?'

'You're probably right. Leave it, then.'

'Sebastian?'

'Yes?'

'You sound bloody terrible. Are you OK?'

'It's all right, Jack. I'll survive,'

'You've done a bloody great job, Sebastian. I really mean it. I should have done it, but I never could. I don't somehow reckon you're going to get the thanks you deserve, but from me at least, you get a bloody medal. Thanks.'

'Bugger off, Jack,' I said. 'I'll ring you later.'

I rang off and limped wearily from the telephone box to the bike. I had pushed it out through the woods. It had taken me more than an hour to travel half a mile. Now, every step was agony. The bullet had jolted straight through the muscles of my outer thigh. It had done no permanent damage, but the wound had now stiffened. Scab tissue split as I moved.

I was still more conscious of the other wound, of the other man's blood. Encrusted now on my shirt-sleeve and down the front of the jerkin, it scratched my forearm and my shoulder. It stank, and every time that I turned out of the wind, my nose was blasted by this deep, dry stench, a cross between stale sweat and rotten fruit.

I had stolen a fawn cashmere coat from Mansell's hall. I had thought that it would keep me warm as well as covering the stains, but my teeth were chattering as I rode up the rough dirt track. I was ill.

I chose something like a vantage point at the top of the hill. A grass field foamed down the hill before me, and no one could approach quietly along the track behind.

The dry leaves smelt good. Fallen blackthorns pricked me. I didn't care. I pulled the coat close about me and curled up into a foetal position. Nothing is colder than sunlight. I needed a short rest-cure in a dream.

I awoke with a clear head and a frost-bitten leg. The sun was still shining, the ground was still warm, but the leg had frozen solid. It weighed ten times as much as any leg should. It was numb, but it ached in my teeth.

231

It took fifteen minutes of excruciating muscular contractions to get up and to totter like a two-year-old child to the bike. Grasshoppers were making a lot of noise and a brisk breeze had got up from somewhere. I judged by the position of the sun that it must be somewhere between five and six o'clock.

I returned to the telephone box, which appeared to have been built for cattle and outlaws. It stood in the middle of nowhere on a little lane between Beckington and Norton St. Philip. As soon as I stepped in, my own smell hit me again, and my stomach pumped like bellows.

'Jack?'

'Bugger off, Sebastian,' his voice like muffled drums.

'What?'

'We don't know you, Sebastian. We've never heard of you or of Mr Heron or of anything.'

I closed my eyes, and leaned my forehead on the list of dialling codes. 'What the hell are you talking about, Jack?'

'Seems that everyone's laughing themselves sick about us. We're naive, see? Everything's under wraps. Official fucking Secrets fucking Act.'

'That's only the prison aspect, for God's sake!'

'It's got nothing to do with prison, Seb. Your friend Carol smart-arsed Heron got scared of you and ran to his friends. His mob lives on. Only difference is, now it's got a special brief.'

'What?' I screamed.

'Steady, Sebastian.' His voice wavered on the brink of a sob. 'What buys votes? Who gives people what buys votes? Who pays Heron and for why? Work on it during the next few months in solitary.'

'Jack ...'

'It's no fucking good, Sebastian. They're even going to hold a courtesy 'D' notice type press conference next month. You want to take on MI5, SAS, the Flying Squad, and probably the CIA and TUC single-handed?'

'Yes!'

'Seb, try to understand. Their activities are not only legal, they're ethical now, as well. They're sanctioned by the arbiters of the dominant ideology.'

'Jesus, where does that put me?'

'In the wrong, Sebastian, in the wrong. You're Rosenberg,

you're Brutus, you're L'homme re-bloody-volté. We're anachronisms, Sebastian, republicans out of step. Time to emigrate.'

'No!'

'Didn't think you would.' He gave a little snort. 'I'm going back to Australia for a week or two, see if Packer or Murdoch will take it. It's got to break.'

'Yes, yes,' I panted. Desperation had induced a fit of Cheyne-Stokes respiration. I felt giddy and sick. 'I'm going to kill every last one of them!' I suddenly shouted. 'I'm going to fight, damn it!'

'More fuel tq your fire,' Jack said grimly. 'Catkin's in hospital.'

'What?'

'Don't worry, it's not too bad. You left her in a bit of fix this morning. They thought you'd seen her. They wanted to know whether you'd left any written evidence. Hit her a few times. I've talked to her, though. She's all right.'

'Send her my love, and thank her,' I said. A cannonball was trying to force its way through my bowels. Suddenly I was overwhelmed by claustrophobia. 'Do your best, Jack,' I shouted, 'I'll see you!' I slammed down the receiver, shoved at the door, and reached the ditch just in time. I puked up everything inside me until there was but a dribble, streaked with blood.

I stood up straight. I felt cleaner now. There was still one job to be done, and then I would rest.

I sent the telegram to Fiona at six-thirty.

DARLING MUST SEE YOU BEFORE RETURN STOP ALL WELL STOP MEET YOU AT NODDING DONKEYS TOMORROW SATURDAY FIVE THIRTY PIP EMMA STOP LOVE YOU ALWAYS ARCITE.

And on the seven o'clock news, I heard of the murder of Lord and Lady Mansell. Sir James was not mentioned.

22

I arrived at the Wookey Hole at half-past four the next afternoon. It was a dull day, and the sky grew darker.

I drew up in the forecourt, and looked around. Before me was the wooden café and the shed which serves as a ticket office; behind me, on the other side of the road, was the long path up to the museum and the massive chain of caves.

I climbed wearily from the bike, and almost sauntered to the ticket office. I didn't feel afraid. I knew what prison was. I knew what being shot at was. Neither worried me. My failure had been total. The evening paper told of the deaths of seven Jews and a stray assortment of wives, children and servants. The old survival mechanism was numb. It was working, but apprehension was just a waste of time.

My leg could have been 1918 wooden. I carried it along with me reluctantly. I had at least managed to wash my clothes the night before in my bath at the George in Norton St. Philip, where I had quite openly taken a room.

I bought my ticket from a pretty brunette. I made some trivial joke about the price, and she laughed. She laughed and showed her teeth and it was like the Latour caves in mid-Sahara. Warmth and smiles and soft reassuring . . . Avaunt, ye spectres!

I wandered across the road and up to the cave entrance. A notice told me that the next tour would begin in ten minutes. Tours bore me. I wanted to be bored. I would have sat and watched 'Crossroads' for the rest of my life if I could have had Fiona stretched out across my lap, purring as I caressed her. I reckoned that I had deserved it.

Then the hopes started. Maybe Heron knew nothing of the telegram. Maybe Fiona would be there. She would smile and rush into my arms. I could press my face into the darkness of her neck and close my eyes and feel her arms clasping me to her, her kisses on my skin.

Maybe, equally, one of Heron's thugs would be there, a man I'd never met with an easy solution to my problems. He could be above me at the end of the gorge, just waiting until the cross on the sights coincided with the centre of my forehead.

I didn't give a damn.

The selection of the Wookey Hole as a meeting place had not been difficult. Heron did not under-estimate my intelligence so I merely had to choose the place which I would really have chosen. It had to be a place known to Fiona and myself, whose location could be indicated in a private code. A pub or a deserted spot in some field would have inspired complete incredulity in Heron, who must have known that I would select no place in which I would be so totally vulnerable. The Wookey Hole, however, was well-peopled, but by tourists rather than by those who would know me.

I had little doubt but that the telegram would have been intercepted and that Fiona, all unwitting, would have translated the bit about the donkeys. They stood, two grey wooden donkeys from a nineteenth-century fair, at the entrance to the fairground museum.

The guide arrived. He unlocked the door, and led me, together with five Americans, into the caves. His deep, mellifluous voice was aided by the accoustics. He guided us from cavern to cavern, telling little jokes, pointing out features of particular interest.

The river Axe had had to get through that rock somehow. It couldn't go over, it didn't want to go round, so it had spent a few million years boring straight through. Where it met an obstruction, it whirled about a bit. When it flooded, it pushed up the roof a bit. It left drops of water on the ceiling and they froze into corkscrew stalactites. It drew from the limestone great cascades of black and orange minerals. It found its way out.

Out of twenty-nine identified caves, they've opened six to the public: the first three, and numbers seven, eight and nine. The rest are for bold divers only. Cables snake through the pools. In the fast-flowing clear water, lit by underwater spots, the riverbed seems only inches away. It's not. It's forty feet down.

The first three caves are huge halls in which men have found shelter since Paleolithic days. They've been the dwellings of hyenas, cavemen, recreants and, at the last, of a potty old woman known as the Witch of Wookey. A good bishop came along and petrified her with a blessing. She's now a stalagmite in the first cavern. Her Gerald Scarfe profile gazes out over the clear blue pool. She is screaming.

The other three caves are smaller and deeper. They've only recently been opened, and a high catwalk runs through them. Beneath lie the waters; above, great vaults echoing darkness.

The tour took us half an hour. I was followed down all the narrow tunnels between caves by an American woman with magenta hair and Cruella De Ville glasses. She gasped, 'Oh, gee, just look at that!' whenever the guide shone his torch on some interesting formation, and grasped my sleeve, 'Honey, please!' as we passed under low rocks. She also persisted in asking the guide and me, 'No, but really, who built these wonderful primitive caves?'

We emerged in open air again. The guide directed us towards the paper-mill at the other end of the streamside path. The rest of the party, thank God, hastened keenly on, leaving me limping. It was that hour at which you are suddenly cheered by switching on the lights and realising that it's dark after all.

It was five-fifteen, and I wanted to be punctual. I hurried as best I could along the gorge and up to the mill, through Madame Tussaud's store-room, where the waxwork heads of redundant celebrities lie disembodied on the shelves, and into the brilliant array of the fairground museum.

The last room, pale grey and white, was almost empty. There were three huge carved peacock seats in brilliant blue and gold, a staring horse's head on a pedestal, and the two grey donkeys with nodding heads and necks.

He was there, leaning across the saddle of one donkey. As I had anticipated, he had done me the honour of a personal appearance. If Heron had an Achilles' heel, it was his consciousness of being a gentleman.

He wore a grey flannel suit, a cavalry tie and Gucci moccasins. Trust him not to omit the one touch of bad taste. He

236

looked pleased with himself. His hair glowed like hammerflush.

I bowed to him as I walked across the room. He smiled, stood straight, and stretched out his hand.

'Sebastian,' he said softly.

'Mr Heron.' I shook the hand.

'You expected me?'

'Of course.'

He nodded. 'You were injured yesterday?'

''Fraid so. A .303 bullet straight through the thigh.'

He winced. 'Beastly,' he said. 'Must have been Tommy's guards.'

'Yes.'

We were talking quietly, but so empty was the room that our voices echoed as if in one of the caves. Heron glanced apprehensively over his shoulder.

'I must say,' he said, 'you've done pretty well so far. Someone had to lose, you know.'

'Yes.'

'But, if you'll forgive any trace of condescension that you might detect, for an amateur, you've done superbly. I wish I had more men of your calibre.'

'*Vous êtes trop gentil, monsieur*. Do I get the Doggie Chox now, or do I have to Die For England first?'

'*Mais pas du tout!*' He smiled again his innocent, healthy, schoolboy smile, and put his hand on my shoulder. 'Come, Sebastian, let's walk around the place, shall we? I've never seen the caves, and I have much to say to you.'

We walked slowly back through the carved wood fairground animals. Horses, ducks, camels and bulls grinned at us through gloss paint. Heron grinned glossily back. Never since I was a new boy at school had I been more aware of a difference in height than now. He was only three inches taller than I, but suddenly I was a fourth former and he my head of house.

'You've heard, no doubt, that we've come out, as it were, that we're official now.'

'I heard. Congratulations.'

'Who told you?'

'Don't be bloody stupid. You can't tap every line to every national newspaper in the country, you know.'

'I say,' he said as we paused before an ornate piece of

237

carving, 'fair puts Grinling Gibbons to shame, doesn't it?'

'It's fine,' I agreed.

I wondered where he intended to spring the surprise on me. It could await me in the next room. It could be in the paper-mill. It could be on the path up to the caves. It amused me to think that he was wondering the same thing about me. I had admitted that I had expected him, and he would not believe that I had arranged such a meeting without some pre-conceived offensive plan.

The funny thing was that I had no plan. I was all but unarmed, and I had no allies. I had just wanted to get over with, whatever 'it' might be. My decision to meet him had been inspired by impatience. I was not going to return to prison, there to await the final call from one of his minions. I had rather that we saw 'it' through, one way or the other.

'So,' he said, as we turned into a corridor lined with glass-fronted wardrobes, 'are you now convinced that we are necessary?'

'Necessary sub specie aeternitatis, necessary because you exist, yes. Necessarily right, no.'

'But come now, Sebastian, you have lived all your life in a country protected by MI6, for example. You cannot tell me that you like their methods.'

'No, but they are within the law, and their activities are perforce sanctioned by law. That is not to say that their methods may be practised by any citizen, but then, nor are those of the law-lords who may order execution or the confiscation of property, but until all men are responsible or until we have a theophany in our Green and Pleasant, someone has to be granted the privilege – and the responsibility.'

'Which describes us perfectly,' said Heron. 'Look, there's that dress that Twiggy wore in *The Boyfriend*.'

'I liked that film,' I said dully. 'It doesn't describe you, because you presumed to stand outside the law. You were thus bound by no law. The hubris of Richard of Gloucester or of Faustus. It does not pass unpunished.'

'The hubris of the rebel, and what do we call the rebel when he has won?'

'Your majesty.'

'Precisely.'

'Or *mein führer*.'

'That's cheap, and well you know it. Every man who believes in anything approaching a fascist cause, a cause both intellectually and morally respectable throughout history, is dismissed with that trite association. You're an inegalitarian who believes in a centralised economy? So was Hitler. He killed Jews, so you must be anti-Semitic, he made war, so will you. It's the standard refuge of the poor, prejudiced intellect in search of a cause. You know it.'

'You're right,' I sighed, you're right. There's not much point in our arguing about this, really. It's merely a matter of priorities, different approaches to the same problem. We both have the same cause and the same degree of commitment. If it's any consolation, I admire your courage.'

But Heron did not want to accept that. He was concerned to persuade me before he struck. For a man of power, he seemed desperately anxious for reassurance.

We had reached the main waxworks storeroom. No one else was there. The next tour would not start for twenty minutes, but we had an audience all the same. Queen Anne, Rod Laver, Clem Attlee and Diana Dors smiled out at us. Churchill and Hitchcock glowered.

I was getting bored with the conversation. I'd already had it with myself. I was getting tired, too, of waiting for the first move.

On our right, as we entered the room, there was a roped-off section, not unlike the average attic. It was littered with props. There were Louis Quinze chairs, a Beatle's collarless grey jacket, cricket bats, sceptres, and all sorts of costume. An original Tussaud cast of a head snatched from the guillotine basket hung above the lumber. He looked disgusted.

I picked on a golf club. It looked like a fairway wood, and it had a label tied around its shank, doubtless telling that someone had won the Open with it. I didn't bother to read it.

Heron sauntered at my left. I didn't hear what he was saying. He was making decisive gestures with his right hand. Even when I was racing fit and fencing every day, I never moved faster. My sound left leg shot out to trip him. My right hand grabbed the club by the handle. Heron stumbled. The club swung high.

Everything happens frame by frame at such moments. The adrenalin-charged brain freezes every shot. There was my hand arising, a surge of pride in those newly developed muscles; there was Heron's hair giving off a pink flash as he turned, off balance. His forearm raised, his pained expression at my perfidy, the clubhead falling fast towards his head.

He couldn't get his arm up in time. He couldn't dodge. He did the only thing possible. He dropped. The club hit a shoulder-blade with a crack which might have been the sound of breaking bone. He'd live.

He rolled hard against my legs and I toppled backward. The wounded leg shot fire at my groin. Automatically, he grasped the head of the club and clung to it tightly. That saved my life. If I had fallen, it would have taken me a full minute to get up again. Heron would not have given me such leisure. His weight held me up.

I kicked at his head as though going for a conversion at Twickenham. My foot crunched into his right cheekbone. His head jerked sideways. 'Ah!' he cried, and blood splashed from his nose. I felt triumphant. I had hurt Heron. Homer had nodded.

I was upright again. Heron's left hand was doing something as he shook the numbness from his brain. He wasn't looking for his handkerchief. I kicked again. I missed. He rolled, his jacket flapped open, his hand emerged. He fired three times. He was moving too fast to have much chance of a direct hit, but I ducked and ran. It was a silenced .38 S&W; three down, twelve still to go. Hitchcock glowered no more. He was splattered all over Jackie Onassis.

I swung round the door-frame and into the paper-mill. I heard Heron splutter and mumble 'By Christ!' in the room behind me. I was doing well. That kick had shaken his brains a bit.

Then I was outside again. The grain of the air filled with dust like charcoat-dust. On my right was the stream. Beyond that, the steeply climbing cliff. To run up there was to cause temporary stalemate. I wanted an endgame. I had to get up to the caves.

The path was dead straight and three hundred yards long. I couldn't keep up Heron's pace, let alone that of his bullets, so I scrambled down the bank and into the stream. The water was icy. It cut through the wound like cold steel on a tooth nerve. I crouched, and waded, looking over my shoulder. I wanted to see death coming.

Death came out of the mill a moment later, tousled, dusty and bleeding. He scanned the scrub on the hillside before him. I felt a thrill of admiration as I saw him there, powerful, agile and brave. I did not want to have to destroy him.

Then I dived.

The water was clear. I saw the dead grey rabbit and the coins half-buried in the silt. There was an old threepenny bit amongst them. I saw the weeds waving at me as if shooing me away. I worried only as to what I would see as I surfaced.

My temple started to throb. I let the air out slowly. My elbow broke the surface. I forced my body down again. The shadow of the bridge approached and I resisted the temptation to arise diagonally towards it. Only when darkness completely enclosed me did I surface.

Everything was still. Birds were singing. I waded under the bridge without looking back. If Heron were waiting above me, following my progress with a gun barrel, there would be nothing left for me to do but to die gracefully. He wasn't. Presumably he knew that there was no way out through the caves and was therefore checking the hillside every step of the way.

On the other side of the bridge, I took a deep gulp of air and pulled myself up onto the bank. I saw Heron and, a second later, he saw me. He was a hundred yards away and he'd lost his cool. He must have been crazed to fire another four bullets at that range. He was running. So, very soon, was I.

I ran into the winding stone tunnel, ducking under the low arches. The clammy cool of the caves was still icier than the water. Heron's footfall behind me echoed around the rocks. I was going through the caves in the opposite direction from that which the tour had taken, so I reached the ninth cave first.

From there on, *déjà vu* took over.

All my life I had been running through that high-vaulted cavern with its roof as dark as ravens' down and its falls of manganese. All my life, the echoes had sounded thus resonant as Heron clattered in and cursed to find me gone. I needed no plans. I was just an unthinking component of a pattern long-since drawn. I knew how it must end.

241

I ducked behind a slimy stalagmite and watched as Heron crouched, both hands on the gun, and I looked round the cave. He ran on into the darkness of the tunnel towards the next cave. His feet struck out the dull echo of iron on the catwalk, just as feet drum in prison. He shot twice at phantasms, and the sound of the shots came fluttering at me like bats down the tunnel as I ran after him into the narrow drum of the eighth cave.

Heron had already run up the steep slope towards the seventh. He was panting and murmuring like the White Rabbit. He must know that I would be waiting for him somewhere like a lover before the show. He, too, was impatient.

I was on the catwalk, twenty feet above the water. The cave was my home. I knew its every contour, its every jagged secret. I belonged there.

I limped along the iron bridge as quietly as I could, until I stood at the entrance to the passage up which Heron had run.

'Carol!' I yelled, and slipped back into the shadows.

My voice clanged around the vaults of the cave. The sound of water lapping soothed the echoes.

Heron clearly wanted no more talk. He hurtled down the slope like the baby grand that Pickfords' men let go. The guide had warned us on the way through: 'Take great care at the bottom. There's only five foot four headroom just round the corner.' It was a sharp, cramped corner, and Heron had no guide. Intent on one end, he swung round the corner and crashed straight into the overhang.

In childhood dreams, I had seen his figure as he emerged, wild-eyed and bleeding. He tottered, and leaned like a drunk on the catwalk railing. As if in a well-rehearsed dance-routine, I stepped forward behind him. I joined my hands and brought them down hard in a double-fisted blow to the nape of his neck. He grunted, shook his head, but otherwise appeared not to notice my presence. He braced his feet, and wouldn't go down.

A child does not discover sex or aggression. They discover him. So did the certain knowledge as to how and when to do this now discover me. I bent down, grabbed his ankles, and pulled.

He went up and over, unresistant. His chest scraped along the top of the railing. He kicked. Then he was gone. There was a deep splash, and Heron sank into the water below me without a sound.

He stayed down for so long that I thought he must be drowned, but at last he surfaced, coughing. The current had caught him and was bearing him away. He was now directly beneath me, his ravaged head just above the water, the rest of him grotesquely white like dead flesh in the underwater light.

God knows what memories, what confused fantasies occupied Heron's mind. He seemed to be totally unaware of danger. His arms waved vaguely at the water, but the current in the Wookey Hole caves is stronger than any Atlantic undercurrent. He had no chance.

I leaned on the railing to watch him. He shook his head, and spoke as though in a trance, 'Sebastian, please . . .'

'Please what, Carol?'

'Come on. Get me out of here. There are cables. Throw me a cable . . .'

'And if I do?'

'If you do . . .'

'You'll kill me.'

'No. Come on, Sebastian, why should I want to kill you?'

'Don't be bloody silly, Carol. You'll destroy me if I don't destroy you.'

He had reached the end of the pool now. His back hit the rock with a force which made me wince. He didn't even seem to notice it. He turned and clung to the rock with both hands, but I could see his legs dragged backward under the arch by the tide, until his body was curved in a perfect crescent. The next few caves were filled to their roofs with water.

'What . . . what do you stand for, then, Foy?' he shouted in the same monotone. 'Mercy, isn't it? Being nice?'

'No,' I told him. I hoped that he would continue in that vein. 'I stand, if for anything, for the freedom of the individual to find his own means to fulfilment, his own means to self-assertion.'

'I'm cold.'

'Forty-eight degrees. You'll die of exposure before the next tour comes round – if, that is, you don't allow yourself to die of drowning first. Either way, you'll be a damned sight colder soon.'

'For Christ's sake, Sebastian,' his voice was high-pitched now and tremulous, 'what have I ever done to you? I only did my best for what I believed in!'

'By God, so you did, Carol. So did I. So do the terrorists.'

'Bloody thugs,' he said. He smiled. I felt his smile rather than saw it, for his face was now like a student's Guevara poster. For a moment I was tempted to throw him a line, whatever the cost. I even looked for the nearest cable. It was a long way off.

I looked straight at him and said, 'Go to hell.'

Suddenly his legs were tugged upward, his face sank into the water and he was sucked under. He was whipped away as if in a wind tunnel.

'Go to hell,' I kept muttering, 'go to hell.'

Somehow, I doubt that he did.

The police were waiting for me in the car park. They claimed that I had been recognised by a tourist who had seen my picture in the papers. They took me in to await the arrival of the Birmingham police. I am told that I spent the whole of the rest of the afternoon in the cells humming 'Singing in the Rain'.

23

I was returned to the Cliff, where the governor sentenced me to a further three months. I was in the prison hospital for the first two weeks and, thereafter, I passed nearly four months in conditions which made me envy battery hens. Thanks to my original pal, Billy, however, and Maurice's influence, I enjoyed physical protection and every privilege of power. I continued to receive passionate letters from Fiona, who had defied her father and intended to marry me on my release.

It may seem strange that I just dismiss four months in a paragraph but, like all ex-cons, I find it impossible to do otherwise. Every day is identical, right down to its colours and smells. The sort of remarkable observation which might identify separate days in a prisoner's diary would be of the order: 'Was constipated today', 'Ran out of burn', or 'Didn't talk about sex'. So a prison sentence telescopes in the memory into one eternal, archetypal day, interrupted only by visits.

Visits lasted only half an hour and we were forced to talk through a grille with officers all around us. It didn't matter. She loved me, she wanted me, and again we made plans for those first days of freedom. Her love gave me the hope and strength and a belief in myself which sustained me as it had throughout the sentence.

I suppose that I knew long before she told me. I had known since first she said she loved me.

It was my last visit. I was to be discharged one week later. I was as excited and anxious as a schoolboy at the end of term.

The screw gave me a thorough frisking and shook my shoes and socks, hoping to find contraband. As always, on failing, he sniffed dubiously, told me to watch it and ushered me into the visiting room.

She was sitting at our usual table. She wore a sloppy pink sweater and a white accordion pleated skirt. There were gold and ivory bangles on her wrists. She wore too much make-up. She made one of her so elegant gestures as I approached. She crossed her forearms and pouted at me. Her eyes smiled.

'How are you, pigling?' she said.

'Surviving, darling.' I sat and leaned forward. Our faces were just two inches apart. Her breath touched my face. I looked down at her lips. 'Only six nights left now!' I said. 'We've made it! How are you?'

'OK,' and she turned to look across the room, casually displaying her profile.

'Have you got the tickets for Rome?'

'Yes.' She flicked back her hair with a long hand.

'Just think. One week from now we'll be in London, and ten days from now, we'll be in Florence. We've made it!'

'Darling,' she smiled.

'Tell me all your news,' I said.

A child locked in a cupboard, crying, *'Come on, let me out. OK, a joke's a joke, but this has gone far enough. Please ...'*

'Oh, not much, my love. Daddy's being an infernal bore as usual. Poor Mummy's being brave, but I wish he'd go back to Lusaka. So does she. Theirs is the happiest marriage in the world so long as he's away.'

'I know, He goes back soon, doesn't he?'

'Day after tomorrow, thank God.'

'People have been known to suffocate, you know.'

'One week from now ... Where shall we go for dinner that first night?'

'I don't know. I don't think I'll let you out for the first week or so.'

'La Belle Dame sans Merci hath me in thrall. *L'homme est partout dans les fers*, but that's one prison that I won't object to. Oh, God, I just can't wait. I just ...'

She was looking at the fat woman at the next table.

'I intend to spend the first day in kissing you very, very slowly from head to toe and back again, stopping at places of particular interest ...'

She frowned.

'*Please let me out. It's dangerous, you know* ...'

'Fiona, what is it? Come on. Tell me.'

'Oh, darling, you do so deserve to be happy. Why should it always happen to you?'

I closed my eyes and steadied myself. 'Come on,' I said, 'tell me.'

'It can't work, my love.'

'What the hell do you mean, it can't work?'

'Everyone's against us, darling. I know that you're going to say that I'm a coward. Maybe I am. I just can't go through with it.'

'Explain, explain!'

'Daddy has sworn that he'll stay in the country if I don't promise not to see you again. He says he'll stop us.'

'How can he, for God's sake? It doesn't matter what he does. We love one another, we belong together. You can't exactly claim that he's particularly important to you.'

'No, darling, but don't you see? He can frame you if he wants to! You've got a record. He will!'

'No, he won't. You know he won't. That's just melodramatic nonsense. Your mother wrote to me only last week telling me how much she was looking forward to seeing me and so on.'

'I'm going to Madeira on Tuesday.'

'You're doing what?'

'We've got friends there.'

'For God's sake, Fiona, I've been here for twelve months. My every thought, my every dream has been of you. I love you. I need you!'

'I love you, Sebastian. Yo don't doubt that, do you? You're the only person that I've ever really loved. You're in my heart. You always will be. But you must not try to see me again. Honestly.'

'Not see you again? What the hell are you talking about. I'll see you all right. I'll make love to you again. I'll go mad if I don't! God, girl, remember those nights when you've been right here with me? Think. Think what we've managed to make! We've conquered prison and spatial restrictions. We've won! And you sit there without a tear in your eye and tell me you're going to Madeira on Tuesday. You can't do this again. I don't

247

think I can face it. Not again.'

'I've got to, Sebastian. Don't try to stop me. I'm so, so sorry. You know I'll always love you, but there's nothing I can do.'

My forehead seemed to press down on my eyelids, to crush my face like a cushion. I didn't know what to do, what to say. The prospect of the loneliness which awaited me was unbearable. I started to smile, incredulous, uncomprehending. It was all happening again.

Then I started to laugh.

On many occasions, in briefings with clients older than myself, I had found myself playing the eager schoolboy or aspirant undergraduate seeking favour, only to recall with astonishment that the clients regarded me as their equal or even their superior. This was the same sort of sudden shock of self-awareness.

I had been playing a part for so long that I had trapped myself in the plot of the play. But Fiona belonged to another Sebastian, a Sebastian who dwelt exclusively in the Savoy or in Her Majesty's prisons. I did not know her, nor could she ever hope to know me, save in bed, where our fantasies coincided.

We had been close when we were apart, as a soldier in the trenches may converse with his god. And now, I realised, my vanity was affronted. I was still clinging to a dream as a refuge for reality. Never once during my stay in prison had she been more than a phantom.

I grew up and I woke up. I did not know, I do not know, whether I liked the new Sebastian. He was a sceptic. He judged Fiona as he would have judged anyone else, on the basis of her generosity, her kindness, her loyalty, her humour. Maybe that was why I was laughing now when I should have been crying as she stood and picked up her coat. I was struggling to control my hilarity as she ran her hand lightly down the grille as though to caress my face and, with a stylish flutter of her eyelashes, whispered, 'Darling.'

A prison officer opened the door for her. She smiled her thanks and passed through.

'Fiona!' I yelled after her. 'Never let them bring down the curtain, my love! You couldn't live through an intermission.'

She stuck her head round the door. 'Don't worry about me, Sebastian,' she called, 'there's no shortage of good parts!'

I grinned at her, 'Intolerable floozie!'

She wiped away something resembling a tear, and was gone.

Billy somehow arranged a party on my last evening. I cannot have been much of a guest of honour. There were sandwiches. There was a bottle of whisky. I remember nothing else of it.

There is a tradition in nick that, unless you eat every last drop of your porridge on the last morning, you're bound to return. Goaded on by my cell-mates, I duly forced it all down. I rolled up my blankets and sat on the chair to await the call. I was apprehensive. Excitement at last seeped through the thick mantle of gloom and vengeful fury which enveloped my brain. I was going to be freed. I was going to be able to breathe fresh air, to see my friends, to go down to the pub, to spend money, to exercise authority.

At ten to eight, the screw arrived. I hastily shouted my good-byes down the landing and followed him through the centre, through the many locked doors, to Reception. I was given my clothes, my money, my books. It felt like Christmas. By the time that I came to sign for them, I was grinning from ear to ear like the village idiot.

The screw led me out into open air and across the courtyard to the front gate. 'Anyone meeting you?'

'No . . . no.' I stopped grinning.

The gate opened. The street burst in. I stepped through, and the noise of the world engulfed me. There were people walking to work. There were cars purring, bicycles tinkling. There was a Woolworths opposite. Its Christmas lights looked warm against the cold grey satin of the morning.

'Don't come back, Foy,' said the officer behind me, and shut the door.

I stood still and shivered. The sky was still black, though the street shone and the skyline shimmered like some dark brocade. It was very cold.

'Sebastian!'

'O me, my heart, my rising heart! But down!' They didn't open till ten-thirty.

'Sebastian, over here!'

I turned. There, in a white Morgan, sat Sylvie. She was waving, smiling. I dropped my books.

Sylvie jumped out, and slammed the car door behind her. She ran over to me. I was transfixed. 'Sylvie, what the hell are you doing? I . . . Oh, God, it's so good to see you!'

I kissed her and sank my face into the musty fur of her collar.

'Darling,' she said, and her hand held the back of my head. 'I read the announcement in *The Times* and I knew you'd be out today and Catkin said—'

'The announcement?'

'Yes. About Fiona. Come on, it's cold.'

She started to pick up the books. Her breath was steamy. The light hair was snapped up by the breeze.

'What's his name?' I asked. 'I keep forgetting.'

'Oh, Charles Fortescue-Arseholes or something, I don't know. He's the original wet little chinless wonder, but he's got a cool 15,000 acres and he'll be Sir Charles soon. I suppose that security was all that she wanted.'

'Some bloody security,' I said, but all the bitterness was gone now. I was free.

'Oh, you'd be surprised how much security there is in stupidity,' she said, and nestled up against my shoulder. 'Come on, let's get away from here. I've got a bottle of champagne and a pile of smoked salmon in the car.'

I was laughing now. 'Lead on, my love,' I said, and squeezed her tight.

'Where shall it be?' she asked.

'Redway.'

'Yes. I thought so. You'll find that there's a lot to be done. The whole place was closed down when your mother died. There've been vandals around.'

'Oh, God,' I said, 'I never gave instructions that the household should be shut up.'

'You never gave *any* instructions, darling.'

The car was warm. The champagne was cold. Chick Corea was making interesting noises on the cassette recorder. I felt refreshed, restored and full of strength. Somewhere along the road, I decided that I loved reality more than any dream. Somewhere a little further along the road, I decided that I loved Sylvie. I haven't changed my mind since.

24

That was eight months ago. I have put off the writing of this account until now, when at last it has become necessary. I have been leading a happy, healthy life here at Redway. The farm manager didn't seem able to cope without my mother there to direct him. There were termites to be poisoned in the stucco and weeds to be cut down in the river. There was re-thatching, repointing and repainting to be done in the staff cottages. I bought six pedigree Limosans from Ireland and planted four acres with hardwood for another generation.

Vandals had expended a lot of energy in the chapel. They had smashed the windows and knocked the heads off monuments. I haven't got round to that yet.

All the staff are back, although I have now shut off the top floor, and Sylvie and I live, for the most part, in the kitchen and the morning-room. Jim took charge of the dogs when my mother died, had my dear old cocker bitch covered by one of the best of the Duke of Sutherland's dogs and, with characteristic scrupulousness, would sell none of the resultant litter in my absence. We therefore share our home with four rumbustious puppies who are rapidly finishing off the work started by human vandals.

We seldom go up to London. I don't want to take the risk. Brinkmanship is no longer my idea of fun. Catkin has come down to see us a few times. She's at law school now, and busily consuming Inner Temple dinners. She'll be here for the summer vacation, which will give Sylvie company and assistance when she most needs it. Sylvie's five months pregnant.

It's been a strange business. Ever since my return, although my need for her is great and my affection for her more peaceful

251

than any that I have ever known, the degree of our physical *communication* has been minimal. I am dissociated from her by twelve months in which all the rough edges were buffed from my soul. She is kind and flattering, and occasionally she gets off on the violence of my need for her, but I know that we are not getting it together. Once, after I had beaten her until she shook and then made love to her as gently as I know how, she said, 'Darling, you know that I like it, but, shit! I've never known such hatred – no, not hatred, desperation – to course through anyone's hands.'

That other night, five months ago, everything worked. It was almost valedictory, and she knew it. She knew as soon as it was over that she had conceived.

Last weekend, Jack Drake came to see me for the first time since my release. He refused to come here, so we arranged to meet at the Golden Ball at Lower Swell.

Sylvie dropped me off on her way to Cirencester. Jack was waiting for me. He was leaner and browner than ever. He looked old. He smiled faintly, but did not move as I came in.

'Pint, Jack?'

'Yeah, thanks, Seb.'

I brought the two pints over to the table and sat opposite him.

'How's it going, Seb?' he said.

'Great. I've become a respectable English country gentlemen now. Sylvie's pregnant. The world is about to be afflicted with another generation of Foys.'

'Congratulations. I'm glad.'

'What of you, Jack?'

'I told you I was going to Australia.'

'Yes.'

'I couldn't get the story published.'

'Nothing?'

'Not a thing. They can't touch it.'

'So we lose and the sods battle on. That's that.'

'It can't be, Sebastian. Heron's gone to new excesses since they went official.'

'Not Heron,' I said.

'What?'

'Not Heron; his successors. I forgot, no one knows. Heron's dead.'

'For how long?'

'Nearly a year now. He went official one day and he went dead the next.'

'Well, well,' Jack grinned. 'You?'

'And good fortune, yes.'

He grunted and placed his glass on the table. 'May not be such a good thing, after all. I've got the names of most of his lieutenants here and on the continent – most of the official ones, that is – and I get the feeling that they haven't got the same iron control over their men. It's not just known terrorists they're hitting now.'

'Never was. Who, then?'

'The mortality rate amongst militant union leaders has been rising somewhat, or hadn't you noticed?'

'No.'

'Bloody obscurantist farmer! Hugh Grey, Jack Lawford, Les Perez, Eric Selfe. Names mean nothing to you?'

'Not much.'

'All accidentally dead in the last six months. Troublemakers. They weren't up to much. Learned their communism from the Manifesto and nothing else and enjoyed the publicity they got for making a lot of noise, that was all. But they were costing certain people a hell of a lot of money, and those certain people didn't like it. The same applies to a couple of university lecturers at Hull. One's dead, the other's in an asylum.'

'Accidently, you said . . .' I offered token resistance.

'Yeah. Car accidents, mysterious disappearances, carbon tetrachloride poisoning . . .'

'Yes,' I said slowly, as the words jogged sleeping phantoms in my brain. 'Yes, I remember that one. Alcohol, smoke and dry cleaning fluid, then sit back and wait for massive brain haemorrhage. That's one of their favourites.'

'Right.' Jack urged. 'And try Eric Selfe's death for size. He was the leader of the Students' Union. Totally brainless and never used a word of English when he could use meaningless anti-imperialist cant. He had a phobia of moths. He made no secret of it. He was scared stiff of them. He died of heart failure. The evidence showed that he had taken a massive overdose of LSD then sat down in a tiny loo in which there just happened to be thirty huge moths. That was some way to commit suicide.'

I shuddered and reached for my glass. 'So what can anyone do, Jack? That's how the country's going. That's all there is to it. Resistance is treason now. Every country has always had an assassination squad. We can't be surprised.'

'You know how they operate, Seb.'

'So?'

'And you've had their training. You believe that they should be destroyed, don't you?'

'I'd like to see them destroyed, yes, like I'd like to see blindness or deafness eradicated.'

'But you're not prepared to do anything about it?'

'Like what? Before you start lecturing me, just remember that I did it. I fought as best I could. I lost. The war is over, Jack.'

'The war's never fucking over, Sebastian, not until people can say what they feel without fear of being silenced.'

'For God's sake, Jack ...' I got up and took the glasses over to the bar for a refill.

I returned, sighed and slumped into the chair. 'So what are you planning to do?'

'I was going to ask you,' he said.

'What the bloody hell have I got to do with it?'

'It's still your battle,' he shrugged. 'I need an ally, and there's no one else whom I can even approach without fear that I'll be wiped out tomorrow.'

'Tidied up,' I said.

'What?'

'The phrase is "tidied up", not "wiped out".'

'Oh.' He sipped his beer, then spoke slowly and quietly, 'You've got the know-how, Seb. They're getting complacent now. A few bullets in the right place, and they're going to have to start behaving again. We'll never wipe them out as an anti-terrorist force, but at least we can assert the law and make them leave political subversives alone.'

'Oh, yes, and why should they, Jack? What's the difference between the communist who threatens the economy by malicious industrial action and another who does it by terror?'

'One's within the law, the other isn't.'

'Ow!' I said. 'Thoroughly hoist by my own whatsit. But look at it straight, Jack. It's all very well being quixotic, but just think what you're suggesting. We've got violent activists being suppressed by violent representatives of law and order. You suggest that we, as representatives of a more fundamental form of law and order, suppress them in turn. Big fleas have little fleas.'

'Don't you understand the difference, Sebastian? These guys have got to be stopped because, unlike the terrorists, their power is such that it threatens the whole system of democracy in this country. What happens if there is a general strike and these people take over, as they surely would? A bloody military dictatorship, that's what. The terrorists play fair in that when they stand up with guns, at least they expect to get shot back. These men have absolute power, like an hereditary Caesar. Absolute power means the end of democracy. You've got a child on the way. Do you want him or her to be born into a country ruled by fear?'

'That's bloody unfair, Jack.'

'I know,' he smiled, 'but you can make it clear to these people that their power is not total. You and I can referee, show them that you can't just "tidy up" a Trevor. We're the only people who can do it.'

'Jack, look at me!' I stood and patted my stomach. 'I'm a veteran! Look, I've got a beer-gut! I'm no active young soldier, and I'm damned if I see why it should be us who have to risk our lives playing Quixote. What the hell can we do? Sure, I could kill a few of them before getting killed myself, but—'

'That's all I ask, Sebastian. We fight for the country as soldiers have fought in every generation, and it's got to be us because we're the only people who know what we're fighting. For every Hugh Grey, we pick off one of their leaders.'

'You're mad,' I stared at him.

'No, I'm not, Seb. I'm just a pragmatist who believes that one or two freedoms are worth fighting for.'

'You're mad.'

'You're getting needled,' he smiled slowly. 'Think about it.'

'Your round times two, you crazy bastard,' I said, and held out my glass.

He stood. 'I don't know,' he said, 'the avarice of these rich English ex-cons . . . Just one thing, Seb . . .'

'Yes?'

'Why are you still alive if you disposed of Heron?'

255

'I don't know,' I admitted. 'I rather think that it's because Heron acknowledged his subjection to one law after all.'

'What law?'

'Rather absurdly, I think he'd have called it cricket. I don't think that he told anyone where he was going that day. He wanted it to be a one to one confrontation.'

Jack nodded. 'I'm told he wasn't a bad guy,' he said.

'Shut up and buy those drinks.'

It's six o'clock in the morning. Last night, I rang Jack and told him that I would call the new foal Rocinante. We are to meet at eleven-thirty at Paddington station. He says I should be back here by tomorrow evening.

Sylvie sleeps on the bed behind me. Her child sleeps within her.

I'm going to leave now. I've got the knowledge, I've got the Browning, I've got a body which I would like to be able to use otherwise, but what the hell. It will no longer do the things that I want it to do, anyhow.

I can see soft leaves framing the broken windows of the little grey chapel. It's mid August. At least I've brought in the harvest.